With all my
Love
Paola

BEYOND OUR WORLD

A NOVEL

PAOLA
ALEJANDRA

Dedicated To My Supportive Family And Friends,
Thank you for believing in me
(You know who you are)

Chapter 1

Sunny skies and chirping birds—two things that never described the beginning of Lola's stories. Long nights and droopy eyes was more like it. Endless hours and little payoff was also acceptable. Nothing she could really do about that. On the other hand, it wasn't like she was the only one who was struggling. There were plenty of Lola's friends who were also finding themselves having to move away for work.

A lot of thought went into how she was going to find the success that she was promised. Exactly who promised that to her was a mystery, because all she could remember was that she had to go to college. If she went to college she would get a good job. If she just worked hard enough, she would get everything she's always wanted. It was supposed to be that easy, until it wasn't.

That's why running around on the hottest day of the year for a life changing opportunity, in downtown New York, was her last shot at magic. Magic, as in crowded walkways always at the peak of pedestrian hustle, claustrophobic maze-like streets, blinding sounds—

1

everything that lures hungry young professionals like Lola and her boyfriend Jason, to try and make it... at least one last time.

"Do you think this is it?" Lola could think of nothing better to ask after interviewing at Tennerin Publishing House. She looked at Jason, waiting for his response while she pinched and pulled areas of her blouse that were adhering to her body with sweat. She just wanted to hear him say that this was the moment that would change everything for them.

"Do *you* think this is it?" Jason countered. His big blue eyes looked at her, enticing her to say the right thing—the right thing for her. Besides her parents, Jason was her number one supporter. Anything she wanted to do never seemed out of reach for him to believe she could do.

Lola gave him a little smile. She knew exactly what he was doing. He was always pushing her to be more confident in her own work. She had a tendency to rely on him too much during important matters—a tendency he was trying to get her to let go of, for her sake. He would frequently tell her that he can't always be there when a decision has to be made.

They both stood there looking at each other, neither one of them surrendering to any kind of awkwardness until a cyclist zoomed past them. As nice of a moment as they were having, it was no match for the sweltering rays that were bombarding them. With little shade to go around, they both made their way underneath a modest cover of leaves from a tree that could barely protect a house cat. In all reality, staying outside wasn't going to do either of them any good. This was especially worrying to Lola who always fussed about Jason's exposure to the sun—but in her defense, his pale skin didn't compare to her naturally tan skin by any stretch of the imagination.

"I'm hungry," Lola told him as she shaded her eyes trying to look for a food vendor. She spotted one only a couple of yards away that looked appetizing enough. "Let's eat something quick and go back to the hotel before you get another spot of cancer." Jason rolled his eyes at her, but followed her lead nonetheless.

After reaching the pizza food truck and having their fill of greasy pepperoni, they began to walk toward the nearest subway entrance. Unfortunately for Lola, they kept bumping against strangers along the way. Her anxiety mounted ever so slightly while going through these exchanges. She wasn't always the best in crowded situations, but she recognized it enough that it became easier to handle the more practice she had. Sadly, this was the kind of instance that made her feel like she had to stop somewhere. There was a small store just ahead that made a great excuse to get out of the crowd.

"Wait," Lola told Jason before he tried to make his escape, not realizing she wouldn't be following. "I'm going to grab some more water." She threw away the empty bottle that she slightly lied about wanting to replace and walked inside the store. She wasn't sure why she had lied to Jason, especially because she knew he would have understood that she was anxious, he always does. It also didn't help that the continuous sweat dripping into her deep brown eyes made her feel like she was being bombarded by her own body.

As soon as they walked inside they almost regretted the

3

decision—it was even hotter in the store than it was outside. Lola was convinced that the smoldering asphalt had somehow found its way over the sidewalk and through the walls. Unfortunately for them, the only air conditioning was placed by the cashier and therefore they had little need to linger.

Lola walked toward the back of the tiny store where the fridges were lined up against the wall. As she walked through the cereal and dog food aisle, she caught a glimpse of someone who looked oddly familiar. She didn't know anyone in the city, but she had a feeling she knew this person. She almost craned her neck to get a better look, but her concentration was broken as soon as she saw the water bottles.

When she reached the broken refrigerator that held the sweating bottles of water, among other sweaty containers of varying liquids, she caught another glimpse of that person she thought she might know. She was wracking her over-heated brain trying to figure out if she really did know that person, and then found herself quickening her steps to get a better view. She stopped by the laundry detergent shelves while continuing to almost creepily observe.

This person who Lola couldn't keep her eyes off of was a woman with short graying-brown hair. The woman was patiently picking apples, and quite a few of them as far as Lola could tell. She was wearing a distinguishable red-beaded necklace, oval sunglasses, and a colorful house dress with two pockets in the front.

Lola watched as the woman continuously picked one apple after another and placed them in her adorable little wicker hand-basket, which to her surprise was not getting full for such a small carrier. From the time Lola started watching the woman, she had put at least a dozen apples in her basket—none of which she could actually see in the basket.

"Lola!" Jason called out as he reappeared next to her. "What are you doing? Let's get out of here. I don't know how much longer I can stay semi-dry."

Lola shushed him without ceasing to watch the woman intently. "That woman looks like my aunt," she finally said, knowing that it couldn't possibly be her. "She looks so much like her, it's freaking me out."

Jason squinted his eyes, making it a little too obvious that they were looking at her. "She really does," he whispered. "Come on, I'm sweating through my shirt."

"Hold on," Lola told him. "I want to try something." She quietly stepped closer to the woman, but not too close. She stopped in front of the asparagus which was obviously wilting judging by the smell. She crinkled her nose, held her breath, and stood firmly, prepared to embarrass herself.

"Tia!" She called out in Spanish. The woman did not move or seem to take notice of Lola calling out. *One more time, just to be sure.* "Tia Mari!"

To Lola's surprise the woman stopped selecting apples and became extremely rigid. Without turning around, the woman slowly began to walk toward the exit and past the register, not even bothering to pay.

"What is going on?" Lola asked herself under her breath. Without giving it a second thought she started to follow the woman.

"Hey, what are you doing?" Asked Jason as he stopped her by grabbing her shoulder.

"I don't know what's going on, but that's my aunt—I know it is," she explained while releasing his grip.

"That's impossible," he assured her. "You know she's back home. I think the heat is really getting to you." He tried to pat some sweat off of her forehead with his bandanna, but she stopped him.

"No, that's her," Lola said as she escaped him and sped out of the muggy store. The sun blinded her for a moment as she searched for the woman she thought was her aunt. Luckily she spotted the red beaded-necklace and continued her impromptu pursuit.

"Tia Mari!" She called out to the woman as she shuffled through the people in her way.

"What are you doing?" Yelled Jason as he chased Lola through the sea of over-heated New Yorkers.

The woman's pace picked up and she was so short that Lola kept losing sight of her. She spotted her again, crossing a major street with the rest of New York City. There were so many people in her way, but Lola still managed to significantly catch up. She finally got so close to the woman that there was no doubt in her mind that this was her aunt. They reached the sidewalk on the other side of the street and with one mile-long stretch of her arm, Lola grabbed the woman's shoulder and turned her around.

She couldn't believe what she was seeing—it was her aunt— right there in New York City. The same aunt who hasn't traveled outside of Nevada in decades—the same aunt who could barely speak English, let alone get around a city like this by herself. Was this a dream? A hallucination? Lola's mind was trying to draw a million different conclusions all at once.

Whatever thoughts that were racing through her mind were broken instantly when she heard a bone-chilling scream coming from the street they had just crossed. She turned around, her hand still on her aunt's shoulder, and was stunned by what she saw. It was Jason. He was lying on the hot pavement in front of a yellow taxi surrounded by people.

Lola felt like her head had swollen up and she found herself running to him without realizing it. She could hear nothing but the muffled noises of everyone around them. Her heart was beating so fast that everything seemed to be moving in slow motion. Her shock turned into panic as she knelt down and lifted his bloodied head from the blistering pavement. She could think of nothing that would help him. Her cries consumed and pierced the ears of everyone watching. She could do nothing and she knew it.

Not moments later, her aunt reappeared and knelt down next to them. She rested her hand on the back of Jason's head as Lola cradled it. Lola could see her aunt's hand holding his head and seconds later, what seemed to be a faint purple light coming from her palm. Lola was too dazed to believe what she was seeing. After a few more seconds, aunt Mari helped him sit up by supporting his head and upper back.

To everyone's surprise Jason opened his eyes wide, like his heart had been injected with a mug full of espresso. The crowd was in awe, the most astonished of all being Lola. She was shaken up and confused, but she didn't care because Jason was alive.

"All right, all right," shouted an unfamiliar voice. "Nothing to see here folks. The boy is fine—he's okay."

Lola looked up slightly from where she was and saw that the voice belonged to her aunt. She didn't know what to say, especially because she had never heard her speak such perfect English in her entire life.

Aunt Mari didn't look at Lola, she just dusted herself off as if nothing had happened and started to walk away. Before Lola could even catch her breath, Jason also stood up and left Lola on the ground without so much as a warning.

Light-headed and bewildered, Lola did not get up right away. She watched her boyfriend follow her aunt back to the sidewalk as the crowd parted for them.

"What is going on?"

Chapter 2

Lola stood up as soon as she could. She wobbled to get on her feet, but straightened out after a couple of steps. "Jason! Jason, where are you going? We need to take you to a hospital!" Lola's shouting proved useless as she wrestled through the crowd of people, inching closer to her fleeing boyfriend.

She was so baffled and slightly heart-broken. Why was Jason walking away from her if she was desperately calling out to him? Why was her aunt just as persistent on keeping her distance and ignoring her?

"That's it!" Lola grunted, completely frustrated. She muscled her way through the crowds with some new found speed, using her shoulders to plow people to the side. As soon as she was able to, she grabbed Jason's hand and spun him around to face her.

"What are you doing?" She asked him with despair in her trembling voice. "Don't you understand that we need to take you to a hospital?" The heat was getting to her and she felt as though she might collapse at any moment. All she wanted was to know what was going on, but she was getting nothing from him. He pulled his hand away with little trouble and continued walking, completely unfazed by her.

"Oh, no you don't," she protested taking his hand once more and trying even harder to make him stop. This proved to be pointless because it only resulted in her being dragged along as she dug her heels into the concrete.

"No more!" Lola screamed trying to hold back tears. "I've had enough of this. I'm calling an ambulance and you are both going to the hospital even if I have to knock you over the head myself." Jason didn't answer, but continued to stare blankly in front of him as he followed Lola's aunt. The scene was outrageous at best—Jason soaked in blood and sweat, and Lola trying to control him—she would have had better luck moving a brick wall.

The searing heat relentlessly beat down on them and to Lola's surprise it didn't affect Jason whatsoever—she on the other hand was losing strength, fast. She was so exhausted and desperate that she could think of no other solution to their defiance besides giving in and hoping they would soon stop.

Not even five minutes later, Lola's aunt finally halted at the entrance of the ugliest building on the block. The building was in no way modern—the classic carved stone edging was enough to give it away. The countless top-rounded windows of the five story hunk of brick also made sure that its age was never mistaken.

As they entered the building there was an immediate coolness that helped Lola level out her thoughts. The only light inside the building was coming from half a dozen windows that were no longer covered up by the black plastic that covered the others.

Lola's mind continued to collect itself and as it did her worries crept back in. She looked around only to see that everything was covered in dust. The smell she was experiencing could only be described as the grunginess you come across when cleaning out the attic.

The carpet, although covered in dust, could still be seen as a dark shade of red. There were multiple sets of black double doors on the back wall and a long balcony right above them that was being held up by decorative stone pillars. Lola had been in enough theaters in her life to know one when she saw it, even if it did look like it was over a hundred years old and moldy.

"It's an opera house," aunt Mari told her. "A very old one." It was almost like she had read her mind.

"This place is abandoned," Lola said, just realizing what was going on. "We shouldn't be here. We can get into a lot of trouble. I'm calling an ambulance." She pulled out her phone with shaky hands, but as soon as she did, it was snatched from her by an emotionally unresponsive Jason, who immediately threw it clear across the long lobby.

"Are you kidding me?" She said, ready to explode. "I am not playing around! Why did you do that?"

"Because I made him," aunt Mari said without missing a beat.

Lola turned around to look at her aunt with eyes that could send an army running for their lives. "What do you mean, you made him?" Lola questioned rigidly, her head tweaking almost mechanically to the side.

"He's not going with you," aunt Mari told her. "Neither am I."

The anger Lola felt after hearing those words was unfathomable—it spilled out of her as a borderline panic attack. She slid her hands down her legs as she bent over to hyperventilate in anger. She couldn't believe how insane this day had gotten in less than an hour. Her head was swelling up with pressure and there was very little she could do to calm herself down. Every sound she heard was muffled as she continued to isolate her mind from all of the frustration. She almost didn't notice Jason retreating and following Lola's aunt to the opposite side of the dingy lobby.

It pained Lola to stand up straight, but she was not about to lose the battle to these unmistakably dehydrated and delusional people that she cared so much about. "What are you doing now?" Lola asked, as if she were talking to mischievous children.

Jason and her aunt had reached the only elevator in sight and were pulling the rusted iron cage-door open. Lola rolled her eyes as any exasperated person would at the sight of yet another annoying antic.

"Don't do that," she told them half-heartedly as she quickly retrieved her phone and then promptly sped over to them. She managed to reach the elevator and lodged herself in the way before they were able to close the gate.

"Both of you—get out—now!" She scolded them.

"I know you mean well," aunt Mari told her. "But you have no idea what's going on."

"All right," Lola agreed. "Why don't you go ahead and enlighten me while we stand in this hundred-year-old elevator, because why the hell not? Seems safe enough. Just another thing to add to our list of lunacy for the day—right next to you being able to speak English and me having a zombie boyfriend."

"You weren't supposed to see me," explained her aunt sullenly. "I had no idea that any of you would be on this side of the country today."

"Okay crazy lady, let's get you to the hospital," Lola said mockingly as she began to dial 9-1-1. She offered her hand to lead them both out, but instead her aunt dipped her own hand into her coat pocket and pulled out a small glass vial that looked like it contained pink glitter.

"Don't worry," her aunt assured her. "He will be okay, and you won't remember any of this."

"The hell I won't!" Lola exclaimed as she shoved her way into the elevator.

"Get her out of here," Lola's aunt ordered Jason. He quickly took hold of her by the shoulders and led her out backwards. She tried to push back but there was almost no budging him.

"That's it!" Lola let out with intense anger. She couldn't let them hurt themselves even more and she had to do whatever it took to make sure that they were taken care of. With slight hesitation she stomped on Jason's foot, fairly hard—and if she was being honest, it was much deserved. He let go immediately and fell to the floor, but not before grabbing the lever in a failed attempt to stay standing. The elevator jolted violently causing the two women to join Jason on the floor.

"No!" Yelled aunt Mari as she lunged for the lever. The

13

elevator plummeted like a terrifying amusement park ride, and less like the smoothness of an actual elevator. The hanging lamp swung back and forth enough times that it shattered the cover, leaving nothing but a flickering light bulb and even more fear.

Lola was out of ideas and the only thought that came to mind was Jason lying on the ground, blank faced. She crawled over and struggled to hold onto him as the pull of gravity tried to stop her. She hoisted her right arm on top of him, foolishly thinking that she would protect him from certain death. Even with her heart climbing out of her throat she was determined to not let any further harm come to him.

Without warning the elevator stopped and all three of them were flung to the roof like a bunch of old rag dolls. At the same time, almost out of nowhere, dozens upon dozens of apples appeared as if they had been dumped on purpose. Right away the air filled with the aroma of the freshly smashed apples that did not survive the impact.

After a few seconds of slight unconsciousness, Lola slowly opened her eyes. Her vision was blurry and her ears were ringing terribly—she was more confused than ever. Lola's aunt was next to her yelling something she couldn't understand while gathering up the enormous amount of apples that spontaneously appeared. Luckily the ringing began to fade away and Lola's vision was correcting itself little by little.

"Look what you've done!" Her aunt bellowed. "I was trying to help you and now we're really in trouble. I can't believe I got myself into this! I should have never tried to save him."

Him!

Lola turned to her other side to find her boyfriend still stoic.

14

"Are you all right?" She asked, panic running through her veins as she smoothed her hands over his head pretending to know what to look for. "Please! Just say something."

"He's not going to say anything," her aunt said, as if it were stupid for Lola to ask him to talk.

There was dismay everywhere—literally, the walls were covered in it. Aunt Mari was mumbling some choice words to herself, while Lola checked Jason for more signs of life. The elevator creaked and settled in a few more inches before a small *ding* indicated that it was now safe to step out.

Chapter 3

"Call 9-1-1!" Lola demanded as she helped Jason sit up against the red carpeted-walls of the century-old elevator. "What are you waiting for?" She was in disbelief that her aunt wasn't understanding the gravity of the situation.

The shattered ceiling lamp was beginning to steady and the flickering slowly ceased. The insanity it was ensuing on Lola began to subside and she started to realize just how much trouble they were actually in.

She looked to her left through the old, rusted gate of the elevator, only to find almost complete darkness. The only light was coming from medieval-looking golden torches attached to the walls of this tunnel. The lights were few and far apart, which made it harder to figure out exactly what was down there.

She barely noticed that the absence of words were replaced with the sound of harmonious dripping water. The cavernous tunnel echoed the sounds of the water that gracefully hit the floor, creating an ominous feeling of helplessness inside of her. A waft of cold, earthy air was the final element that brought Lola to the realization that 9-1-1 might not be enough to get them out of this one.

"What have you done?" Lola asked her aunt, holding back tears, continuing to comfort Jason by resting her hand on the back of his head.

"I didn't do anything," her aunt responded as she stopped picking up apples. "Your ludicrous stunt brought us here and broke any chance we had of getting back—at least any time soon."

"No," Lola yelped in disbelief. She stood up frantically and started pulling the elevator lever back and forth thinking that somehow that would fix it. The lever made clicking sounds as it was manhandled from one side to the other.

"Stop. Stop. Stop," aunt Mari told her, reaching for the lever to prevent Lola from continuing.

"We have to keep trying!" Lola urged her as she fell to her knees without letting go of the lever—her long dark-brown hair no longer in a ponytail, but now curtaining her face. Her aunt squatted down next to her, but made no effort to comfort. She watched Lola sob for several seconds before deciding to be just a little sympathetic.

"Your name is Lola, right?" Her aunt asked, looking like she was meeting her for the first time. Lola peeked through her hair, enraged at the nonsense her aunt was asking.

"Of course that's my name," she responded with agitation. "What else would it be?"

Aunt Mari took a deep breath as if she were about to deliver the most devastating news. "I'm not who you think I am," she explained. "I'm not your aunt. My name isn't even Mari—it's Sonia." Several seconds of silence went by before anything else was said.

"Enough," Lola whispered delicately, dropping her gaze from obvious exhaustion—tears finally spilling out one at a time. "I've had enough. I'm not doing this with you anymore. Just please give me a couple of minutes to figure this out."

"You can't fix this," insisted the woman who was clearly her aunt, but was suffering from a delusional mental state.

"Don't tell me I can't fix this!" Lola screamed desperately. "You are being crazy and you need to let me think of how I'm going to get us all out of here—"

With a shushing sound and a snap of her fingers, Sonia silenced her. A soft glowing red light appeared inside of Lola's throat. Mesmerizingly, the glow ran from her throat and down her left arm to her hand where it transcended her skin until a marble-sized ball of radiance was visible between the two of them.

Lola's mouth fell wide open. She had watched this woman snap her fingers and produce a ball of light that caused her to lose her voice. It sounded impossible, but somehow she knew that tiny sphere was her voice.

Sonia promptly grabbed the little marble of light between her fingers and pushed it into a tiny bottle, which she quickly corked. Lola was speechless, and not just because she was missing her voice.

"Now do I have your attention?" Sonia asked, as she shook the bottle in front of Lola's face.

Lola stared at her with a frozen, frightened expression, but decided to concede as she slumped back against the elevator wall next to Jason.

"If you listen you will get this back," Sonia told her, putting the bottle into her dress pocket.

A single tear fell as Lola felt defeated and cornered by someone who practically raised her as a child. How could aunt Mari have hidden something so significantly impressive all these years? Did she not trust her family? Was she the only one who didn't know?

"I need you to pay close attention," Sonia started saying, still crouched next to them. "I've kind of messed up, and now you can't go home—at least not yet."

Lola's bewilderment was unmistakable by the look on her dumbstruck face—she had no idea what Sonia was talking about.

"Your boyfriend is in very bad condition," she continued explaining, clearly struggling. "You saw what happened, you're not stupid—you know that nobody walks away from an accident like that without a miracle. If you want to save his life you have to do everything exactly as I tell you. I promise I will explain as we go, but we don't have much time now. Do you understand?"

Lola nodded furiously, scared out of her wits and tears silently streaming down her blood-rushed cheeks.

"You can have this back when we leave the tunnel," Sonia promised, patting the pocket that contained Lola's voice. "If I tell you to do something, you do it—don't hesitate, don't stop, and don't you dare react to anything you see—you will never get your voice back if you do." Lola nodded again, this time wiping away remnants of her tears and mascara.

"Get up," Sonia told her. "Get him up too."

Sluggishly Lola managed to stand up pulling Jason with her. Her arm stayed intertwined with his as it usually had in happier circumstances. Sonia quickly picked up the rest of her apples and put them back into her little basket, where they disappeared. Lola couldn't figure out why Sonia was so concerned about her apples or how she was making them vanish, but after everything that had happened, Sonia's devotion to her apples was the least of her concerns.

"Exactly as I say," Sonia reminded her one more time as she struggled to open the iron elevator gates.

They all stepped out of the elevator with Sonia leading the way, as Lola protectively guarded Jason. Lola took a peek back at the elevator and it looked completely out of place in the gloomy tunnel, but she had neither the voice nor the energy to question it.

As they began their walk down the dreary tunnel, Lola began to take notice of her surroundings. Her eyes scanned the space for any imminent danger that might be lurking around. If there was anything more to be scared of, she could bet it was in that tunnel.

Although she could barely see anything in front of her, she was at least able to tell that the tunnel was constructed out of jumbo bricks. As she continued looking at the walls, she could've sworn there was a dark purple gleam to them as if they were made out of glass. She was so concentrated on whether or not she was imagining the shine of the bricks that she hadn't noticed that Sonia was slowing down.

Lola opened her mouth to ask why they were slowing down, but nothing came out. Her anxiety rose at the thought of so much vulnerability. She looked over at Jason, but he didn't look back at her like he usually does with his reassuring side smile. He was facing forward with uncommonly good posture and zero expressions. His face had flashes of illumination as they kept walking past each set of torches, and Lola started to realize how much taller he was compared to her. Six inches of height never seemed so intimidating to her before today. The more they walked and the more she kept looking up at him, the more she felt like she was shrinking. How in the world was she supposed to protect him when she felt like the size of a squirrel?

Lola hated that she wasn't in control of this situation. Between Jason's obliviousness and Sonia's command, she felt useless. She had to do whatever Sonia demanded if she was ever going to speak again, and despite how calm Sonia's threats were, they were still threats. It was at that point that Lola realized she had to come up with a plan to escape, but not before Sonia fixed both her and Jason. Right as a slight speck of an idea started to form, Sonia began to slow down again.

"Don't cry, don't sweat, don't run away," Sonia ordered. It was evident that she could see, or at least sense that something was coming up, something that Lola couldn't. The more they walked, the slower the pace became and Lola could feel that Sonia was also getting nervous. They took a few more steps and all at once, like a rush of

21

unexplainable adrenaline, it became very apparent why it was for the best that Lola didn't have her voice.

Chapter 4

As dark and mysterious as the tunnel was, there was no mistaking what was right in front of them. Lola's jaw was close to coming unhinged at the sight of a terrifyingly real...angel! He was positioned directly behind a very tall podium, and the lack of lighting was only helping him look more petrifying. She wanted so much to believe that this celestial being was not actually there, but at that point there was little that would convince her of that.

She stared at him intently, dragging her eyes over every one of his features. The angel had long copper-colored hair that effortlessly sat behind his ears, a chiseled warrior-like face that looked completely unhappy, pure-white feathery wings that spanned at least five feet, and he was wearing a floor-length brown robe accompanied by a sword on his hip. He was nothing like the angels Lola pictured in catholic school as a child. Not only did she believe the angel could smite them without warning, but now she was sure they were dead. Why else would they be standing in front of an angel that possessed the face of pure judgement? They had obviously died when the elevator fell. Now all she could think of was what would happen to her family. She had accidentally abandoned them and didn't even get the chance to say goodbye.

"Sonia!" Boomed the angel's deep authoritative voice. That definitely didn't snap Lola out of her despair. "What are you claiming?"

Sonia handed her basket to the angel without hesitation. She looked cool and collected, almost as if she had done this before.

"Seventy-four apples," she told the angel. She stepped back from the podium as the angel peered into the basket for no more than a second.

"Who are they and why are they here?" Asked the angel looking directly at Lola and Jason. His slight accent sounded almost Russian, but it was hard to tell.

"They're my mannequins," replied Sonia, clearly confident that she had a legitimate excuse for having two strangers with her.

"Is one of them broken?" the angel asked arching one eyebrow. Sonia swung around to look at them only to find that Lola was still gawking at him and his wings. She reached for Lola's face and lifted her jaw into place while giving her a stern, burning look.

"I don't recall you leaving with any mannequins," the angel continued to speculate. He leaned in over his podium to take a closer look.

"Well, that's because they were in my basket in case I needed them," Sonia was oozing confidence, so much so that Lola's nerves had begun to settle. "They're new. I decided to test them out on this trip.

I'm working on getting them to talk at-will for better camouflage, but obviously they're not working out too well."

"What happened to the male?" He asked. Jason looked like he had gone through a meat grinder—his clothes were completely mangled and he was covered in blood.

"I'm testing out the look," Sonia answered as if it were true. "He keeps other people away, but you know what, you're right—he is a little distracting."

"He looks familiar," said the angel, probably trying to catch her off guard.

"Does he?" She asked, pretending it was humorous. She turned around to face the two of them, holding one hand under her chin as if she were deciphering a puzzle. "What do you know? He kind of does look like the baker's son." She played it off as if she was amused by her own work. "They all sort of blur together after a while."

The angel did not looked convinced for a second. "The female is undoubtedly modeled after your niece. Do you not think it dangerous to use a mannequin that looks like her next to yourself in Terre One?"

"Oh—well—I made sure to check that there would be no one that would recognize me in the vicinity," Sonia assured him in her continuously tranquil manner. "There's really no need to fuss, they're just mannequins. Watch." Sonia turned around and made direct eye contact with Lola. "You, slap him."

Lola's eyes widened but Sonia promptly mouthed, *now*, through gritted teeth. Lola's hesitation was almost unnoticeable. She rigidly turned to face Jason and quickly landed a believable slap to his left cheek, which warranted no response like expected.

"You see?" Sonia asked in a false irritated voice. "They're just hunks of flesh. Honestly Sebastian, this is a little embarrassing for you. I mean, I could be half way back to my lab right now. Don't you realize how much work I still have to do to convince the council to let me proceed? To be wasting my time like this is quite frankly mediocre of you."

Sebastian looked taken aback, but nodded his head and almost acknowledged Sonia as being superior. "My apologies, Sonia," he said with a hint of wounded pride in his voice. He handed her the basket and replaced his wings to their resting position.

"Thank you Sebastian," she said exuding confidence. "You two, let's go." Lola did not hesitate that time. She nonchalantly took Jason's hand and followed Sonia past Sebastian and his podium.

As soon as he was out of sight, and more importantly out of earshot, Sonia reached into her dress pocket and produced the small glass bottle that held a familiar red glow. She unstoppered it and took Lola's left hand so she could dump the contents into it.

Even though she still didn't want to believe, Lola could not help but be astonished. The little ball of warmth floated above her hand and its energy called to her.

Sonia put the bottle back in her pocket and immediately smashed her hand down onto Lola's hand to make the energy ball go back where it came from. The light traveled up Lola's arm, past her shoulders, and into her throat.

"I'm giving this to you early, but just because you have your voice back does not mean you *should* talk," Sonia told her.

"Are you kidding me?" Lola asked bewildered, trying hard not to freak out. "How am I supposed to stay calm if you don't tell me what's going on? What the hell was that back there? Am I dead? Are we all dead?"

"You're not dead," Sonia said with a snippy attitude. "Don't look back, just keep walking or you'll look suspicious."

"I'll look suspicious?" Lola asked sarcastically as she gestured her arms to the empty space. "If anyone here is suspicious it's you! Since when can you speak English? You might want to start talking, *Sonia.*"

Sonia stopped in her tracks and hung her head in exasperation. She rubbed her eyes and let out a heavy sigh knowing that this was going to take a lot of explaining. "Your boyfriend is gravely injured," she whispered.

Lola nodded as the solemnness crept back in. It was hard to believe that he was actually hurt, given that he was standing right there without a single moan from ache. She could see his chest rise as he breathed, but she knew things weren't right.

"I will answer your questions," Sonia assured her. "But for any of this to work—to help him—you have to believe every single thing that I tell you. I am not pulling your leg, I am not trying to insult your intelligence, and I am not your aunt. Do you understand?"

Lola gave her one more quick nod as she put on her brave face. Sonia nodded back in acknowledgment and then continued to

27

walk forward. Lola once again took Jason's hand and cradled it in hers as they followed.

"So, if you're not my aunt, who are you?" Lola asked, still thinking there was no way this wasn't the same person that used to braid her hair.

"I'm Sonia," she answered. "Technically I'm not related to you either." Lola didn't understand how this could be possible, but she didn't have to wonder long because Sonia knew what she was going to ask next. "What you really want to know is why I look exactly like your aunt." Lola stayed quiet not wanting to miss anything Sonia was about to tell her.

"You and I live in completely separate places, and by that I mean different dimensions," Sonia said that so casually and almost convincingly.

Lola stifled a laugh by pressing her lips tight, but that only made them curl up. She even had to close her eyes before asking, "Are you crazy? "Do you expect me to believe you've mastered inter-dimensional travel and you do it just to buy apples?"

"You really don't have a choice, do you?" Sonia retorted. "Besides, you have to believe me for this to work, remember?"

As demented as all of this sounded, Sonia was right. Lola didn't have a choice, especially now that she didn't know where they were. She was going to have to rely on Sonia without question, although she still wasn't completely sure they weren't dead.

"Fine," Lola conceded still being completely unconvinced. "Just tell me what you did to him."

"It was a spell," Sonia said like it was no big deal—like she wasn't an inch from falling off the edge into cuckoo land.

"Spell?" Lola asked, because she obviously heard wrong. "Like magic?"

"Like magic," Sonia confirmed. "I'm controlling his mind and body so that he remains unconscious and can't feel the pain. I've also regulated his vital organs to work at a fraction of a normal pace, to slow down the process of him dying."

"Why can't you stop him from dying if you really *can* do magic?" Lola asked as she played along with the lunacy.

"Because that requires more work and I don't normally carry that potion with me," Sonia replied.

"So, we're going to take him to a hospital, right?" Lola asked enthusiastically assuming that was the only logical idea.

"No," Sonia responded immediately. "No one can know you are here. If we take him to the hospital they will report me for bringing you to our dimension and they will let him die." Lola's face froze in horror. She couldn't possibly be telling the truth. No hospital would just let someone die.

"Why would they do that?" Lola was becoming more terrified by the second.

"Because we are not supposed to interfere with the lives of people outside of our dimension," Sonia told her. "There's always a chance that interference could cause catastrophe, which is precisely why I am helping you. I hate to admit it, but I was a bit careless this time around by not checking to make sure none of you would be in

New York. I have to set things right without the authorities finding out."

Lola kept silent after hearing this. She wanted to trust her instincts that were telling her this was all impossible, but she couldn't bring herself to be convinced of that—not after everything she had just seen. She stared down at the rocky path feeling defeated and lost—the dimness of the tunnel also wasn't helping her morbid mood.

"Do you believe me?" Sonia asked cautiously, but also not really caring whether Lola did or not.

"I really don't have a choice, do I?" Lola snarked.

Sonia concealed a little smirk at Lola's words. "Do you have any more questions?" Lola had a million questions. How could she not? Everything was happening so fast that she could barely keep up.

"Why was that angel questioning you?" Lola asked. "Also, why did you tell me to slap Jason?"

"Didn't you see?" Sonia said. "He wasn't believing me. Besides, I couldn't very well have him slap you, now could I?" Sonia asked, as if it were common sense. "You were giving us away with that stupid look on your face. We had to convince him you were mannequins."

"Right," Lola said pretending she knew what she was agreeing to. "And mannequins would be what, exactly?"

"Exactly what it sounds like except ours move, look like real humans, and are occasionally used as camouflage in Terre One," Sonia explained without missing a beat. For her this seemed tedious, almost like talking to a child. Her patience was thinning, and Lola could surmise that she wasn't used to this kind of attention.

"I'm assuming Terre One is where I'm from," Lola said catching on.

"Yes."

"Yeah, I guess that name makes sense," Lola said with unwarranted smugness.

"Can you watch the attitude around here?" Sonia said. "The last thing we need is some of your first-world cockiness following us around." Just as her insult landed, she held out her arm in front of them. Lola didn't know why they had to stop. All she could see was exactly what she had been seeing—a dull, water dripping, brick tunnel with no end in sight.

Making her way to the wall, Sonia reached for the torch closest to them and pulled it out of its holder. She held the bottom end of the torch to her face and ran her thumb over three rings that were molded onto it. Lola kept a close eye on every one of Sonia's movements, as an inexplicable chill ran up her spine. Her eyes kept darting back and forth and she was nervously hoping Sonia knew what she was doing.

"All right," Sonia started to say as she visibly tensed up. "As soon as we pass through, speak to no one. Are we clear?" Lola nodded quickly, as a knot in her stomach started to form. "If someone starts to speak to you, pretend to be sick and cover your mouth or something. Stay close and don't make eye contact."

Hearing all of Sonia's instructions was giving Lola palpations. She was hard to scare but all of this—the tunnel—Jason's injuries—not knowing where they were—it was sure doing some damage to her psyche.

Sonia pushed both of them back to make room for something. She pointed the flaming torch at the ground and started walking to the other side of the vast tunnel in a straight line. It only took seconds for her efforts to pay off. Three quarters of the way down, she struck her goal. A burst of violet flames ignited in front of her, creating a singular narrow strip of fire reaching the ceiling.

"What the hell?" Lola said as she jumped back. She pulled Jason to her but almost immediately realized it wouldn't have saved him from anything. He towered over her, and although she wasn't that short, what could she really do to protect him right then?

"Come—quickly," Sonia ordered as she waved them to her. "We're going to step through to get to the other side, and yes I know it's fire, but we'll be fine. You're going first." Her eyebrows smoothly indicated at Lola.

"What? Why?" Lola asked all jittery.

"So that I can make sure you don't run back the way we came," Sonia told her as she pulled her by her elbow and led her toward the fire. Lola assertively yanked her arm away and pulled Jason back with her.

"You will be fine," Sonia said. She punched through the fire and Lola instinctively yelped. "See?" It looked like another everyday occurrence for her. "One more thing," she said as she grabbed Lola by

her shoulders and forced her to face the flames. "Do not freak out."
Without a second thought she was shoved through the purple inferno.
There were elegant violet flames all around her and not a single ounce
of pain. Within two seconds she was out and nowhere near the dingy
tunnel.

Chapter 5

Lola came through to the other side with no more than a couple of misplaced hairs. Sonia had pushed her through what seemed like dangerously painful fire, only to emerge completely unharmed. Her eyes were still shut. She didn't want to risk opening them, not knowing if she was still engulfed in flames.

"Oh for crying out loud!" Sonia said as she threw her arms up in the air. "Just open your eyes." She was beginning to feel more and more like a babysitter at her wits' end. "And don't think about running back. You'll never find your way out."

Hoping with all her might that she was out of harm's way, Lola slowly opened both eyes. She had them shut so tight that they had begun to water, but as soon as she had taken a peek, she was immediately astonished. Everything she witnessed was unreal and beyond explanation. All around them was lush, vibrant grass that made the rolling hills look like something out of an exquisite oil painting. Off in the distance she could see the unimaginable sight of brilliantly colored mushrooms the size of houses—there was an apple-green one with yellow mix-matched stripes and a smaller cotton candy-pink one right next to it.

Actually trying to concentrate didn't help Lola's brain soak up the information any faster. The harder she tried to take everything in, the more the air around her started to buzz—or was that actual buzzing? Lola could swear the irritating sound was coming from the flapping of the humming birds that danced by.

Her mind was working on fumes and everything her eyes were absorbing was not helping. She had to crouch down and stare at the gravel beneath her for balance. As she lay both hands on the sandy packed dirt, she could feel its realness. She was a vivid lucid dreamer and had been since she was a kid, so she knew when she was dreaming…this wasn't a dream.

"Are you done?" Sonia asked, looking around like she had something to hide from patrons walking by. "You're embarrassing me."

Lola stood up slowly, but even then, her head felt woozy. One more deep breath and she would be ready to make the first step.

"Come on," Sonia told her. "We can't waste time."

They began to walk down the path that led to both the tunnel they had just come out of, and apparently a nearby town. Lola, still transfixed, looked behind from whence they came. She saw a dark tunnel the size of a five-story building that was made from the same glistening, glass-like purple bricks she had seen when they were inside. It was beautiful but disorienting at the same time. The mountain that contained the tunnel was odd for the mere fact that it looked out of place—a small detail that really made Lola wonder where they were.

The entrance of the town was only a couple of yards away. Lola quickly assumed they would be going to the main part of the town just by what she could see from the outside, and because there was plenty of pedestrian traffic heading the same way. There was a beautifully made sign on the way that said:

Welcome to Lunding
A Wonderfully Magical Place To Call Home

She could see the old European-influenced shops from where they were walking. They reminded her of pictures she had seen of quaint German towns like Rothenburg. There were people walking by in garments Lola had only seen in cartoons where becoming a princess was a common occurrence. Words could not escape her, even though her mouth was embarrassingly drawn open. The entire scene was remarkably ethereal.

"I need you to take a deep breath," Sonia told her as she demonstrated exactly how deep the breath needed to be. "Are you going to be okay?" Her biggest worry at that very moment was that Lola would lose her mind trying to rationalize everything that she was seeing.

"Where are we?" Lola stuttered—her eyes' rapid blinking was also in need of some control.

"For now, let's just say you're still on Earth," Sonia said calmly, almost as if Lola were a delicate child. "I can explain more later, but right now we have to go." She grabbed Lola by the elbow and gently pulled her along. Jason needed no help in following. He had even broken away from Lola by that point.

As Lola was being pulled through the old-timey town, she took in as much as her eyes could capture. No one was dressed like them and nothing looked normal or modern except for the concrete sidewalks that lined the cobblestone streets. Those streets were overrun by several horse-drawn wagons—some carrying fruits, others carrying flowers, and the rest carrying who knows what.

The shops they passed were undoubtedly charming and almost made Lola feel like the people were going to break out in song around the fountain in the square. All of the buildings had triangular roof tops and windows of all shapes. Some of those windows were adorned with planters hanging just outside of them. The best part was that each shop was a different color, and some were more than one color due to the eccentric trim around the windows and doors.

"Good afternoon Sonia," they kept hearing from every passer-by. Sonia acknowledged these people with frank nods and nothing more. She was on a mission to get off of the streets and out of public view, and for good reason. Jason was getting a little too much attention with his bloodied face and shirt.

Lola was tranced as she gathered sight after sight of bright colorful aspects of the town. The weather was perfect—the sun peered from behind cotton-white clouds, and that only added to the marvelous atmosphere. Every couple of minutes she would even get a whiff of freshly baked bread which made her drool, but only slightly.

She was so submerged in her surroundings that she almost ran into a festively adorned light pole. She had barely missed the pole when she noticed that the entire town was decorated with elegantly hung bunting fabric in blues, golds, and whites. They also walked past several florists and she noticed that they were all selling an assortment of beautiful blue and white bouquets that had been lightly dipped in gold glitter and were held together with gold ribbon.

As she kept looking around, Lola hadn't realized that Sonia had let go of her and that she was unconsciously following. They walked through the tunnel underneath the town clock tower and as soon as she emerged on the other side someone grabbed her by the hand and pulled her in for a tight hug.

"Mara! When did you get back?" Asked the perfect stranger that was now holding onto her. The stranger's dainty English accent still lingered in Lola's ears. The young woman stretched out her grip to get a better look at Lola.

Lola could usually lie convincingly on the spot but was absolutely caught off guard at that moment. She shrugged her shoulders and made a weird sound without talking.

Apart from a huge smile, the young woman had short black hair and a beautiful deep olive complexion. If Lola hadn't heard her speak, she would have guessed she was from India.

"What are you wearing?" Asked the young woman with a chuckle. "Have you been in Terre One all this time? What in the world were you doing there? I thought you were supposed to be—"

"There you are!" Sonia exclaimed, having finally found that Lola wasn't behind her. "Penelope, dear, how are you?" She asked not intending to let her answer. "Mara can't talk right now, her throat hurts —you understand. You'll have to catch up later. Bye-bye." Sonia resumed to pull Lola down the sidewalk without stopping. Lola looked back at Penelope and gestured to her throat apologetically.

"I'm starting to think you want to get caught," Sonia said exasperated. They reached an ugly building and stopped in front of it. This building did not have the same festive exterior that the others had, and in fact looked like a regular building she would have seen back home. The exterior walls were light gray and completely boring. In truth, it was disturbing the appearance of an otherwise adorable looking town. It was probably the same reason it was at the very edge of the town, right before the road broke off onto a scenic route. Sonia led them both Lola and Jason inside and then to the elevator.

"I think I've had enough elevator rides for today," Lola said coldly.

"Well, lucky for you we have stairs," Sonia said in a snarky tone. "Would you like to take them?"

Lola was not amused by her poorly delivered joke. She really was nervous about the elevator, but she couldn't make Jason go up the stairs with her, not in his condition. Rationalizing the odds of another elevator disaster made her decision to take it, easier. They rode the elevator to the third and last floor, only to find more gray sterile walls. Sonia walked to one of the two doors in the hallway and unlocked it. As they walked in Lola noticed the sign next to the door that read:

Sonia Cruz, Lead Researcher of Magical Sciences

As they entered, the first thing they saw was a receptionist's desk with nothing on it but a phone and a blank notepad. To the right of the desk was another door. Sonia opened it to reveal a laboratory. To no surprise, it was just as clean as every other part of the plain-looking building.

Every table in the lab was equipped with what Lola imagined was everything a proper lab would need. She identified what were beakers, vials, and all the other middle school things they were allowed to touch—but she had no idea what most of the other equipment was used for. As they continued to walk in, Lola noticed that the lab seemed to take up half of the entire third floor—granted, the building wasn't very large to begin with, but either way it took up a lot of space.

"So this is yours?" Lola inquired, already knowing the answer. "What do you do here?"

"Right now, I'm saving your boyfriend and that's all you need to know," Sonia said curtly.

"Why are you being so secretive?" Lola wanted to know, at the risk of sounding like a brat.

"Because you're not supposed to be here," Sonia's voice elevated slightly as she answered. "Because everything you see can be taken away from me if anyone finds out that I brought you here and that I was careless enough to not check that I wouldn't be recognized!" She took a deep breath having slightly lost it in her explanation. Lola could see a strike of fear that was fueling Sonia to the brim. She didn't say anything more, she just waited for Sonia to get a grip before asking anything else.

While Sonia tried to calm her nerves, Lola registered something that she hadn't before. There was something so different about who Sonia was as opposed to her own aunt. Probably no one could tell by looking at her at that very second, but she seemed like an extremely poised and intense person. She also acted like someone that would turn her nose up at you if you walked opposite of her on the sidewalk. Her demeanor was that of a stuck-up know-it-all that had a lot to lose—so why wasn't she being nicer? Lola was sure, she herself would never be this mean if she wanted someone to keep a devastating secret.

As those thoughts ran through her head, Lola walked Jason over to a chair. She looked at him intently as he sat down. Just watching him made her eyes foggy—he was still all bloody and bruised. His wounds had stopped bleeding thanks to Sonia, but they were still open.

"Can we use any of this stuff on him?" Lola asked, not bothering to look over at Sonia.

Sonia rolled her eyes but then walked over to a cabinet and started pulling things out. She gave Lola some antiseptic and soft towels. She also pulled out a vial with what looked like dark blue syrup, but Lola didn't pay it much attention—she was more concerned with making sure Jason was cleaned up. As she gently dabbed his wounds with the now wet towels, Lola became aware that Sonia was staring at her.

"Is everything okay?" Lola asked a bit creeped out. Sonia didn't answer right away, she just kept looking at her.

"Yes, it's just…" Sonia lost her train of thought for a second. "I've always been so fascinated by the fact that there is never even the slightest difference in appearance when it comes to the people from

41

both of our worlds," she said, continuing to look at Lola as if she were examining for a flaw.

"Yeah, it's weird," Lola said inching back a little, making sure not to make any sudden movements. "I still can't believe you're not my aunt." She continued to disinfect Jason's wounds hoping Sonia would look away. She was making her uncomfortable.

"Yes," Sonia said. "Other dimensions we've visited show differences in our doppelgängers, but not yours for some reason."

"That's…interesting," Lola said with a lump in her throat, still feeling like she was being dissected by Sonia's eyes. She was watching as Sonia absentmindedly played with the vial that she was holding. "Is that for him?"

"No," Sonia said after having to think about it for a second. She was distracted by something, but Lola couldn't tell by what. She walked over to the cabinet again and put the vial away. As she turned around to face the two of them, her pensive eyes looked past them and her forehead furrowed.

"Are you going to tell me what's going on?" Lola asked. "Where's that potion you were talking about? Let's heal him already so we can leave."

Sonia didn't produce the potion Lola was referring to, and for good reason. "I don't have it," she said.

"You told me you had it," Lola said rigidly. "Can't you just get some more?"

"I can't just get some more," Sonia told her with a hint of condescendence. "But I can make more."

Even before asking, Lola knew that she wasn't going to get the answer she wanted, "How long is that going to take?" Sonia didn't answer her right away, but she didn't have to—Lola understood that Jason wasn't going to be out of harm's way any time soon.

"You're going to have to stay for longer than I originally led on," Sonia told her. "But that doesn't mean we're not on a time crunch. I can't have anyone finding out that you're, *you*."

Even knowing somewhat the full extent of the consequences still made it difficult for Lola to grasp why being there would put them in so much danger. She found it hard to believe that a hospital would really let a person die just because he's not from around there. At the same time, she had to remind herself that as crazy as it sounded, she really was in a different dimension and couldn't risk assuming that this dimension exhibited humanity the same way as her dimension— although it wasn't hard to beat.

"Well, if I'm not supposed to be me, who am I?" Lola asked with little ardent curiosity. If anything, she probably already knew what Sonia was going to say.

"Mara," Sonia exhaled. "My niece." A pained expression crossed Sonia's face as she said her niece's name—it was hard to not notice.

Lola wasn't inherently a nosey person, she rather liked straying from the gossip, but this time she could tell it would find her regardless of her indifference. "So even though we're not related, I still look like your niece?" Lola asked, needing more clarification. In her view, there must be something relating them one way or another for Sonia to have the same family she did.

Sonia walked over to a desk that was consumed by papers and various academic instruments. She leaned toward the other side of the desk to pick up a poster that looked like it had fallen off. She unrolled the poster and tacked it to the white wall in front of them, covering up other papers in the way. The poster itself looked unusually plain, except for all the notes written on the margins—each with arrows pointing to a specific horizontal line segment. The lines were nothing more than that, just lines. Each line was labeled starting with the first one, *Terre One*. Below that was the line labeled, *Terre Two*, and so on.

Lola counted six black horizontal lines on this plain white poster. There was something there that she wasn't catching onto. She just kept staring at it hoping that by some chance she would all of a sudden know exactly what these lines were and why Sonia was showing them to her.

In the meantime, Sonia was rummaging through a desk drawer for something of importance. When she emerged she was holding a tiny black remote. She aimed it at a projector that was fixed above them and tried to turn it on, but nothing happened.

"I'm sure to everyone else it's pretty obvious what this is, but I could use some more information," Lola said, referring to the poster with the lines. Unfortunately, her slightly smug tone wasn't doing her any favors. She would never admit it out loud, but being a know-it-all herself, was something she occasionally took pride in. Not knowing what was going on reversed some of that pride. Smugness just happened to be a product of defending her intelligence.

"Patience must be your most prominent virtue," Sonia mocked, having heard the smug tone. Sadly, Lola was the only one there to catch the irony of her statement.

Lola walked over to the poster to see what was on it. Sonia's handwriting was hard to make out. One of the notes said, *intergalactic travel*, at least that's what she thought it said. Another one that was pointed at the fifth line segment read, *underwater colonization*—but again, hard to tell.

Lola kept scanning the poster to see if she could make out any more of the scribbles. The note at the top that had an arrow pointing at Terre One said, *Henry/unborn*. She had no idea what to make of any of this and just as she was going to ask about "Henry," she decided not to. She saw Sonia smacking the remote on her hand as she tried to get it to work, so it was probably not the best time.

After a few more taps, the remote finally turned the projector on. The image flickered like an old monitor. They were looking at computer files, only they weren't projected on the wall, they were projected in midair, like a hologram. Sonia used the remote to scroll through the files before clicking on the one she was looking for. The projector opened up an image of Earth—it floated freely in front of the lines poster.

Sonia set the remote down and walked over to the hologram of the planet. She put both hands in front of it and acted as if she could touch it, then she spread her hands over it like she was zooming in on a

45

computer screen. She kept zooming in until they were overlooking a town.

Lola's dumbfounded expression said it all. "How did you... never mind—magic—got it. What am I looking at?" At that point, Lola had no problem attributing everything unexplainable to magic—it was going to make this journey a lot easier for her.

"This is a bird's-eye view of the town," Sonia answered, slightly amused at Lola's astonishment. The hologram was mesmerizing. They could see every mountain peak, every tiny house, and every person going about their busy day.

"Are we still in the United States?" Lola asked, thinking it was a fair question.

"Iilerria," Sonia answered, with a pinch of pride in her otherwise serious manner. "Geographically you could say we're still in the United States, but don't say that out loud—we're in Iilerria."

Sonia motioned her hands above the hologram to zoom out. They were now looking at a satellite view of the United States—or Iilerria, in this case. The image multiplied and stacked on top of each other. Each image lined up with one of the line segments on the poster. Sonia placed her hands on each side of the hologram and proceeded to compress it and then ball it up like a piece of paper.

"Do I have to have magic to do that?" Lola asked, secretly hoping she would get to try it.

"It helps, but honestly I don't know," Sonia said. "We've never had someone from Terre One try it."

"Are you a witch?" Lola asked quietly, trying not to offend her. Even before she said it she had a feeling she should have phrased her question better, but it kind of just came out.

"Yes."

"Is everyone a witch?" In the back of her mind, Lola could sense the kid in her jumping up and down in amazement of the magical splendor, but she was an adult and as such had to act like one. Although to be living something that so many people, including herself, always dreamed of, was nothing short of a miracle to her.

"No, not everyone is a witch, but many people do use magic," Sonia told her. "Magic here isn't like any of the made-up stories that you've heard all your life. Even though it's still not fully understood, we don't see it as some completely mystical entity. To many of us, it's a science. We use it for medicine, transportation, environmental studies, and things you couldn't even imagine."

"You'd be surprised, I have dreams like this all the time," Lola responded trying to be witty to no avail. "So if the magic here is so amazing, why does everyone look like they rolled out of a Jane Austen novel?"

Sonia gave her a confused look. It was evident that she didn't understand the reference, but rather than inquire she just looked at her unblinkingly. She gave Lola a look that suggested that she wasn't planning on asking her to elaborate.

"Why does everything look so old-worldly?" Lola gave in with a slight attitude. She found it very difficult to get along with Sonia at any given moment. In the few hours that she had known her, she

47

realized that there was probably nothing she could do to get Sonia to be friendly toward her—even though this whole situation was mainly her fault.

"I'm not surprised that you would think so highly of yourself and where you come from that you wouldn't overlook the aesthetics of our town," Sonia said with a crooked smile. She looked to be rejoicing in some sort of teachable moment that was about to come, but before she continued, Lola cut in.

"I was actually asking out of curiosity," Lola said, a bit annoyed. "I happen to really like what you and your town have going on. I was just wondering why it isn't as modern as our world."

Sonia didn't take Lola's comments as her being bested, she merely continued as if Lola had not said anything. "We learned long ago that over-consumption would be the destroyer of our world. For the most part we take only what we need. We've been able to study your dimension for hundreds of years and we've seen what you've done to yourselves—and for what? For faster cars? For food you throw away? For land that makes your leaders feel more like rulers? It's fascinating, but also sad."

"Yeah, you're preaching to the choir here," Lola said, feeling a little ashamed by association. "If you're so much better than us, why keep studying us at all? What's the point?"

Sonia took a deep breath before answering. She almost started to speak but then stopped herself for a second thought. "No dimension is without their tribulations," Sonia confessed as her gaze trailed back to her basket of apples. "You have something we desperately need."

Before saying another word, she walked over to the line poster. She pointed at the first line and said, "There's a reason your dimension is named *One*." The projector spit out an image of an apple orchard.

Lola turned to look over at the apples in Sonia's basket, but they failed to give her the epiphany that pieced everything together. "Apples?" She asked thinking she was going to be wrong. "You desperately need apples?" At that same moment the low sound of booming bells rang out.

"I don't have time to explain," Sonia told her as she scrambled around for a purse that was laying around. "I'll explain when we get back."

"Get back from where?" Lola demanded as she rushed back to Jason.

Sonia nudged her toward the door as she pulled out some keys. She grabbed her basket with the apples and locked them in a pretty modern-looking safe.

"Wait!" Lola squeaked. "We have to help Jason."

"He's staying here," Sonia said, now pushing Lola out of the door.

"I can't leave him here," Lola insisted. "What if something happens to him?"

"Something's already happened to him," Sonia shot back. "Besides he's not going anywhere and I'm the only one who has access to my lab." She pointed a finger at him and said, "Sleep." He immediately closed his eyes and slumped in the chair.

"I can't leave him!" Lola protested.

"He'll live," Sonia assured her as she locked the door behind them. "For now."

Chapter 6

As they made their way out of the drab gray building, they were rejoined by the alluring aroma of freshly baked bread and a slightly less distinct scent of freshly cut flowers. Lola was no longer holding on to a glimmer of hope that this was all a dream. The fact that everything seemed so authentic—the people, the tug from Sonia's hand, and her unfamiliar brutish personality—that's what was making her acceptance of this, all the more real.

Sonia pulled her in the opposite direction of the town. It was interesting to Lola how easily the town was cut off as soon as they exited—there was no gradual dwindling of shops or anything. The only thing that led way to the exit was the cobblestones slowly sinking deeper into the ground until they met that sandy gravel road. On each side of the road were several of those horse-drawn wagons Lola had seen throughout the town. They were smaller up close and could only fit about four people, not including the driver.

"So you don't have cars?" Lola asked sort of surprised that they wouldn't at least have a faster mode of transportation.

"No," Sonia said nonchalantly. "They're more of a novelty since we have better ways of traveling long distances."

"Do you have airplanes?" Lola asked trying to seem like she wasn't that interested in the response.

"No," Sonia said, growing tired of these inconsequential questions.

"How about—"

"Please no more questions," Sonia blurted as she rubbed her temples. "Try to enjoy the view, or something."

They walked over to one of the wagons and climbed in. Sonia told the driver where to go and before Lola could take her seat, the wagon started moving. She fell forward over the seat, enough to have her upper body hang on the outside of the wagon for half a second. She saw that the back of the wagon had been decorated with a big white and blue bow with glittery gold trimming. Lola didn't think much of it until she remembered that everything in the town was decorated like that.

"Do you have a holiday coming up?" Lola asked, straightening herself out from the fall and looking back at the town's festive blue and gold decorations.

"I said no more…" Sonia sighed with exaggeration. "No, it's not a holiday." She must have realized it wasn't too fair for Lola to be told not to ask questions. "The Governor's son is returning and apparently it's a big deal to those of us who care, of which I am not one."

At that moment it occurred to Lola how oddly Sonia spoke. It was completely out of place for her to hear that manner of speaking, especially since she was used to her aunt only talking in Spanish. She wanted to ask more questions but refrained.

They rode the rest of the way in silence. Lola knew better than to ask where they were going—she figured that if it was of dire importance she would have been told. Instead she decided to take Sonia's advice and enjoy the view. In any other instance, Lola wouldn't mind just enjoying the perfectly green landscape and clear blue skies, but she couldn't stop thinking about Jason—at least, not right away.

Along the way they passed by the most peculiar-looking houses. These cozy, yet strange houses, didn't make sense. They looked almost normal until you spotted the crazy shape of the chimneys. These chimneys twisted up into a toppled spiral and were capped off with what looked like a triangular cover. They could even see smoke coming out of a few of them, only the smoke would come out in the shape of a spiral and dissipate in the same form. She couldn't grasp why they would need to be shaped like that in the first place. There had to be some sort of explanation, or maybe she was just trying too hard to use this as an excuse to not think about Jason.

"This place just keeps getting weirder and weirder," Lola commented, thinking she had done so to herself.

"You haven't seen anything yet," Sonia said with a less than beguiled smirk.

As they neared to a stop, Lola's heart started to pound in her chest and any attempts to calm it were certainly futile. When the wagon did stop, it was in front of a pink house. Lola stared at the spiral chimney and then scanned the rest of the cute house before deciding that this was probably not going to be a pleasant visit. The vibrant-colored houses that were running down the street reminded Lola of the pictures in her old story books.

The pink house itself had a luscious garden in the front yard that looked very well kept. It was blooming with every color of flower you could imagine and even some that were just plain unnatural in her world. As they walked past the playful garden, Lola got a closer look at their splendor. She saw the bees buzzing all around the flowers and could have sworn she saw a line of them flying in unison to a humming tune—not buzzing. The humming, she quickly found out, was coming from some cute little hummingbirds that whizzed by. It sounded melodic and peaceful—she imagined it would be perfect for falling asleep to.

"Is there something wrong?" Sonia asked cunningly noticing that Lola had caught onto what the creatures were doing.

"Nah," Lola said, almost as if she had given up. "At this point I'll just welcome the weird."

"About that—" Sonia told her, halting in front of the house steps. She turned around and looked Lola straight in the eyes. "I don't know who's home right now, but if you don't make a scene you can keep your voice."

"This is your house?" Lola asked genuinely surprised. "A little too cheery for you, don't you think?"

"We won't be long," Sonia continued to say without minding Lola's sarcasm. "We just need to change—and for the love of all that is magic, do not say one word."

They walked up the steps toward the front door and Lola noticed that the white porch railing looked unkempt and weathered—something that would never fly at *her* mom's house.

"Once we get inside, immediately go up the stairs and into the first room on the right," Sonia instructed. "Change your clothes fast." Lola nodded and prepared herself to do as she was told. Sonia opened the white wooden door slowly and winced at what she saw inside. There was someone in the living room—someone Lola knew all too well—her sister.

"Mara?" Asked the girl on the couch, surprised to see her. "Oh my gosh! What are you doing here?" She got up from the couch and raced to the front door to give Lola a hug. "Why didn't you tell us you were coming back?" Lola said nothing, but she didn't need to because her eyes practically bugged out at the sight of this girl.

"Evie, you ruined the surprise," Sonia interjected, her fake smile not doing anyone any favors, especially her.

Lola said nothing, she just stared at the girl who looked like her sister and smiled—her brown wavy hair and round cheeks all too familiar. Before anyone could say anything else, they all heard a thundering sound coming from a back room. The loud noises startled both Lola and Sonia. It sounded like someone was manhandling some pots and pans.

"Mom's making dinner," Evie said trying to stifle a giggle. "She accidentally made all the spoons disappear yesterday. She used some Make-Many on the only spoon she could find, but it didn't work out too well. She left the bottle unstoppered and it spilled all over. It's a sea of cookware in there."

"Evie?" Yelled a woman's voice from the back of the house. "¿Quién es?" She asked in Spanish. The woman came out through a swinging door of what was no doubt the kitchen. She didn't look up right away because she was wiping her hands with a towel, but when she did bring her eyes up she almost fell backwards.

"Mara?" Asked the woman, just as bewildered as Evie had been. She quickly went in for a strong hug and a peck on the cheek. "I can't believe you showed up without telling us you were coming." She held Lola by the shoulders as she examined her. "What in the world are you wearing?"

Lola's expression was unmistakably shocked. She was looking at her mom, or at least a woman who looked and sounded exactly like her mom. Before she could say anything, Sonia saved her from disaster.

"Don't you want to go change, *Mara*?" Sonia asked Lola as she pushed her up the stairs. "Martina, you're crowding her. You know she traveled all the way from Cavalerian. I'm sure she feels gross and smells bad, don't you Mara?" Lola did not agree with Sonia's sentiment whatsoever, but out of fear of being silenced again she said nothing.

"Oh, don't be ridiculous Sonia," expressed Martina. "It's not like she traveled by land—"

"Actually," interjected Lola uncharacteristically meek. Sonia's face froze, fearing the absolute worst. "I did this time. It was…fun?" She looked over at Sonia, her face still petrified, like she was waiting for the other shoe to drop.

"Oh, fine then," conceded Martina not believing the excuse completely. She pulled Lola in for one more kiss on the cheek. "Go take a nap. I'll let you know when dinner is ready. You need to eat— you're skinnier than the last time I saw you." She walked back into the kitchen as the clinking and clanking of the pots protested her entrance. Evie returned to the couch almost sloth-like, and Lola attempted to go upstairs.

"Don't take a nap," whispered Sonia. "Get dressed, we have work to do." Lola nodded and kept going up to Mara's room. When she reached the top of the stairs, she saw that the frame around Mara's bedroom door was pink and the knob a fake gold-painted metal—an odd way of decorating for someone in her twenties, but okay. She opened the door and found that the room had obviously been preserved from when Mara was a child. The walls alternated from pink to lavender, and from the ceiling hung a delicate sheer canopy above a white four-post bed.

Lola stepped in slowly as if she were trespassing on sacred land. This was the room of her parallel self—a room that she was expected to recognize, and one that could reveal all sorts of secrets…it was perfect! It reminded her so much of her own room back home at her mom's house, except for the giant mahogany wardrobe that just barely matched—although not really.

She began to touch everything in her reach—the trinkets, the paintings, the furniture, even the makeup that was left behind on the exquisite white standalone vanity. She ran a hand along the comforter that was covering the bed and couldn't resist laying down. As soon as she did, it felt like she had been drained of energy. She had experienced the worst, most exhausting day of her life and it was finally sinking in. Even though Sonia had said not to take a nap, Lola didn't think she could stop herself from doing so. She could feel her energy wavering and the ebbing light succumbing to a shadow of sleep. Only a few more seconds of silence and she would fall victim to her exhausted state.

Just at the brink of losing consciousness, she heard thunking that she was hoping she could pretend to ignore, which she did until the final thunk almost knocked her out of the bed from fright. The double doors of the wardrobe swung open violently, causing Lola to feel a reserved surge of adrenaline. She screamed out loud and sprung off of the bed to scan the room for anything that could attack her. She saw nothing. She climbed onto the bed as she grabbed a pillow for protection.

"Sonia!" Lola called out, but when she did a pink and black blur bolted out from underneath the bed and jumped back into the wardrobe. Lola heard the stomps of someone running up the stairs. Sonia swung the bedroom door open with a warrior-like expression on her face.

"What happened?" Sonia asked running out of breath.

"There's something in here!" Lola responded as she pointed at the wardrobe. "In there! I think it was trying to hurt me."

Sonia walked over to the wardrobe cautiously and stuck her head inside. She then took a hold of what seemed to be the culprit and pulled it out from under some dresses. "Is this your monster?" She asked with an irritated look on her face. She was holding a pig—a small adorable pig with black spots.

"How was I supposed to know?" Lola asked exasperated but delighted at the sight of such a cute little animal. "That thing is fast—way too fast for a pig." Sonia put the adorable, non-threatening pig on the floor and it proceeded to glare at Lola, which she found to be slightly funny. "Why is he looking at me like that?"

"Because he knows you're not Mara," Sonia said frankly.

"How does he know?" Lola asked. She thought no one was supposed to know the difference, but somehow this piggy did know. How was that possible?

"This is Pigsby," Sonia started to explain. "He's Mara's valiant. I have no idea why he isn't with her, but regardless of that, he knows you're not her."

"But how does he know?" Lola knew pigs were smart, but she also started to think Sonia was messing with her.

"That's not important now," Sonia responded. "Just get dressed. I'll take him with me. Come Pigsby." She left the room as the fat little pig pranced out behind her.

Lola plopped down on the bed feeling like she was on the edge of defeat. She sat up as quickly as she could in an effort to not fall asleep. Forcing herself to get off the bed felt unusually cruel, so she bargained with herself and enjoyed the comfort of the bed while she took off her shoes. She ran her toes through the scruffy carpet not having realized her feet were sore—it felt so soothing.

At long last she got up and walked over to the wardrobe hoping she would be able to find a pair of clean pants. When she looked inside, she thought to herself that it couldn't possibly hold more than a couple of hangers of clothes. In front of her she saw only dresses. She rummaged thoroughly, wishing that pants would jump out at her, but nothing did. On her final attempt to magically shake out a pair of pants, she pushed the dresses back and forth not knowing they would somehow disappear.

She had pushed the hangers to the right, but instead of them hitting the end of the wardrobe, the clothes just kept going into the oblivious darkness. She was taken aback and stepped away, praying that nothing would pop out at her. Before continuing to look through the wardrobe, she did double-takes of the whole room feeling like she was being pranked. After several seconds of reasoning with herself, she reached into the pitch blackness of the wardrobe and pulled back the first thing she could feel—it was another dress.

"I really hope I don't regret this," Lola remarked to herself as she stepped into the wardrobe. She held an arm straight out into the darkness where she should have hit the solid wood panel, but didn't. She couldn't see anything, not even the clothes she had just pushed in there, but she could still feel the fabrics swaying against her arm. With a deep breath she started walking into the unknown part of the wardrobe with her arms still extended. She could feel clothes brushing against her. Before too long the top of her head made contact with something that was hanging above her. She grabbed it and even in the darkness she could tell that it was a chain that belonged to a light fixture, or at least she hoped it was.

Lola tugged on the chain and all at once everything around her became illuminated by several tiny crystal chandeliers. She was momentarily blinded but could see a glimpse through squinted eyes. She saw that the walls were crimson red and they were adorned with framed pictures—probably family portraits. In fact, it was surprising that Lola could see any of the red at all given how many frames were covering it up. She couldn't believe what she had stumbled into. The beige carpet inside the wardrobe looked brand new, or like the owner maintained it constantly. Above the unusually long clothes rod, was an equally long shelf. There were stacks of colorful boxes up there. Maybe they were filled with even more pictures that couldn't fit on the walls.

"This isn't a closet, it's a freaking hallway," Lola said to herself as she riffled through the absurd amount of clothes—mostly dresses and a good number of ball gowns. "What's with all these puffy gowns? Is this girl in pageants?"

Thanks to some quick digging, Lola was able to finally find some pants, although not what she was expecting. They looked like horse-riding pants, but with a little extra volume on the sides. Her blouse options weren't much better either. Unfortunately for her they all looked like they belonged to a very clean pirate. They had long flowing sleeves that cuffed at the wrists and the bottom of the shirt bubbled above her already full hips.

Lola made her way out of the closet, stumbling without fail, and changed into Mara's borrowed clothes. She slipped on a pair of

61

black, calf-high boots that definitely completed the pirate look. As she watched herself in the mirror, she couldn't help thinking about how funny Jason would have found this to be. He would have told some stupid joke or commented on how sexy the clothes were. No matter how hard she tried to focus on actually saving him, she couldn't stop thinking about him dying. She rubbed her right eye before it could produce a tear. There was no time for a crying session.

She returned downstairs within seconds of getting dressed. Sonia was impatiently waiting for her and she didn't try to hide it. She had changed her clothes as well, only she had opted for a pastel green dress.

"Come on, come on, let's go," Sonia hurried Lola. She grabbed the handle to the front door to make their quick exit, but before she had the chance, someone on the other side beat her to it. The door opened as if in slow motion and standing in the way was an older man with a graying beard and a familiar bald head that Lola hadn't seen in years. Sonia immediately looked like a fever had smacked her right in the face and she started to exude intense panic.

All day, Lola witnessed things that she never believed to be possible—magic and angels—but to this point, nothing had been able to stop her heart the way the bearded man just did.

"Dad?"

Chapter 7

Lola hadn't seen her dad in years, but yet there he was—right in front of her as if he had never been gone.

"Mara!" The bearded man said, surprised to see Lola. "Why didn't you tell us you were coming home?" The man held out his open arms and Lola instinctively gravitated toward them. The two embraced in a hug that Lola was sure she would never have the will to pull away from.

"What did I do to deserve this sort of welcome?" Asked the man as Lola clung tightly.

"I missed you," she said barely audible, as she dried small tears on his faded brown jacket.

"I missed you too, princess," he said, resting his chin on the top of her head. "When did you get back?"

Lola said nothing. She continued to hug him without noticing that there was anyone else in the room. She was lost in the moment, but she didn't care.

"Just about an hour ago," Sonia said in response to him. "We were actually on our way out." Sonia tugged Lola toward the front door. "We'll be back, though."

"I'm glad to see you two are getting along again," he said with a sigh of relief. "It's about time we had some peace in this house."

"Manny!" Hollered Martina from the kitchen. "Is that you? Come help me in here."

"Don't be late for dinner you two," he said to them as he placed a kiss on Lola's forehead and then walked toward the kitchen. He had a hard time getting through the doorway, but managed to noisily push his way in.

Sonia quickly pulled Lola out of the house before it was too late and shut the door behind them. "Let's move," she ordered.

"No," Lola whispered sternly, her eyes fixed solely on the neighbor's tree in order to maintain some type of composure and focus. She was bemused that Sonia thought she could get away with not explaining. Sonia stopped and turned to face her, clearly irritated. She stared at Lola knowing exactly what was about to happen. "That's my dad," Lola said in a shaky voice. "I'm going back in there." She turned around and tried to go in the house, but before she even made it to the steps, Sonia grabbed her.

"Stop it," Sonia demanded. "He is not your father. You need to stay focused."

"No, you stop it!" Lola yelled at her, almost sounding like a toddler. "You expect me to ignore the fact that I get a second chance to be with my dad? Are you crazy? I can't believe—" Lola stopped speaking, having realized something truly unsettling. "That's why you were in a hurry, isn't it? You didn't want me to see him."

Sonia didn't admit to anything, even as she was being stared down, but she wasn't going to get Lola out of there if she didn't explain. "You don't think I knew you would react this way?" Sonia asked. "I was trying to protect you. That man is not your father, and you can't get swept away thinking that he is. Your father is gone and for that I am sorry, but you cannot replace him with the man inside that house. He already has a daughter that looks like you."

Silent tears streamed down Lola's face. Sonia's words were harsh and although true, in that moment Lola really didn't care that the man who looked like her deceased father wasn't actually him—she just wanted to pretend it was him.

"Listen to me," Sonia said, possibly about to make up for her abrasiveness. "I know what you're thinking, but you can't stay here. Have you forgotten that you have your own family? Are you really going to let your actual family grieve for your loss if you don't return? Don't do that to them. Be strong. I know you can do it." That last bit of encouragement looked hard to swallow. Sonia really was terrible with empathy, but she was also right. These people were not her family and Lola needed to do everything she could to get back to the ones who were.

She gave Sonia a firm nod, but didn't look at her. She felt like her chest had received a pounding which made it hard for her to take a step forward, but she did anyway. There was a pit in her stomach that felt like it was burning, and she just wanted that feeling to go away.

They took a wagon back to the town, mostly in silence, until Lola spotted yet another bizarre sight. She could see something poking out from behind a grassy hill. It looked like black decaying branches, but she wasn't sure.

"What's over there?" She asked morosely without looking away from what appeared to be dead trees.

"An apple orchard," Sonia told her, without even turning to see what Lola was asking about.

"Maybe you should try watering the trees," Lola said in a monotone voice. Feigning a joke was far as she could go.

"That won't help," Sonia said as she sighed. "That orchard is over one hundred years old. It's one of tens of thousands of orchards all over the world—all failed."

"Do you know why?" Lola asked. The topic had slightly piqued her curiosity.

"No, we don't," Sonia answered, her voice leaving trails of irritation at Lola's questions.

"I'm confused," said Lola. "I saw those street vendors selling all sorts of fruits. Where do you get all of those from?"

"There's nothing wrong with our soil—it's our world," Sonia said, as if Lola should have already known. "It won't give life to the life-giving fruit. I've spent my entire career trying to figure it out... just like everyone else."

"Life-giving fruit?" Lola said. Almost immediately she imagined a tree that could grow infants, but there's no way that's what Sonia was talking about.

"Yes, life-giving fruit," Sonia said with a scowl. "Do you really think we would endanger the exposure of our existence for anything less? The apples you keep on your kitchen table cure forty percent of all diseases and ailments in this world. I know it's hard to imagine, but we've had cures for diseases like dementia for the last twenty years."

"That's impossible," Lola said, completely flabbergasted. How could her dimension have missed something like this?

"For your world, it is impossible, but for us it's completely different," Sonia continued to say. Lola could see a spark in her eye as she said it.

"So, is that your job?" Lola asked. "Getting apples for hospitals or something like that?"

"No, I'm working on something else," Sonia told her as the wagon began to slow down without stopping. They arrived at the edge of the town near Sonia's lab, within a couple of more seconds. When they got to the building where the lab was, Sonia stopped Lola from entering. "Wait outside," she instructed her.

"No, I want to see him," Lola protested.

"I'll let you come in to see him after I'm done getting the apples," Sonia said. "I can't have you knowing how I open the safe."

Lola gave her a crooked, untrusting look. "Fine," she agreed. "But hurry up... please." She waited outside of the building like she was told and began to watch the people walk by. Everyone showed signs of being in a good mood. They kept smiling at her, and each other, as they passed.

"Mara!" Called out a friendly voice from close by.

It was the young British woman from before. *What was her name?*

The young woman approached her fast. "What are you doing out of bed?" She asked Lola. "Aren't you sick?"

Lola was afraid to speak but there was nothing she could do to avoid the situation now. "I ate an apple?" She responded, shrugging her shoulders and trying to think on her feet.

"You ate an apple?" Asked the young woman in a horrified tone.

Lola shrugged her shoulders again and smiled not knowing what else to do. The young woman started laughing as if Lola had done something worth laughing at.

"Mara, you're such a prankster," her English accent danced delicately out of her mouth as it reached Lola's ears.

Lola tried to scope out an exit, but before she could make a speedy retreat, they heard the sound of horns from a short distance away. They were coming from a road Lola had passed on her way here.

Both women looked toward the noise and saw a band of decorated men and women riding in on horses. Some of them were holding flags and some were playing their horns. It sounded like they were preparing to fight—either that or it was a victory march.

"They're back!" Yelped the petite English woman, her brown eyes appeared to be smiling on their own. "This is so exciting!"

"Who's back?" Lola asked. She was hoping she wouldn't get stuck in the middle of a parade. If she got lost from Sonia, she would be in so much trouble.

"You really have been gone a long time," said the young woman.

The sound of the horns became louder and people started to gather in the street to wait for them. Everyone stopped what they were doing and started cheering. Handkerchiefs began to wave in the air and children climbed on parents' shoulders for a better view. Soon, Lola and Mara's friend were completely surrounded by the welcome party and were quickly made part of it.

"What's going on?" Lola yelled over the noise. Mara's friend, who's name Lola still couldn't remember, pointed at the men and women riding in on their horses and then continued to cheer with the crowd. Each rider was decorated in royal blues, golds, and whites. Flowers started flying as the riders gallivanted past the crowds like heroes.

As the last of them rode in, Lola quickly found out exactly what Mara's friend had been so excited about. At the end of what seemed to be a military parade, was the person everyone was cheering for the loudest. He was riding in on his white horse with a smug smile on his disgustingly good-looking face. His hair swished around as he waved at everyone and caught the occasional flower like a pompous showboat.

Mara's friend was staring at Lola with a mischievous look, like she knew what she was thinking—but even Lola didn't know what to think. Before she knew it, Lola had the misfortune of locking eyes with the handsome chestnut-haired man.

"Mara?" He called out as if he were caught off guard.

Lola didn't say anything, but also didn't look away. They watched each other as his horse continued to follow the rest of the squad. The entire time his expression failed to collect itself, almost as if he had seen a ghost.

The crowd followed the riders while Lola and Mara's friend stayed in place. As the noise subsided, Sonia finally came back down from her lab.

"Penelope, what a wonderful coincidence running into you twice in one day," Sonia said, her tone suggesting otherwise. "Looks like I missed all the commotion...pity."

"Adam's back," Penelope told her with a giant grin on her face.

"Is that right?" Sonia said passing a glance at Lola. "Yet another pity," she mumbled.

"Sorry, what was that?" Penelope asked.

"I said, I expect we'll have a ball soon," Sonia told her with a gritted smile. In Lola's opinion, she was the epitome of an evil stepmother if she ever saw one. Luckily Penelope didn't catch on.

"That's right!" Penelope exclaimed. "I forgot that Governor Gartwick promised a ball as soon as he came back." She looked at Lola with beaming eyes, expecting the same excitement from her.

"Oh, wow—I can't wait," Lola said trying to fake enthusiasm, although lazily done.

"I know you're being pissy on purpose, but it does not excuse you from going," Penelope told her. "I will talk to you later, and I expect a little more excitement next time." Penelope walked away, but not before giving Lola another hug.

Lola didn't bother occupying her thoughts with a ball she wasn't planning on attending. She was way too busy trying to get back home with Jason, safe and sound. "What took you so long?" Lola asked Sonia, her attitude all huffy.

"I wasn't that long," Sonia said, thinking that Lola was immaturely exaggerating—which she probably was. Her basket was hanging from her arm and Lola could see all the tiny apples rolling around in there.

"You wouldn't let me go upstairs with you so I wouldn't see you open your safe, but you'll carry your apples around in a common basket?" Even now, Lola had a hard time containing her smart mouth comments—it was her go-to defense mechanism, whether she knew it or not.

"You have to be authorized to handle apples here," Sonia told her smugly, regarding herself with very high importance. "Besides, no one here would take them. They wouldn't have the slightest idea how to use them."

Thinking back to just a few minutes ago, Lola realized why the idea of eating an apple seemed comical to Penelope. She couldn't help thinking how stupid she must have sounded. Fortunately for her, she had more important things to think about.

Leaving Sonia behind, Lola entered the building and made her way to the top floor to see Jason. She almost couldn't get there fast enough. When she got to Sonia's lab and saw him, she immediately became overwhelmed with despair. He looked awful! He continued to sleep on the chair like Sonia had ordered, his limp head hanging to one side.

She walked over to him and pulled up a chair in front of him. She took his hands and cupped them in hers, trying desperately to hold back tears. "I'm so sorry," she said to him, her sullen brown eyes focusing on his beaten-up face. She looked at him intently and could hear his regulated breathing flowing out of his mouth. She knew she couldn't stay long because every minute she spent there was another minute that he was slowly dying. "I don't know if you can hear me, but I promise I'll take you home soon," she said, giving his hands a squeeze.

Before leaving, she gave him a simple kiss on the lips, took a deep breath, and wrenched herself away. When she made her way out of the building, she found Sonia sitting on a nearby bench. She could tell that Lola was going to be distracted.

"Are you going to be able to focus?" Sonia asked.

"Let's just get started."

Chapter 8

As they made their way to their next destination—Sonia leading the way and Lola bombarding her with questions—they noticed that the previously excited crowd had gone back to their peaceful routine. Lola almost felt like asking what that whole arrival was about, but ultimately decided against it. It was of no importance to her, so why bother? The only thing that mattered was knowing what they were going to do next.

"What do we do first? How long is this going to take? How much time does Jason have? Where are we going?" Even if Lola had an itinerary, it still wouldn't be enough.

"We have to deposit and preserve the apples first," Sonia said, her patience no more there than it ever was.

"Well, how long is that going to take?" Lola asked. She would have gladly agreed to be an apple mule for the rest of her life if it meant speeding up this process.

"It won't take long," Sonia answered. "Just be patient, we have enough time."

Those words gave Lola a moment of peace… but only one. As much as she would like to rest, she was not going to do so until she and Jason were back home.

They arrived at their destination fairly quickly, although, Lola thought the town was bigger than it actually was. This part of the town looked just as whimsical as the other parts she had seen, except for the building that they were actually going to enter. This building was another complete eye-sore in the fairytale town. It also looked like they had reached another extreme of the town because Lola could see the main road leading out past all the town buildings. She kept her gaze on the out-going road and stalled when she saw where that road led. Not too far away in the distance she saw it—a castle, but not like any other castle she had ever seen in real life. It looked fake, like a giant-sized trinket or something out of a children's book.

"It's beautiful isn't it?" Sonia asked, noticing that Lola was drifting toward it.

"Yes," she answered softly.

"All right," Sonia said. "That's enough, let's go inside." She had to pull Lola to get her attention. The building they were about to enter had the same sterile feeling that Sonia's lab had. The only noticeable difference was the large sign announcing the nature of the establishment:

Iilerria Government Laboratory of Magical Sciences

On the wall by the entrance there was a plaque that clearly stated that only authorized personnel were allowed to go in. Sonia pulled out an ID badge and scanned it so that the doors would unlock for them.

Once inside, they both immediately felt colder—as if the AC had been on full blast for hours. The long white room they had entered held a receptionist desk at the very end. There was nothing to interrupt the haunting white, except a single potted plant halfway from the entrance. The planter was very odd and not like any planter Lola had ever seen before. It was a red oblong-shaped pot with molded rings around it.

They reached the bulky white desk at the end of the room where there stood a tall receptionist sporting an equally white lab coat. If it weren't for her dark burgundy hair, she would just about disappear.

"Good afternoon," greeted the woman behind the desk.

"Good afternoon Charlotte," Sonia acknowledged her. "I'm here to make a deposit. Seventy-four."

"Seventy-four?" Inquired Charlotte the receptionist. "Hardly worth the trip, don't you think?"

"Yes, well they're not really in season," Sonia replied with snark (no one seemed to be on her good side).

Charlotte smiled stiffly and reached under her desk to push a button. "Have a nice day," she said with a smile that resembled that of a plastic doll.

They made their way to another set of big doors and Sonia scanned her ID badge again so the doors would open. This new hallway was just as clean and white as everything else. It was lined with door after door on each side and none of them had any signs, but oddly enough each door did have a potted plant in front of it—the same type of plant that was in the lobby.

"Please don't tell me we have to try every door until we find the right one," Lola said, concerned that they would be looking for the right door for hours.

"I know which door I'm looking for," Sonia said after she rolled her eyes.

As they passed each door, Lola continued to look at every planter along the way. They were all different—different color, different shape, different texture, not a single one remotely resembling another.

They must have passed at least twenty doors before they stopped. When they did stop, Lola quickly noticed the same oddly shaped planter that was in the lobby, across from the door that they were just about to enter.

Lola was waiting for Sonia to unlock the door, but she didn't need to. It was already unlocked. As they walked in, Lola immediately noticed how much bigger this lab was than the other one Sonia had. It was also much darker as far as the lighting went. There were no windows and the lights had a blue tint to them. The glass containers, instruments, and burners she saw, reminded her of equipment a mad scientist might have. To top it off, there was a giant table that held all this equipment in the middle of the room.

"This is impressive," Lola said, hoping this wouldn't turn out to be a scene from a sick horror film.

"This is my government issued laboratory," Sonia explained. "All government issued laboratories in the region are in this building."

"This might be none of my business, but shouldn't you at least lock your government issued lab?" Lola asked. "Aren't you afraid that someone can just come in here?"

"No," Sonia answered. "Just like they're not afraid that I will go into theirs."

"You must really trust each other," Lola said. Even though she had only known her for a couple of hours, it was surprising to her that Sonia would trust anyone but herself.

"No, not really," Sonia said, ending the conversation and leaving Lola to dissect what the hell was going on.

Sonia walked over to the giant table and grabbed a clear box to dump all her apples into. The apples only filled up the box a third of the way, but to be fair they were still the size of quarters.

Lola's eyes kept wandering around the room. She saw an assortment of vials and containers with luminescent liquids in a cabinet. She took a closer look and found that they were all labeled. The neon blue one was labeled *Dormious*. One of the pink ones was labeled *Mémoiré* and looked like it was a glittery powder. The one that really caught Lola's eye was gold and gave the impression that it was thick and goopy—it was labeled *Manifold*.

"Don't even try to touch those," Sonia told her. "Don't touch anything unless I tell you to touch it."

"What does this gold one do?" Lola was so curious about everything in the room—she couldn't help it.

"It makes multiples of certain things," Sonia answered.

"Is it the same stuff that spilled on the pots back at your house?" Lola asked, recalling what Evie had told her when she first met her.

"Yes," Sonia said as she put on a pair of goggles. "It's commonly referred to as the 'make-many' potion. Mostly because people don't know how to use it and they end up making too much of one thing."

Sonia continued with what she was doing by putting on a pair of sturdy looking rubber gloves and then pouring ice-blue liquid into the clear box with the apples.

"Wait, am I missing something?" Lola asked as if she had just pieced together the most obvious mystery. "Why don't you just use this potion to make more apples? Why are you going through all of this trouble?"

Sonia took the clear box and walked over to a large thick door. She gestured to the door so that Lola would go over and open it. As soon as she opened it, she realized it was a freezer. It held stacks upon stacks of these clear boxes full of apples.

Sonia placed the sad, almost empty looking box, next to the hundreds of full boxes. They closed the heavy door and Lola followed Sonia back to the table. Sonia reached underneath the table to get something out of a mini fridge that was not noticeably visible. She pulled out a slice of an apple and placed it front of herself gently, almost as if it were made out of glass. Then she walked over to her potions cabinet and brought back the vial filled with the gold liquid.

She had yet to say another word. Lola could sense that what she expected to happen, was not about to happen—Sonia wouldn't have stayed this quiet, for this long, unless she was trying to make a point.

Using a pipette dropper, Sonia slowly added a minuscule drop of the potion onto the apple slice. Like magic, the singular apple slice turned into two apple slices right before their eyes. Lola smiled and was amazed that it worked—it was unbelievably beyond words.

"That was incredible," Lola expressed, still smiling from ear to ear.

"Keep watching," Sonia said unflinchingly.

Lola watched the slices intently. Within seconds, the duplicate slice began to rot. It started decaying in the middle and then moved rapidly throughout until it resembled a chunk of coal.

"What happened?" Lola asked thoroughly fascinated.

"I wish I knew," Sonia said as she threw away the rotted slice. "It's the same reason they won't grow—the same reason they're so powerful. Believe me, we've tried everything we can think of."

"That's why you keep going back, isn't it?" Lola said completely intrigued.

"Yes," Sonia said. "We need them, and decades of trying to grow them has amounted to nothing. They're just unnatural here."

Lola couldn't help thinking how she would have loved to have stumbled upon this place in different circumstances. The revolution of scientific discovery that would ensue in her world would have no end, and the thought of being the reason for a discovery of this magnitude almost made her heart race. Being on the verge of success always gave her a rush.

"Is this how you're going to save Jason?" She asked, hoping the answer would be here and they could take care of this whole mess right now.

"Yes, it's part of it, but not entirely," Sonia told her, somewhat crushing her hopes of a speedy recovery for Jason. At the same time, her mind started to work and she began pulling drawers open in search of something. She continued to rummage but didn't find what she was looking for.

"Come here," she ordered Lola. "Before we start, you need to understand something. The things we need to gather won't come easy. We can't use a conventional curing potion, that will take too long to heal him. We need something faster. Something that is only used in extreme circumstances."

"Is it dangerous?" Lola asked, her voice quivering.

"The potion? No," Sonia answered. "Gathering what we need, that's debatable." Her laissez-faire attitude was giving Lola anxiety.

"This doesn't sound right," Lola whimpered. "I want to take him to a hospital."

"I already told you, they won't help him," Sonia reminded her. "Now, listen to me. If you do as I say, you will be out here before you know it. Just trust that I am doing what is best for everyone in this situation."

It took her a minute, but eventually Lola reluctantly nodded in agreement. She knew that she really didn't have any other options.

"Good," said Sonia. "The other part of this is that you have to keep pretending to be Mara. The people you are getting these things from need to believe that." Lola didn't like this plan. This whole operation was sounding sketchier by the second.

"Why does it matter who they think I am?" Lola asked. "You're going to be the one doing all the talking." She looked at Sonia, but Sonia didn't say anything. After a quick moment, Lola let out a deep sigh having just realized a vital part of the plan that Sonia hadn't yet revealed. "You're not coming with me, are you?"

"No."

"What do you mean 'no'?" Lola asked in a husky tone.

"I'm not coming, because if these people see me, they won't give you anything," Sonia confessed.

"Oh, I see," Lola said, her sarcasm resonating throughout the room. "That doesn't make me distrust you at all!"

"It's the only way it will work," Sonia told her, looking only slightly guilty for not telling her sooner.

"What makes you think they will give *Mara* anything? They'll probably assume I'm working with you." Lola's temper was getting the better of her, but she felt justified.

"No one would believe that Mara would be working with me," Sonia said, a bit heated.

"Why?" Lola asked sternly. "What did you do?"

"Why do you assume I'm at fault?" Sonia retorted. Any normal person would have looked offended at such an assumption, but Sonia didn't—her scrunched up face looked more snobbish than anything. Lola was coming to understand that Sonia had a hard time hiding her true colors, even when she was trying.

"So, you didn't do anything wrong?" Lola asked, already knowing the answer.

Sonia pursed her lips and turned away—kind of immature for her usual self, but at least it gave Lola some insight into her relationship with Mara.

"How am I supposed to be Mara if Mara is supposed to be mad at you and I don't know what I'm supposed to pretend to be mad at you about?" Lola asked.

Sonia hesitated for only a moment before speaking. "All you need to know is that Mara asked me for help, and I was too busy to give it to her."

"You're so full of it," Lola said, taking a jab at her.

"Hey! That's not fair," Sonia said, slightly insulted and sounding like a teenage miscreant. "I was working on something just as important, if not more. I'm done talking about this. You know enough to get by." She turned her back on Lola, pretending to busy herself by collecting items from several drawers. It was so easy to tell what her weaknesses were, but Lola couldn't figure out which weakness was more detrimental—Mara or her pride.

"So, your niece is mad at you and these other people I have to get things from don't trust you?" Lola said as if she were thinking aloud, wondering if any of this was actually going to work in the end. "Anything else you want to tell me?"

"It's easy to judge if you're looking at it from the outside," Sonia said, composing herself slowly.

"You might as well tell me something if you don't want me to mess up this act," Lola insisted. It was probably going to be much harder for her to go on without knowing what all of the animosity with these people was about.

After several seconds, Sonia took a deep defeated breath and went to open one of the drawers next to her. She pulled out a framed picture and the way she looked at the it made it seem like the picture itself had wronged her in some way.

"This is who you're looking for," she said as she handed the frame over to Lola.

Lola looked at the picture and there were three women, each one of them holding an apple. Two of the women, Sonia being one of them, were smiling like they had just won a prize. The third woman looked to have been forcing a small smirk.

"Who are they?" Lola asked, her anger subsiding as she realized how hard this was for Sonia.

Sonia took back the picture and lingered on it. She tried to hide a pained expression, but Lola could tell it was there. "They used to work with me," she finally said. "I mean, we used to work together. We were working on something big. Something that people have been trying to understand for thousands of years without luck, but we knew we had something."

"Is that why you need the apples?" Lola asked. "Are you still working on that?"

"Yes, I'm still working on it," Sonia told her. "But I'm working alone."

"What happened?" Lola's curiosity was starting to boil. She carefully assessed whether or not she was overstepping her bounds, but even if she was, she felt comfortable enough to ask.

Sonia turned to her with squinted eyes and lips pressed together, as if to say, *you're asking too many questions.*

"If I'm going to continue to be Mara, you should tell me things that Mara knows," Lola said, knowing she was right.

Sonia's droopy eyes gave her away. She knew she had no choice but to tell Lola what she was trying to hide. "There's a very terrible thing that happens to some families in our dimension because of your dimension," Sonia said, soft hearted. "As far as we know, your dimension overpowers all other dimensions that we've discovered. You take our…" Sonia stopped. It was like her voice had ceased to exist.

"What do we take?" Lola asked cautiously, not wanting to startle her.

"Our children," Sonia said as she pretended that was the end of the conversation.

"Your children?" Lola's eyebrows furrowed intensely. She felt a ping of guilt even though she did nothing wrong, but she could feel how much it affected Sonia.

Sonia quickly scrambled in the cupboards beneath the table. She pulled out a rolled-up poster and fixed it to the top of the table with objects holding each corner. It was the same poster she had shown Lola at her other lab, the one with the six horizontal lines.

"This is you," she said pointing to the top line that was labeled, *Terre One.* "This is us," she placed her finger on the line below the first one. "For as long as history has been recorded we have lived in fear of losing our children. It was only until the last two hundred years that we found out where they were going—they were going to Terre One."

"Wait," Lola said. "I'm so confused. Are they running away, or something?"

"They don't leave by choice," Sonia told her. "They just disappear."

"How do you even know you're blaming the right dimension?" This started to sound more implausible to Lola by the minute. "There are plenty of other lines on this thing. Go blame some of them."

"We have proof we've gathered from your world," Sonia said, seeming a little too happy to make her point. "It was discovered by one of our first interdimensional travelers to your world." Lola listened on the edge of disbelief, but was intrigued nonetheless. "If you had grown up here you would know the story like the back of your hand," Sonia continued to say, her tone mystical. "We all grow up listening to it.

"His name was Rupert Heart. Records show him as being the fourth man to travel to Terre One. At the time of his journey no one knew that our lookalikes lived there, so when he recognized a man that was identical to his own neighbor, it was an epic discovery. That was the discovery that led to one of the most gruesome truths about your world."

Lola was riveted, so much so that she had unknowing taken a seat while Sonia was talking. She also had an inkling that Sonia was hamming it up.

"It didn't take much observation to find out that the same man that looked like Rupert's neighbor had two children who were completely identical," Sonia said.

"You mean, he saw twins?" Lola asked. She almost thought Sonia was being facetious, but then quickly understood that there was much more to it than just an ordinary pair of twins.

"Yes," Sonia said, as if Lola was being obnoxious. "He saw twins, but it was hard to understand at first. Twins don't exist here. This was the first time anyone from our world had seen identical lookalikes in the same dimension. It became even more difficult to take in when they started piecing things together.

"Rupert remembered his neighbor's wife being pregnant several years before, but because of the anomaly, one day she woke up and was no longer pregnant."

"What anomaly?" Lola was having a hard time keeping up. To her it sounded like the woman had lost the pregnancy.

"That's what I'm trying to solve," Sonia said, getting really close to Lola's face. "The anomaly. The women—here—they can go months being pregnant and then out of nowhere the pregnancy disappears. I know what you're thinking, but they're not miscarriages —it's far from that. These babies are being born in your world. We are where your twins come from."

Lola looked horrified—her eyes were wide, and they had a hard time blinking. She could feel the pain in Sonia's voice and see the heartache in her eyes.

"Okay…" Lola said, trying to process all of this new information.

"We don't know how or why, but every time a set of twins is born in your world, it's because a child was taken from ours." Sonia was visibly drained from explaining. "Triplets, quadruplets, it's all the same. Your world takes children from multiple dimensions."

Lola was frozen. There had to be an explanation. "This can't be true. I mean, how do you explain fraternal twins?"

"Women don't always choose the same mate in every dimension," Sonia said.

Both of them stayed silent for more than a few moments. Lola was trying to comprehend what she had just been told, and Sonia was settling her thoughts.

"You're trying to stop it," Lola muttered. "You and those other women in that picture—that's what you're trying to do."

"What we *were* trying to do," Sonia said stiffly as she got out of her chair and ransacked the drawers once again. She pulled out a very large parchment, tore off the bottom corner, and then started scribbling on the back. When she flipped it over, Lola could see that it was a map, or at least part of one. It looked gorgeously detailed and old-worldly, like something Sonia should not have ripped up.

"I almost forgot," Sonia said as she flipped the parchment over again. She stood still for a moment with her eyes closed and then snapped her fingers. A small purple light started shining out of her right temple. It was similar to the one that had emerged from Lola's throat when her voice was taken.

The marble-sized light traveled from Sonia's head, to her arm, and down to the palm of her hand which she then planted on the parchment. Sonia lifted her hand and both of them watched as the light disappeared into the parchment and lines began to sprout from it—a picture started to appear. As it drew near the end, Lola saw that it was a picture of a doll.

"That is what you need to get first," Sonia said. "This is—"

"A doll?" Lola interrupted.

"A special doll," Sonia corrected her. "It's made out of the purest, magic-crystalized ginger in the world. It's virtually indissoluble. It's harder than diamonds and tastes like nothing you've ever tasted before. The only thing that can penetrate it, is a precious tea leaf that grows alongside it. The only problem is that the tea leaf blooms only once every four years." Sonia sounded a bit maniacal, but mostly like she was geeking out about this amazing rarity. Lola was glad she was seeing some excitement in her after their solemn talk.

"So all Jason has to do is drink this tea and we can go home?" Lola asked with some relief.

"No, that's not what I was trying to say," Sonia said. "It's not the tea that will make him better, although eventually we need that too. It's what's inside the doll that we need." Sonia grabbed the framed picture on the table and pointed to the women on the left. She had long dirty blond hair and straight clean bangs to match. She wore a big full smile, just like young Sonia. "Her family owns the ginger fields that grows next to the tea."

"Are you going to tell me what's inside the doll?" Lola asked, half expecting a "yes" answer.

"There really is no point in explaining because it will take too long and it won't help you get it," Sonia said. "All you have to know is that it's an important ingredient for Jason's potion."

Lola nodded her head and decided she didn't care for it to be explained as long as it worked. "I'm guessing this ingredient isn't something you come across easily if it's trapped in a weird doll."

"Look at you—such a smart girl," Sonia said mockingly. "Let's just say it's experimental."

"Of course it is," Lola remarked. "So I need to get the doll and the tea?"

"She doesn't have the tea," Sonia said. "There's only one place we might be able to find it, but we'll get to that when the time comes. Just focus on the doll for now." She pointed to it on the parchment. "It's small, no bigger than your pinky. You won't be able to steal it, so you have to convince Gwen to give it to you."

"You're implying that eventually I'll have to steal," Lola said matter-of-factly.

"Focus," Sonia urged her. "This is happening tonight." She turned the piece of parchment over and pointed at a large plot of land that showed rows of trees. "You're going to enter from here. Gwen's house is at the very end of the orchard." As Lola studied the piece of map, a sudden change to it took her by surprise. One of the minuscule drawn-on trees disappeared.

"Don't worry about that," Sonia told her. "Those trees fall all the time." She started to look nervous as she said that. She grabbed her apple basket and walked over to a glass cabinet that held dozens of fluorescent vials. She started picking through them and dropped a couple of the vials in the basket. Lola started to walk over but Sonia stopped her. "Stay over there. I'm working on getting an unbreakable cabinet and I'd rather not take any chances." She walked back over to the desk and set the basket right in front of Lola. "I'm not saying that you'll need these, but better safe than sorry." Sonia pulled out a vial with light blue liquid. "Some of these vials are meant to break and some are not," she said as she put the vial in Lola's hand. "This one is not. This freezes anything you pour it on in a matter of seconds." The label on the vial read *Géla*.

Sonia reached into the basket again and pulled out a murky, almost black, liquid. "This one *is* meant to break," she said. "It creates a smokey veil, but don't worry because it's not actually smoke. The only problem with this is that you can't see through it even if you're the one who uses it, so be careful. As a matter of fact, be careful with all of these. I really hope you don't have to use them." She continued to go through the vials as quickly as possible. "The purple one makes people fall sleep, the green one creates a vacuum for sound——," and so on.

"This one," Sonia said pointedly, holding a vial with light pink powder labeled *Mémoiré*. "This one makes people forget whatever you tell them to forget. It's called mem powder. Only use this as a last resort. I almost don't want to give it to you." She put all of the vials back in the basket and handed it to Lola. "Come on, let's get out of here."

"You haven't told me how I'm going to convince Gwen to give me the doll," Lola said. "What if she doesn't give it to me?"

"I'll think of something for you to say before we get there," Sonia told her. "Just don't lose that basket."

Lola hugged the basket close to her chest as she looked down into it. The vials were shrunken inside just like the apples had been—they rolled around at the bottom of the basket as they walked out of the lab. Lola wondered if she really could be trusted with the responsibility of this magic. What if she actually had to use it and something went wrong?

"Wait," Lola said following Sonia to the door. "You didn't explain what Mara has to do with any of this."

"I guess I didn't," Sonia said, and then just walked out.

"Sonia?"

Chapter 9

After leaving Sonia's government lab, they didn't stick around town. The two of them made their way back to Sonia's house for dinner, as they were so lovingly told to do by Mara's dad.

The entire way back, Lola was anxious to see him again—she had a lump in her throat the size of an orange, or so it seemed. She even tried to have something prepared to talk to him about, but that didn't make sense since he wasn't actually her dad. She literally knew nothing about him.

As they arrived at the house, Lola's heart started to thud rapidly in her chest. The anticipation of seeing the man that looked like her father was almost too much for her to handle, but to her surprise he had been called back to work. Lola couldn't tell if she was relieved or upset at the news that Mara's dad would not be there for dinner.

Eventually, it was dinner time and everyone that was still at the house came together. From what Lola could tell, Mara's brother Jesse, liked to drop in for dinner on nights he wasn't working. He looked exactly like Lola's brother, but no surprise there.

The entire meal was spent listening to gruesome stories of Jesse's work. Lola tried to figure out exactly what his job was and gathered that he probably specialized in treating injuries caused by dragons, or something to that effect.

"You should have seen this beast," Jesse recounted. "She was all over the place. She even managed to torch one of the oldest mushrooms in the state. We already got flak for not saving the giant thing. First she knocked it over and then she burnt it to a crisp!"

Lola listened, quite entertained. She couldn't fathom the idea that dragons existed, let alone that her parallel brother was working around them.

"At one point…," Jesse said stifling a laugh with a sip of water. "At one point she got so mad that she tried to fly away and the gust from her wings launched the guy we were trying to save." He let out a boisterous laugh. "He landed on my partner, Vince!" Everyone started laughing. Lola wasn't sure if she was laughing at the story or at Jesse's own uncontrollable laughter.

"The guy's fine," Jesse continued. "Vince is fine too, but you should have seen his face when I got that guy off of him."

Lola enjoyed dinner a lot more than she thought she would, but was also glad when it ended because she had a hard time answering all of their questions. She avoided most of them by saying that she was still working on it. When everyone was finished clearing their plates, Lola started to head upstairs.

"Find a small bag for the vials and then bring it back down for me," Sonia told her. "It will be less noticeable than your basket. I'll enchant it to shrink your things. Also, don't go to sleep."

"Are you kidding me?" Lola said. "I'm exhausted!" She looked at Sonia with a desperately immature pouting face, until she got what she wanted.

"Fine," Sonia consented. "But as soon as everyone else is asleep, I'm waking you up, so don't get too comfortable."

Lola vigorously made her way up the stairs. She didn't want to waste any time that could be spent sleeping by trudging, as if it made a big difference. She opened the pink bedroom door only to find that the spot she was coveting was already in use. Underneath the blanket lay a relatively small lump, but not small enough to not be noticed. The adorable head laying on the pillow rose up to look at Lola. It was the piglet from before, the one that had scampered out of the endless wardrobe.

Lola quickly looked around for a small purse that she could give to Sonia, before even thinking about touching the bed. Just looking at the bed activated a siren's call in her head. When she found a purse, she rushed it to Sonia and then rushed right back to the room. She walked over to the edge of the bed and sat down gently, trying not to disturb Pigsby. The little pig just stared at her. She wanted so badly to lay down, but she also didn't want to get attacked. She slowly slipped off her boots and scooted farther onto the bed. Without invading Pigsby's space too much, she curled up and almost instantly fell asleep.

It couldn't have been more than an hour or two before Lola was being woken up by Sonia. She could have easily argued that she had only gotten five minutes of sleep, but she knew that wouldn't make a difference to Sonia. Unbearably, Lola somehow managed to open her eyes and it only took being shook two times.

"You look terrible," Sonia told her, straight-faced. Her arms were crossed, her menacing demeanor failing to do its job.

"Good morning to you too," Lola said, groggy and definitely not in the mood.

"It's not morning," Sonia said, hardly believing that Lola could be that confused.

"Yeah, I know," Lola pulled the covers over her face as she let out a tired grunt.

"You're letting Pigsby push you around, are you?" Sonia commented, having seen Lola squirreled up in the corner of the bed.

"What choice do I have?" Lola grumbled.

"Well, get up," Sonia ordered. "We've got work to do."

Lola sat up, honestly surprised that she was able to do so. She turned her head over to face Pigsby, who was now standing on the bed looking at her. If it was ever possible for a pig to look snooty, his face was it.

"You keep quiet," Sonia told Pigsby. "Or I'll tell Mara you were sleeping in her bed again." The little pig turned to her and shook his head, then he rubbed his snout on the bed in objection to her threat. Lola could swear it was more of a scoff than anything, but that was nonsensical.

95

"You know what?" Sonia said, her eyes still on Pigsby.
"You're coming with us."

Pigsby let out a little oink in disapproval. His little noises were
so adorable, Lola almost found him appealing.

"Oh yes you are!" Sonia told Pigsby. "You have been a little
slob ever since Mara left, so you're coming with us." The tiny pig
oinked and oinked, but Sonia was not going to let up. "Do you want me
to tell Mara you've also been sleeping on her gowns? If you don't say
anything, I won't say anything." Pigsby seemed to understand that and
made his way down a tiny ramp that was leaning on the other side of
the bed.

"Where did you get that ramp?" Sonia scolded him. Pigsby
ignored her and continued to leave the room. He tugged on a white
scarf that was hanging on the doorknob and managed to open the door
to make his way out.

"Spoiled pig rigged the room," Sonia muttered. Lola, on the
other hand, was still too tired to have been astonished by the intelligent
little creature. "All right, get up. We have to get going."

"Let me at least splash some water on my face," Lola said.
She put the boots on again and wobbled to the door right next to the
bedroom. She opened it and was immediately greeted by her own
reflection. Sluggishly she opened the faucet and hunched over the sink
waiting for the water to get slightly less cold. She cupped her hands and
splashed the water all over her face a couple of times, then she looked
up and stared at herself.

"These stupid bags," she said to herself as she stretched the skin under her eyes. "What twenty-five-year-old has bags like these?" It wasn't hard for Lola to find fault in her appearance, she even thought her olive skin was starting to look a bit pale.

After a good ten minutes of trying to get Lola out of the house, they finally managed to make their way toward the orchard that Sonia had mentioned beforehand. The brisk air helped Lola wake up a little more, but remembering why she was doing all of this helped her wake up a lot more.

The night was tranquil and quite lovely. Lola couldn't recall the last time she had been able to see so many stars. The scent in the air was calming, like it had just rained. Pigsby trotted in front of them, like a snobby child forced to go somewhere bothersome. His little legs moved quickly as Sonia and Lola took a normal stride.

"What's the deal with him?" Lola asked, as she gestured to Pigsby.

"He's Mara's valiant," Sonia answered.

"And that is?"

Sonia looked at Lola sideways, which clearly meant she was getting to that part. "A *valiant* is an animal that is magically and spiritually linked to a person. Many people in my world have them."

"Do you have one?" Lola asked, trying to imagine what animal it could be.

"Yes," answered Sonia. "She's a rat. Her name is Madelyn. Don't ask me where she is because I don't like people knowing."

"Why not?" Lola pried. What could be the harm in knowing where her rat is?

"Valiant's aren't pets," Sonia started to say. "They're like a part of you that freely walks the earth. They protect you, take care of you, sometimes even hide things for you."

"What kinds of things?" Lola asked, imagining Pigsby digging a hole to hide one of Mara's slippers for some reason.

"They hide memories, mostly," Sonia said as if she were bored. She knew what Lola was going to ask next, so instead of waiting for her to ask, she beat her to it. She seemed to be a big proponent of not wasting time, which Lola had noticed.

"We find our valiants by accident," she told Lola. "We run into each other at some point in our lives—usually as children."

"How did Mara and Pigsby meet?" Lola could hear herself becoming more of an irritating presence the more questions she asked, but she couldn't help it. From her perspective, not knowing certain information could be detrimental to their plan.

"They met at my father's ranch," Sonia said. "Manny and Martina were so proud the day Mara found her valiant." Lola might have been wrong, but she thought she saw a twinge of Sonia's own pride when she said that. "My father raised cows mostly," Sonia continued her story, looking somewhat nostalgic. "But he also had every other farm animal you can think of, so it was only a matter of time before Mara linked to one of them. She loved riding the horses and we were sure one of them would be it." Sonia chuckled recounting her memories of Mara. There was something about Mara that visibly affected her, and it wasn't hard to miss.

"There was one summer she was so excited to visit the ranch that she was annoyingly antsy," Sonia told her. "As soon as we got there, Mara ran out ahead of everyone and headed straight for the horses—like always. She liked to take a short cut through the fenced area where the cows slept and accidentally stepped on one of their tails. The cows went mad, and Mara was stuck in the middle—and mind you, she was about six or seven years old. She was not a large kid either.

"She screamed when the cows started closing in on her, and that's where Pigsby showed up. Martina was frantically trying to get to her and when she did, there wasn't a scratch on her." Sonia's face had drawn a pleasant smile, that she didn't attempt to hide.

"Pigsby saved her," Sonia said, as she watched him continue to trot ahead of them. "He created a shield around them both, and they found him in her arms. Apparently, he got loose from the pen when my father opened it. Troublesome little runt was only five weeks old."

As she too watched Pigsby, Lola could see why he might not like someone pretending to be the special person he had once saved. She also couldn't help thinking how nice it was to see a softer side of Sonia—it was refreshing. After that, they walked in silence, but it was nice. Lola's mind focused on taking in the earthy aroma that was going around. She had a lot more questions, but she was exhausted and wanted to preserve every bit of energy she could—especially because she didn't know exactly what she would have to do to get that crystal doll.

When they got to the entrance of the orchard they stopped. "Do you have everything?" Sonia asked.

"I think so," Lola answered patting herself down. She had her little purse of potions that she switched out for the basket. She also had a flashlight that she insisted on bringing, even though Sonia thought she wouldn't need it.

"Remember," Sonia said. "Only use the potions if you absolutely have to. I doubt that you'll have any trouble with Gwen—she always did like Mara."

"So, what's the plan again?" Lola asked on the verge of breaking out in a cold sweat.

"Just tell her you're there for the doll," Sonia said, like it would really be that easy.

"That's your master plan?" Lola asked, almost ready to shoot her. "How do you know that will even work?"

"Like I said," Sonia reiterated. "She trusts Mara and it helps that Mara does actually need what's inside the doll. I know for a fact that Gwen has been helping with her endeavors. I just hope she hasn't already given her the doll."

"This whole plan reeks of plot holes," Lola said, her voice was trembling. "What if Mara has already asked for it? What happens then? She'll find out I'm not her. She'll report us and Jason is as good as dead!" Lola was visibly shaken up. She looked around wildly, clasping her forehead as if she would be able to find the solution somewhere in the dark.

Sonia grabbed Lola by the shoulders, trying to calm her down. "Hey, listen to me. Remember what you have in that purse?" She shot Lola a look of reassurance. "What's inside that purse that will help you if she finds out you're not Mara? Think about it."

Lola's breathing slowed down gradually as she swallowed the lump in her throat. "The…," she started saying. "The… Mémoi…"

"The Mémoiré powder," Sonia helped her say. "The mem powder, okay? Just pour a little bit into your hand before you knock on the door. If you think she suspects anything just blow it in her face and tell her to forget you were ever there. If it *does* all go according to plan, just drop it before you go inside. It's that easy."

Lola nodded her head, continuing to steady her breathing. The plan seemed easy enough—nothing a little improvising couldn't fix.

"You know, it doesn't help that she lives behind a bunch of dead trees," Lola remarked.

"She was our botanist," Sonia said. "The closer she lived to the orchard, the better. I wouldn't be surprised if she's still trying to figure out how to grow the apples. Anyway, you're ready. Just walk straight through. Don't turn left, don't turn right, just straight."

"Yeah, I got it," Lola said, not sure if she was about to throw up from the nerves.

"Also, take him with you," Sonia told Lola, pointing at Pigsby. The little oinker looked peeved. "It will help relieve any doubt she might have about you." Pigsby was not on board.

"Do as she says Pig, or I'll board up that bedroom door and you'll be sleeping in the living room like a pet," Sonia threatened. To that, Pigsby let out a loud oink in disapproval, but did as he was told.

The two of them began walking into the orchard, just as straight as Sonia had instructed. "You'll protect me, right?" Lola asked Pigsby. The little pig snorted at her as he took the lead. "I guess that's a no."

Chapter 10

Their walk through the orchard took a little longer than expected. Even though the sky was clear and the moon was full, Lola still used the flashlight she had taken with her. Neither she nor Pigsby said a word the entire time, although Pigsby couldn't talk even if he wanted to… or could he? The silence between them didn't matter to her, there was plenty to listen to. The sounds of the crickets and leafs rustling was soothing to Lola, but that's not the only thing they heard. There was some movement among the trees, and then out of nowhere they heard a wolf howl in the distance.

"Whoa, what was that?" Lola asked thinking Pigsby would make some sort of attempt to communicate. Then they heard it again—this time it sounded closer. The movement in the shadows had become more apparent and Lola began pointing the flashlight all around her.

"Are you seeing this?" She asked as she continued to point the flashlight in every direction. Pigsby was paying very little mind to what was going on around them, even though the movement in the distance caught his eye too. "Okay," she assured herself. "If the pig isn't freaking out, I won't freak out."

Soon after, the ruckus stopped and didn't see the moving shadow anymore. Lola made a mental note to herself to ask Sonia for bear spray for their next mission. Fortunately for her sake, they were finally able to make out a light at the far end of the path.

The closer they got, the more she noticed that it was a single lantern that was illuminating their way. It could have been her lack of sleep, but that lantern seemed to light up everything in front of them—unlike a normal faint lantern.

From only a couple of yards away, the cottage became visible. It looked even scarier than she thought it would. It was almost completely enclosed by a wall of tall healthy bushes, which didn't match the decaying orchard in front of it at all. As they arrived, Lola noticed the path to the door of the cottage began under a wooden-lattice archway that was covered in plump vines. Rather than continue to go in, she stopped right underneath the archway to take a few deep breaths.

Looking around she saw that the cottage itself did not look to be well maintained at all, but oddly enough it didn't take away from the beautiful garden that engulfed it. Even though it wasn't light out, Lola could still tell how luscious the greenery was. The night was so clear that the moonlight bounced off of the dark-red cottage bricks in patches that weren't covered by vines and abnormally large leaves.

The peculiar cottage had two triangular rooftops on each end, separated by a rectangular rooftop in the middle. The windows looked antique, but not well maintained like all of the other windows Lola had seen in town. It was definitely spooky by all accounts.

Pigsby was getting tired of waiting for her and he made sure Lola knew by ramming his head into the back of her calf. With the little oinker's help, she finally stopped procrastinating. The front door was only a few feet away from the archway, but something started to happen that made Lola want to stand still. Little buds of lights started shining all over the garden. They were all different colors, like a rainbow of lightning bugs, although they looked a lot larger than that.

Lola took smaller steps as she approached the door. She was mesmerized by the dancing luminescent creatures but kept going anyway. When she got to the door, she didn't knock right away because she was too busy tracing the little light patterns in the dark. Thankfully, Pigsby was not shy about reminding her to keep going. With a second nudge, Lola got the hint.

Just as she was about to knock on the door, she remembered to take out some of the mem powder. She reached into the small purse and pulled out the vial with the powder. She poured a little bit of it in her hand and then put it away, her clenched fist holding the loose granules tight. She was afraid she would mess this up, so much so that she almost forgot the powder was in her hand only seconds later.

Pigsby waited almost impatiently for Lola to knock on the door, but before she even attempted, the doorknob turned. The door opened and standing in front of them was not the woman Lola had seen in the picture. This woman was wearing a black hooded-cloak and was hunching slightly, but aside from that she was much older looking than the person she was looking for. Her skin was paler than any person she had ever seen, her face had more wrinkles than a woman of her supposed age should have, and her nose was long and curved downward.

"Mara?" The old woman asked. She looked Lola up and down, and then she looked at Pigsby. Her eyes were squinted as she glided them over Lola's face. Her lips pursed waiting for Lola to speak, almost as if she were trying to catch her in a lie right off the bat.

Lola took a silent breath and said, "Gwen, I'm here for the doll." After that she just stood there with determined eyes, hoping she wouldn't flinch.

After what seemed like more time than was needed, the cloaked woman scoffed and turned to go back into her house. Lola looked at Pigsby and watched him scurry inside. She exhaled hugely and dropped the mem powder on the plants outside of the door. As relieved as she was that the woman was actually the witch Gwen, she still couldn't help noticing how old she appeared compared to Sonia.

Putting her thoughts aside, Lola was on the verge of following Gwen inside when a red light dropped on her shoulder. She was just about to swat it away when she got a closer look—it was a tiny person! Was it a fairy? It had to be a fairy. It had wings and its skin was a rich pink.

This is fine…this is normal…just make it get off and go inside.

Trying hard not to injure the creature, Lola shook her shoulder and even blew on it to make it go away. She immediately went inside after it flew off, not wanting any more of them to land on her.

The inside of the cottage was almost completely covered in vines, various plants, and flowers. Lola could still see some of the gaudy pea soup-colored wallpaper underneath the vines. They walked into the parlor where there were two armchairs facing each other. Gwen took a seat, and before Lola could take the other, Pigsby had already settled in by pulling down a blanket for himself that was draped over the top of the chair.

Gwen looked at Lola with a raised brow, but Lola just turned to Pigsby and said, "Go ahead and rest—you deserve it." Her gritted teeth were only visible to him and her sarcasm went unnoticed. She sat against the chair wanting to make sure she was at arm's length of Pigsby in case he blew their cover. "Poor thing—he's tired."

All three of them sat in silence for what seemed like several minutes, but was probably no more than a couple of seconds.

"Mara," Gwen said in a scratchy voice. "What do you want?"

Fake confidence surging through her, Lola took no more than a second to answer. "You know what I want."

"Well, why don't you just tell me again?" Gwen was looking Lola down, wanting to see if she would crack.

Lola's heart rate started to elevate quicker than anticipated. She was keeping her composure on the outside, but it almost seemed like Gwen was on to them. "You know why I'm here," she gulped. "Let's not waste time—not now."

"So, it has gotten worse?" Gwen asked, granules of skepticism still in her voice.

At that moment, Lola decided that if she treaded lightly, she might be able to pull this off. "Please Gwen, you know it has." She knew calling her by her name was risky, not knowing what her relationship with Mara was actually like, but she said it convincingly.

Gwen settled into her chair, as she took in a deep breath. "You've thought this through then?" She asked Lola. "You're positive it will work?"

"Why else would I be here?" Lola said, knowing she was close to getting what she needed.

Gwen placed her hand over her mouth and stared past Lola, deep in thought. Lola didn't have the faintest idea whether or not Gwen was actually going to give her the ginger doll, but either way she had to maintain her straight face.

"It will take me a couple of minutes," Gwen finally said. "But you can have it." Lola beamed at her, but immediately stopped when she noticed Gwen's expression. Gwen's matted ashy-blond hair covered her eyes a bit, but even then, Lola could tell they were a vibrant green, just like in the photo.

"Thank you," Lola told her sincerely, her stomach muscles unclenching. "This is really going to help."

"Don't thank me yet," Gwen said. "Athena has to go find it first. I asked her to hide it, but she forgets everything." She stood up from the armchair and as she did, she called out Athena's name, whoever that was. She waited by the entrance to the kitchen and the seconds later she crouched down for something. A fluffy white rabbit had appeared. It was wearing an adorable forest-green vest.

Gwen stroked the cute bunny before asking her to go look for the ginger doll, but it didn't leave right away. "I told you she would forget where she put it," Gwen said as she struggled to stand up from her crouched position. "I imagine you're not in too much of a rush." She straightened up as much she could and then followed the rabbit through the kitchen, leaving Lola to wait for them.

Lola sat there, her lips turning into a cocky grin. She couldn't believe she actually might be able to pull this off. While she internally complimented herself for this tricky feat, she almost didn't notice that something was crawling on her—or rather, climbing on her. She jumped up and almost swatted the bug until she saw it flinch. It wasn't a bug; it was one of those fairy things that were outside—this one was blue. It was wearing a cute little blue dress with matching tights and had an expression of complete wonder on her face.

The pinky-sized fairy kept staring at Lola, and Lola stared back unabashed. It even got close enough to Lola's face to start feeling around. The fairy seemed fascinated by her skin like if it were a weird texture, or maybe just because she wanted to make sure Lola was real.

Lola didn't know what to do, so she sat back down and just let the fairy climb all over her. When it got to her hair, the fairy used it like rope to get to the top of her head. It tickled as the fairy gently tugged her strands. When it reached the top of her head, she could feel it walking around and then suddenly there was a tiny prickle of pain. The fairy had plucked out some of Lola's hair. Without thinking about it, Lola went to rub the area where the hair had been pulled, which made the fairy fly out of harm's way.

"That hurt, you little punk," Lola said still rubbing the top of her head.

The fairy didn't seem to want to make amends, it just fluttered around Lola like it was looking for a safe place to land—or like it was trying to drop a tiny fairy bomb. It eventually landed on her purse and Lola didn't think much of it until it burrowed inside.

"Hey, get out of there," Lola said as she opened the mouth of the purse—but as soon as she did, the fairy zoomed out carrying one of the potions. Lola jumped to her feet with agility unfamiliar to her, and tried to chase the fairy. It was zipping around so fast that she could barely keep up. The potion it had taken was the murky black one, the one that could fill this whole place with imitation smoke.

"Give me that!" Lola demanded as she lurched in every which way trying to catch fairy. Pigsby was hardly participating—he was still curled up on the armchair and looked almost amused by what was going on. Unfortunately for Lola she quickly lost sight of the fairy. It would emerge for a second and then disappear again—over and over.

"Help me find it," Lola implored Pigsby, but he did nothing. "If I have to make a run for it, guess who I'm leaving behind."

To that Pigsby did get up, although huffy about it. He sniffed around the floor and the base of the walls until he found a hole close to a corner of the room. He oinked for Lola to come closer. Just as Lola was approaching, they both saw the little fairy pop her head out of the hole and then go back inside, only to shut a tiny door in their faces.

They were both surprised to find that the hole wasn't just a hole, but Lola didn't care. She got down on the floor so she could stick

110

her hand inside and grab the potion. The little door knob was difficult to open but when she finally got it, she was scared to actually stick her hand inside.

"Do you think it's just fairies in there?" Lola asked Pigsby, afraid that there might be something more, like cockroaches. Pigsby oinked, but Lola couldn't tell if that was a *no* or a *yes*.

Without much of a choice, Lola reached into the tiny doorway but as soon as she did she felt a rush go through her, almost like she was on a rollercoaster. She found herself in a completely different room soon after. She was standing in front of a doorway that was unfamiliar to her. She inched closer to the outside of the doorway only to find something giant and pink standing right outside. It had scared Lola so much so that she ducked back inside and at the same time she heard a loud oinking sound. She cautiously peeked out again, and from afar she could see that the giant was Pigsby.

It took her all of five seconds to figure out what had happened —especially since she recognized the surroundings Pigsby was standing in.

It was that fairy! She tricked me, or shrunk me, or... damn it!

Lola looked around the room, which had walls the color of a creamsicle, and only saw a round foyer table in the middle with a vase full of flowers. On the other side of the table was another doorway, but the room behind it was dark. Lola didn't know how long she had until Gwen came back with the doll, so she couldn't waste time worrying if it was safe to go into a strange room, as ridiculous as that rational sounded.

Before stepping into the room, she stretched her left arm out on the inside wall to feel around for a light switch. She was able to find one and when she turned it on she saw that darned fairy—only she was standing on the ceiling. As a matter of fact, everything was on the ceiling. Lola looked up, and in that split second fell to the ceiling, or at least it felt like falling. She stood up immediately and now everything looked to be right side up, except for the doorway she had just passed through. She also noticed that they were in what seemed to be the living room of the mouse hole—or fairy hide out, in this case.

The fairy was in the middle of the room next to a ratty old armchair. She was holding the vial in her hand only it was now proportional to her body.

"Give that back!" Lola demanded. "It doesn't belong to you."

The blue fairy said nothing and shrugged her shoulders like she had no idea what Lola was talking about. That's when Lola pointed at the vial in the fairy's hand and mimed that she wanted it back. The fairy understood that, but instead of giving it up she shook her head and held the potion to her chest like she was hugging it.

"Oh, come on!" Lola let out in frustration. She took a step toward the fairy, but as soon as she did, the room started to shift and she lost her balance. She barely missed hitting the tarnished coffee table and instead used it stand up. "Did you do that?" The fairy was almost dog-like in that she looked like someone was trying to take away her favorite toy. "Don't do that."

Lola tried again to walk toward the fairy, but the room shifted like a tumbling barrel. The fairy, meanwhile, was having no problem because she was hovering off of the ground with her wings. The armchairs and table were now almost completely inverted while Lola was stuck in the divot of a rotating corner of the room.

Getting up, Lola decided to make a run for it. The room started tumbling again, but she kept going. Almost immediately she could feel that there was a trick to it, as if some magic was helping her. As long as she kept going, her feet would hit a flat surface. Having realized that Lola figured out how to keep from falling, the fairy panicked and flew to the next room, and the next, until there were no more rooms in which to escape to—all the while, Lola was dodging furniture that rotated her way.

The last room they went into was small and had barely any furniture. Lola saw the fairy go into a closet on the other side of a tiny bed. She opened the door and there the fairy was, determined to keep the vial.

"Give it to me," Lola said through gritted teeth and panting.

The fairy shook her head and pouted her lips. She even threw in a raspberry meant to insult Lola. None of that worked of course, and Lola reached at her to snatch the vial away—to Lola's surprise, it wasn't that hard to do. The fairy seemed to lack a lot of strength and was almost fragile, which also made it easy to lock her in the closet. She figured that being weak wouldn't stop the fairy from going after her again, so she ran back to the outer doorway as fast as she could. The rooms continued to tumble like she was a bingo ball trapped inside.

When she reached the mouse hole that had gotten her into this mess, she stepped outside and instantly felt that same stomach-dropping rush. She landed in the middle of the parlor where Gwen was sitting in her armchair, waiting with a rabbit on her lap. She didn't say a word, but she didn't have to—Lola was ready to explain the second she saw her.

"I'm so sorry," Lola started to say. "I didn't mean to drop in like that, but I was running away from this blue fairy—she stole my potio... possession—and I went after her to get it back—and I shrunk, and fell on the ceiling, and locked her in the closet—and... I'm sorry."

Gwen observed Lola without so much as a twitch. "Well, it's not like I haven't told you before," Gwen said. "Watch your stuff around them—although, it doesn't bother me if you go after her."

Lola blew out a sigh of relief. She was worried that Gwen was going to be mad enough to kick them out, but luckily that wasn't the case. She sat down on the armchair that Pigsby was curled up on. He oinked at her angrily, but having been so winded from chasing the fairy, she wasn't paying much attention. On the other hand, something she did notice was an old weathered box sitting on the table in front of them. The box appeared to have been made of cardboard material. It had water damage that was unmistakable, and one of the corners was peeling enough to see the ridges in between.

They both looked at the box—Lola not knowing what to say and Gwen probably holding out on letting her take it. Lola didn't dare touch it, but she still put on a bold face because she was determined to leave with it.

Giving in, Gwen picked up the tattered box and opened it— she tipped the contents into her hand and a doll shaped lump fell out.

She held it between her thumb and index fingers as she brought it up to her face.

"Did I ever tell you why I started making these dolls?" Gwen asked, knowing she had not told Mara this story before. "My father taught me. He would use the tea leaf allotted to him, to sculpt into the crystal ginger that grew on our land. He did this just like his mother taught him when he was young. He would make one for each of my sisters and I—and when we each had one, we would get together around the table, drop our respective dolls in the tea, and drink while we listened to another rendition of the same story we heard every four years."

Gwen reached over to the bookcase next to her chair and pulled out a photo album. It was tattered and a bit dusty. Lola imagined it had to have been in Gwen's family for generations. She handed it over to Lola and beckoned her to take a look.

The first page had two pictures on it. They were so worn and faded that it made Lola nervous to keep looking at them, fearing they would spontaneously combust. One of the photos was of a man and a woman digging in the soil. The photo next to it was of the same couple, only the woman was holding a ginger root and the man was kissing her on the cheek.

Flipping carefully through the album, Lola saw more family photos of different people on the same farm doing the same thing— digging out ginger roots. There were also photos of people delivering crates of this crystal ginger to different facilities. In one of those delivery photos, Lola saw a sign hanging on a building that said, *Happy*

Well Being Day. The photo next to that one, was of people lining up to receive the ginger and tea leaves—probably the same tea leaves she keeps hearing so much about. When Lola closed the album, she looked up at Gwen and saw that she was smiling sweetly to herself. She probably didn't think that Lola had seen her.

"That's the story he told us," Gwen said shaking off the smile and eying the photo album. "It was always about how important our family is to this world—about how many people live better lives because they can drink the well-being tea with our ginger. Although, everyone knows it's really the tea that does all the work, but we loved listening to him tell it anyway."

Gwen's story really put Lola in a good mood. She could tell how proud Gwen was of her family and why she might have found a calling to study plants.

"As roundabout as that was, I need to know that you're not going to sully my family's name and do something too stupid with my doll." Gwen's face went from mildly happy, back to skeptical. "That pertains to absolutely everything you're about to do, including obtaining the tea. We both know the next harvest isn't for another six months. Are you planning on telling me where you're getting it?" Lola wasn't anticipating this question, nor did Sonia mention exactly how they would be getting the tea.

"You know where," Lola said. Thankfully she was getting good at answering vaguely with just the right amount of sternness.

"And you're planning on doing that how?" Gwen asked. "Stealing it? Although I guess you would just ask your boyfriend, wouldn't you? Do you think he would actually give it to you?"

"Come on, it's me we're talking about," Lola answered. "If you're giving me the doll, why wouldn't he give me the tea?" Lola was starting to push the boundaries of remaining vague and it looked like Gwen might be catching on. The two looked at each other. Gwen squinted her eyes as she ran her gaze all over Lola's face—probably looking for any sign of nervousness.

"I should really get going," Lola said as she tried to get up from the chair, but when she did she fell right back into it. She looked over at her arm and saw that there was a single vine wrapped around her wrist. She tried to pry it off, but was having trouble doing so. Her breathing quickened as she started to think that maybe she had finally been caught. She looked at Gwen as friendly as possible, almost like this was a little joke. Gwen gave it a moment, but then clapped her hands once and the vine let go.

"I forgot those little buggers are strong," Lola lied as she rubbed the part of her wrist that had been entangled.

"They must have forgotten who you are," Gwen said. Her tone had lowered suspiciously, and her lips pursed slightly as her eyes squinted.

Lola got up and cautiously walked over to where Gwen was seated. "Thank you," she said as she extended her empty palm.

"I want it back, *Mara*." Gwen said softly—a warning if Lola ever heard one.

"Of course," Lola breathed out. Gwen placed the crystalized ginger doll into Lola's hand. Lola closed her fist tight and then placed the doll in her little shrinking purse.

"Let's go," she ordered Pigsby. They walked to the front door, but when Lola looked back she saw that Gwen had gotten up from her chair and was now standing in the middle of the parlor. From the front door Lola could see the blue fairy had reappeared and as she did, Gwen held out her hand. It was hard for Lola to see what was happening, but out of nowhere, vines began to slither out of the walls like snakes in a garden. They met Gwen half-way, as if forming a pedestal, and then somehow they emitted a bowling ball-sized sphere of light. Gwen dusted her empty hands into the ball of light and then peeked toward the front door.

"Mara," Gwen called out before Lola crossed the doorway. "Don't screw it up."

"Right," Lola assured her and closed the door behind her.

Chapter 11

Lola couldn't believe she had just pulled off that plan—she was certain getting that doll from Gwen would not work in her favor.

"I did it! I actually did it," she started laughing to herself silently, she was so elated. They were still standing right outside of Gwen's front door, so she tried to keep the celebrating to a minimum. "Can you believe it worked?" She chuckled as she asked Pigsby quietly. She turned around to gauge his response, but that's when she saw him in a daze. "Pig? Are you okay?"

Pigsby was shaking his head like he was trying to get something off of him. He kept moving around disoriented until Lola noticed what he kept running into. His head was hitting an unreasonably large leaf covered in pink luminescent dust—the same dust she had dropped earlier.

"Oh no," she gasped. "Oh no no no no—" She quickly got him away from the rest of the loose mem powder and tried to make him focus. The little pig started to squeal like he was in danger. "Shhh, it's me," she tried to reason with him. Pigsby squealed louder and louder so she picked him up and ran him away from the cottage so that Gwen wouldn't hear. Once they were far enough away, Lola started to dig into her little purse looking for something that might help. She kept fumbling as she tried to position the flashlight well enough to see what she was looking for. She mumbled to herself trying to remember what color potion did what, and then she found it.

She pulled out a vial containing a purple powder, unstoppered it with her teeth, and unthinkingly dumped the entire contents on Pigsby's head. The little pig stopped squealing and quickly entered a blank haze. His balance was wobbly as he swayed from one side to the other until he finally swayed too far and collapsed on the ground. Lola immediately checked to make sure his adorable pot belly was indicating signs of life. She watched as it went up and then back down steadily, then she too let herself fall to the ground. She hadn't realized that in making sure that Pigsby was still breathing, she had forgotten to do the same for herself.

As she sat on the cold hard dirt, she thought of nothing. Her mind was so empty. She was coming down so hard from the adrenaline rush of getting caught, that she could think of absolutely nothing. She sat there leaning back on her hands as her fingernails dug into the damp earth. It was hard to tell how long she had stayed frozen, but she really didn't care.

She came back to her senses when Pigsby gave a loud sleeping snort. Having had time to catch her breath she wrapped her arms around Pigsby and cradled him. He was heavier than she was anticipating, but what else could she do? When she stood up she didn't even bother to dust herself off, she didn't fix her half-way untucked blouse, she didn't untangle her purse strap, she just began to walk.

It wasn't supposed to take too long to get back to Sonia, but Lola was convinced she was never going to reach her. It couldn't have been more than a mile walk, but there was no way of telling. As she looked from left to right, the bitter darkness appeared endless. It also didn't help that she was trudging at a snail's pace and hauling a well-fed teacup pig in her arms. All-in-all, Lola had no idea how much longer she would have to walk through the rows of dead trees, which was starting to worry her.

"This sucks," she said to herself in a low groan, but before she could continue complaining, she heard a terrifying howl. She stopped at once and looked around furiously, but not for long. She didn't need another sign to know that she had to pick up the pace. She cautiously, but vigorously, continued on the path. Then she heard the unknown creature howl again. This time she didn't stop to look around because she could tell from the direction of the howl that she was ahead of it.

Without further hesitation, she started running. She kept looking behind her to make sure she would have an opportunity to dodge if she had to. When she turned back to look where she was running, she could see the clearing out of the orchard, but at the same time she saw fast blurry movement out of the corner of her eye. She had no choice, she did the only thing she could think of, even if it meant compromising her location.

"Sonia!" She yelled chillingly. "Sonia!" Her throat felt soar and her arms were close to giving out from holding Pigsby. "Help!"

The blur was getting close and Lola's entire body was burning out. She was almost there and with her last mustered piece of strength she yelled, "Sonia!"

From outside of the orchard, Lola saw her—Sonia started running in her direction. She was so excited to see her that she started to feel like she could keep going.

Sonia quickly realized they were not alone. As she continued to run toward Lola, she reached into her own purse, pulled something out, and smashed it on the ground. A flash of white light bursted and erased everything around them. Lola tripped as she tried to shield her eyes into Pigsby without dropping him. She told herself to get up, but she couldn't make it.

As soon as she was able to open her eyes, she saw that she was back in Central Park. She was laying on the picnic blanket. The sun was shining on her face and she could feel small beads of sweat on her forehead. She sat up slowly as she shielded her eyes from the sun. Looking around she noticed that neither Pigsby nor Sonia were there with her.

She was in the same location she and Jason had been that morning. The same group of friends they had seen before, were still playing frisbee—the kid whose ball had interrupted them earlier was still running around—but there was no Jason.

She stood up quickly. Something wasn't sitting well with her. There was an air of uneasiness all around, but it quickly went away when she ultimately did spot Jason. He was walking toward her with two bottles of water in his hands.

"Hey, you're awake," he said as Lola went to give him a tight hug. "I was only gone for ten minutes," he chuckled.

"You were gone for a lot longer than that," Lola said to him.

"Well I guess it was closer to twelve minutes but..."

"No," Lola interrupted his joke. "In my dream—you got hit by a taxi and I had to save. We went to this other dimension and I was being chased by a monster while carrying a pig, and..."

"Whoa," he said as he handled her one of the bottles of water. "You have the craziest dreams. You should think about writing some of this down." He teased her, but Lola wasn't going along with it.

"It's not funny, it was scary," she scowled. "You were dying, and I could barely do anything to help you... I couldn't... I... I'm... I'm dreaming," she said, realizing what was happening.

"Yeah, it was just a dream," Jason said. "Don't worry about it."

"No," Lola was coming to a conclusion she knew was true. "This—this is the dream—you and me here, it's a dream."

"I think I should get you out of the sun," he told her trying to move her toward a shady tree.

"You're not real," Lola told him blankly.

"Lola, you're freaking me out," Jason said to her. "Let me take you into the shade."

"I know when I'm dreaming," she said. "I can see the haze. I can tell."

Jason looked at her with a smirk, like she had won. He sat down on the blanket and patted the space next to him, asking her to join. Lola sat beside him and opened the bottle of water to take a drink.

"Why didn't you just tell me I was dreaming?" She asked sounding a bit annoyed.

"You always figure it out," Jason answered. "I thought you might enjoy me *not* dying for a couple of minutes." Lola looked up at him and they were no longer in Central Park. She peered past him and saw that they were now on the beach. They were sitting on white sand as the sun was setting. "Let's go in the water," he suggested as he stood up.

"I can't," Lola said. "I have to wake up."

Jason was now at the edge of the water, the bottom of his pant legs were getting soaked. His eyes were shut serenely as he took a large breath. His hair whipped back as an unfelt breeze pretended to go through it. Everything here was fake.

"This is nice and all, but I really have to go," she told him after getting close enough for him to hear.

"I know," he said as he continued to walk into the water. Lola would have been scared had she not known this was a dream. Instead she just watched as he eventually disappeared and all she could see was the glistening clear blue water reflecting the orange sunset.

"I have to wake up," she very quietly muttered to herself. She made her way to the water and continued going until she too disappeared.

When she opened her eyes once again, she was looking at a white ceiling and pink walls. She could feel the cushion of a bed underneath her and the weight of a mildly heavy sack on her left arm. She sat up slowly, rubbing one sleepy eye at a time. She slipped her arm out from underneath the some-what heavy sack, but when she did, she noticed that it was Pigsby who was on her arm. She was back in Mara's room. Unfortunately, she was also still wearing the pirate-looking get-up, only it was completely covered in dirt. After taking a quick sniff, she decided it would be best for her to take a shower before she did anything else.

She got up and went to open the door to drag herself into the bathroom. Her head seemed to weigh more than usual and she could barely bring it up to look ahead. Every part of her body was fighting against her will to stay up. She almost didn't care how she got back to Sonia's house, although she was hoping she would get an explanation once she saw her.

As she was taking off her clothes, she could see the twigs and leaves tangled in her mangy brown hair. There were also scrapes and bruises all over her body, and weirdly enough, looking at them made it hurt even more.

Her time spent in the shower was fairly long—even long enough to warrant a knock on the door.

"You're not drowning yourself, are you?" Sonia asked jokingly, although her tone was dry. "Hurry and finish. The fun isn't over yet."

Lola wrapped up her shower begrudgingly. She would have gladly stayed there for hours if she could. She went back to Mara's room and decided to barrow a simple navy-blue dress that tied up in the front. While she was in Mara's wardrobe, she saw another one of those baggy pirate shirts and decided to take it for Jason.

As she got dressed, she noticed that Pigsby was still asleep. She was surprised that she didn't feel like sleeping anymore even though she was still very tired. It was probably time for her to get the day started anyway, especially since the sunlight that was coming in through the window made her think it was early afternoon.

When she opened the door to go downstairs, she heard the chatter of two different voices. Walking down she saw that Mara's brother and sister were in the living room watching TV, noticeably bored.

"Mara!" Evie said as soon as she saw Lola. "Do you want to go do something today?"

"Something besides sleeping," Mara's brother said mockingly. Evie swatted her brother in the chest for that comment, but he returned the favor by grabbing a pillow to retaliate and throwing at her.

"I'll get back to you on that," Lola told Evie as she hurried into the kitchen to look for Sonia. The path to the kitchen smelled mouthwatering and she could hear even more people in that direction. She pushed open the swinging door and saw three people in the midst of their conversation.

"Buenas tardes bebé," greeted Mara's mom in Spanish. She was cooking whatever it was that smelled so alluring.

"Hi Ma," Lola said without thinking, then immediately felt odd about it. Sonia chocked on her coffee at Lola's words, while Lola tried to play it off like everything was normal. She sat down at the small kitchen table with Sonia and Mara's dad, who was also drinking coffee in addition to munching on some sweet bread.

"Buenas tardes," Lola said to Mara's dad, Manny. She didn't have the courage to look at him right away.

"Buenas tardes mija," he said back with a sweet smile and sip of his coffee.

"You're lucky your dad had a late night," said Martina. "You would have had to make your own late breakfast if he hadn't. Do you want an omelet?"

Lola nodded her head as she tucked her arms between her legs and hunched over. She noticed that the kitchen wasn't very big, but it felt comfortable. She also saw what looked like at least four dozen pots and pans hanging from hooks all over the walls.

"Get your plate Mara," Martina told her, but before Lola could ask where the plates were, Sonia snapped her fingers. A single plate danced out of one of the cherry-wood cabinets and landed right in front of Lola. Alongside the plate came a fork and a knife from a nearby drawer. No one seemed to notice that Lola hadn't gotten the plate herself, nor did they care.

Martina carried the hot skillet over to Lola's plate and slid the omelet onto it. It looked just as fluffy and scrumptious as the ones her own mom made.

"Gracias," she thanked Martina.

127

Almost as soon as the omelet hit the plate, it was gone. Lola was hungrier than she had thought. After taking her last bite, she sat back in her chair with her hands over her belly enjoying the smell of the coffee.

"Mara," Manny called Lola. She didn't respond, but instead kept slumping in her chair trying not to move more than she needed to. "Mara," Manny said again, that time a little louder. Lola sat up immediately to look at him. Sonia was looking at her slyly, making sure she was ready to snap her fingers if she needed to intervene.

"You should help me fix up the wagon today," he continued to say. Before Lola could say anything, Evie burst into the kitchen.

"She can't!" Evie said excitedly. "She's going into town with us."

"You are?" Asked Manny and Sonia at the same time.

"I guess—" Lola muttered.

Everyone had eyes on her. Sonia's eyes said, *you are not doing that*—while Evie's said, *too late, I decided for you.* Lola really didn't know what to say and she was hoping Sonia would say something for her.

"She already promised to help me in the lab today," Sonia said in a smug tone like she had just won the prize of Lola's company.

"Well, she promised me that we would hang out when she came back," Evie said, sounding like she was double crossed. "You said we would hang out the last time you called." She was looking at Lola with fierce eyes.

Lola started to feel her dress collar constricting as she faced everyone in the room. She didn't know what to say. All she really wanted was to check up on Jason and she was starting to fear that she wouldn't even be able to do that. She reminded herself that playing the part of Mara was crucial to making sure everything worked out. After taking an enormous breath Lola knew exactly how to handle this situation.

"The lab is in town," she said a little shaky and awkwardly, speaking to both Evie and Sonia. "I'll help there first and then meet you afterwards."

Evie seemed to take this compromise very well, given her little squeal of excitement as she rushed out of the kitchen to get ready. Sonia, on the other hand, didn't hide her disapproval—it was quite apparent from the way her jaw locked up, but the damage wasn't over yet.

Lola looked over at Manny, trying very hard to contain her composure. She was convincing herself that this was all in an effort to keep her cover, but she knew better. Even with Jason's life in the balance, she couldn't resist the chance to spend just five minutes with her dad again, even if Manny wasn't really her dad.

"Can I help you with the wagon later?" She asked cautiously.

"Of course, Mara," he said, his fatherly tone sounding quite proud of the way she had handled the situation. Lola smiled from ear to ear while fighting to keep a single tear from leaving her right eye. That was Sonia's cue to get her out of the kitchen.

"It's getting late," she said to Lola, grabbing her by the shoulders and making her stand from her chair. "Go put your shoes on and don't forget your purse."

Lola gave Manny one more smile and thanked Martina again for breakfast. She really thought that the situation couldn't have gone better, and although she was doing everything she had to do to heal Jason and leave, she had a feeling it was still going to take longer than anticipated.

Sonia pushed Lola out of the kitchen hastily. Lola almost let herself be guided to wherever Sonia was taking her, but then she remembered she still didn't know what had happened last night.

"How did you get me back here?" Lola asked after turning to face Sonia.

"Shh," Sonia hushed her until they could get to the living room. She looked up the stairs to make sure no one was coming down, and then quietly explained. "I was going to drag you as far as I could, but then I found a wheelbarrow. I enchanted it to push itself here," Sonia said sounding impressed with herself. "That's pretty much it."

"A wheelbarrow?" Lola's lips pursed comically. "How thoughtful of you."

"You're welcome," Sonia said, taking Lola's sentiments as a compliment and completely missing the tone.

"What was that thing that was chasing me?" Lola could tell Sonia was leaving that part out on purpose. "And what was that flash of light?"

"You ask too many questions," Sonia said.

"I'm pretty sure we decided I could ask a million questions," Lola countered. "You know, because I'm not from around here."

"Okay. Okay." Sonia tried to keep Lola quiet. "Why can't you just be happy you're alive?"

"You're the reason I'm here," Lola whispered angrily.

"How long are you going to throw that in my face?" Sonia said as if she should be cut a break by this point. "Just go get ready."

Lola left Sonia in the living room to go back to Mara's room. As she put on a pair of practical black boots that she found, she was also thinking of what excuse to give Evie so that she didn't have to hang out with her for too long. She didn't want to get too distracted by Mara's obligations to her family—unless of course it meant spending time with her father's lookalike, but even then she couldn't get carried away. She had no idea how much longer Jason had to live, which obviously made the healing potion priority number one.

Within minutes everyone was ready to go, even Mara's brother, Jesse. Evie was especially excited for some reason. She had a giant suspicious grin on her face that wasn't going away.

"Don't take too long," Evie told both Lola and Sonia. "I want to get all of our shopping done today. I have to buy new shoes to match the gown you gave me, but I also have to get the gown hemmed first. " Evie kept going on and on about all of the shopping they had to do, so Lola just assumed she was going to a fancy party. She figured it was a very important party for her to be so riled up about it.

"I can't believe you haven't said a word about it," Evie said to Lola as they got into a wagon, presumably the one that wasn't broken. "You should be the most excited person in town!"

Lola furrowed her brows trying to figure out why she of all people, should be the most excited person in town.

"Yeah, I'm pretty excited," she said to Evie still not knowing what to be excited about.

"Seriously, don't even try to play it cool," Evie said. "Everyone knows you're dying to go to the ball."

Sonia exhaled in annoyance and rubbed her temples. It was clear that she was planning on keeping this information from Lola as long as she could, but Evie took care of blowing that detail wide open.

Lola's mouth dropped and she immediately turned to face Evie. "What do you mean, the ball?"

Chapter 12

The wagon ride into town was a bit daunting. Lola didn't know how to register the whole idea of a ball on the list of things to do in conjunction with trying to save Jason. Her mind kept going in different directions and it wasn't stopping.

What if I have to go to keep my cover? What if it takes up time I don't have to spare?

Her head started to spin, and her worries were slowly turning into a headache. It also didn't help that Evie chatted endlessly about the ball and who was going to be there.

They arrived at the entrance of the town within minutes. They each exited the wagon and made plans to meet in about an hour. As soon as Evie and Jesse were out of sight, Lola rushed Sonia inside to her lab. Even though it had been less than a day since they left Jason, with everything that had happened, it felt like he had been alone for a lot longer.

Lola wasted no time bursting in as soon as Sonia unlocked the door. All she wanted to do was make sure that he was still breathing.

She put her hands on his face and patted his cheeks a bit. She didn't notice any type of fever or clamminess—or *anything* strange for that matter. She looked down at his clothes that seemed even more dirty and bloody than they had been yesterday, except today they completely reeked.

"Can you give us a minute?" Lola asked. Sonia gave her an exasperated look but consented to stepping out anyway. Once she was out of sight, Lola began to take Jason's shirt off. It was proving difficult to do, not only because he was unconscious, but also because the stench that comes along with being hit by a car and traveling to a different dimension was pretty foul. She decided that instead of taking it off, she would use the holes in the shirt to rip it off.

After tearing the bloody shirt piece by piece, she couldn't help but go wash her hands vigorously. Unfortunately, her slight germaphobia took over which incidentally made her decide she should at least clean the blood off of him—it might even help the stink go away.

Finding something to clean him with was unusually difficult despite the fact that they were in a laboratory. She thought there should have been at least one rag. She searched through the cabinets and drawers, but all she was digging up was equipment. At one point she even discovered what looked like the corner of a broken mirror. It was tinted blue glass that reflected her face perfectly, but for some reason made it look like there was fog around her. It was extremely odd and it wasn't reflecting any of her surroundings, just her face.

As captivating as the mysterious piece of mirror was, Lola chalked it up to something magical that she didn't care to ask about since she had more important things to do.

Finally, she was able to find what she prayed was just an ordinary sponge. She soaked it in the sink and then tested it on her own skin before using it on Jason. The sponge felt harmless enough, so she pulled up a chair and proceeded to clean up as much blood as possible, being careful not to actually touch any of the blood with her bare hand.

Jason was in terrible condition. The left side of his head was completely covered in caked-on blood. His chest and abdomen were black from the pavement, as well as bloody. Lola began with cleaning his chest gently in small circles, hoping that it wouldn't cause him any pain. Thinking about him suffering on the inside by himself, almost brought tears to her eyes. The closer she got to sponging off the grime, the more she could see that something was completely wrong—or maybe right.

She wasn't positive that what she was witnessing was real so she quickly wiped off the rest of the grittiness from his abdomen. She was so focused on cleaning him off that she didn't notice that she was getting some of the dirtiness on her hands.

"Nothing," she whispered to herself in disbelief. She stood up quickly and rushed to the sink to rinse off the sponge. She tripped over her own feet going back to him, but she continued as if she hadn't. She started patting the sponge on the side of Jason's face where all the blood had accumulated. She began at the top where she believed the source of the blood had come from, but when it was dabbed clean, she saw nothing. She kept cleaning where the blood had spilled over into his ear and down to his chin and neck, but she saw nothing.

A large smile crept over her face and she even had to hold herself back from jumping for joy. She grabbed Jason's head and gave him a joyful, but gentle, kiss.

"Sonia!" She called out. "Come in here." Sonia walked in and saw a gleeful Lola double checking her boyfriend's head.

"What are you doing?" Sonia asked. She was taken aback by the fact that Jason was shirtless, like she had missed something entirely.

"Look!" Lola told her without paying attention to her question.

Sonia walked over and looked at Jason but didn't understand what Lola wanted. "I don't see anything."

"Exactly," Lola said in a breathy voice. "There isn't a scratch on him." Sonia's eyes widened and she immediately tensed up, something Lola didn't miss as she waited for her reaction.

"Look at him," Lola demanded cheerfully. "He's fine! There are no bruises, or cuts, or anything." Sonia didn't look impressed, but Lola stopped noticing because she was already digging into her little magical purse. She reached in and grabbed the long-sleeved pirate blouse that she pulled out of Mara's wardrobe earlier. The blouse looked like it was meant for a doll until it reshaped itself into a full-sized garment. Lola draped the blouse over Jason's head and excitedly began to dress him.

"I can't believe it," she said out loud. "You did it! You healed him." She was having a little trouble putting his arms in the sleeves

136

while she talked. "Now we can go home. You can take us straight to that elevator. Let me just finish cleaning up his face and we can go." She was so elated she didn't even hear Sonia.

"You can't go," Sonia said, but not loudly enough.

Lola walked over to the sink to rinse off the sponge again. She was jittery and it was very plain to see from the way she clumsily washed the sponge and then unsteadily kept cleaning Jason's face.

"You can't go," Sonia said more forcefully.

Lola stopped immediately but didn't look up at Sonia. Her shoulders slumped over, and she hung her head as she took a deep breath. "What do you mean, we can't go?" Lola asked dumbfounded. "If anyone wants us out of here more than me, it's you."

"I only patched up his external wounds," Sonia said. "His internal ones are much harder to heal. We still need the potion—" Sonia was cut off by Lola violently kicking over her chair and letting out a deep-pitched resentful grunt.

Sonia stood expressionless waiting for Lola to calm down. Much like Lola's own aunt, Sonia was evidently not an emotional person or someone who really empathized all that well. She didn't feel comfortable comforting others even though it was clear that Lola needed it.

"We have time," Sonia told her. "He won't die, I promise."

Lola still didn't look at her, but she took her time calming herself. She wiped her nose on her sleeve several times before having the strength to stand up straight again.

"I just thought…" Lola started to say, but then gave a low sigh. "I just thought it was over."

"It will be soon," Sonia assured her. She walked over to the toppled chair and set it right. "Go meet up with Evie. I know you might not want to, but you have to keep up the persona and that means going to the ball as well." Before Lola could protest, Sonia explained. "One of the ingredients is behind the castle walls and unfortunately—or fortunately, however you want to see it, Mara is the only one who can get it."

"Of course she is," Lola muttered as she rolled her eyes. She couldn't help thinking that this was seeming more and more like the cheesy story of a beloved heroine, only she was the stand-in while Mara got all the credit.

"Go," Sonia insisted as she shoved a wad of colorful notes into Lola's hand. "I have to plan our next outing anyway and I don't need you here asking more questions."

"Your sympathy is endearing," Lola commented, harshly sarcastic. She gave Jason one more kiss on the forehead before heading out. "Can you at least get him a pillow and lay him on the ground? He needs to rest properly." With that she left Sonia's lab and went to look for Evie.

Once outside, she looked down at her hand and realized Sonia had handed her some money. The bills were bright and cheerful looking.

She began to walk farther into the middle of town because Evie had told her to meet her at a place called Élégance Boutique. The closer she got to the center of the town, the more crowded it became. Shopkeepers were dashing around with their produce and products, all in the same direction.

Lola walked to the center of the main plaza in order to get a better view. She stepped into a little gazebo that was there, which was the only thing parting the ocean of people and looked around until she spotted the sign of Élégance Boutique. She also got a look at where everyone was flowing toward. There seemed to be some sort of tunnel almost all the way across from the Élégance Boutique. There were four guards standing watch over two particularly wide doors that resembled those of a very large basement. The vendors and merchants went down the stairs of the tunnel, two at a time.

For a moment, all Lola wanted to do was just stand there and breathe. She wanted to mindlessly watch as everyone bustled around her. People watching was something she often found relaxing. After several minutes she realized the commotion was most likely due to the impending ball.

Begrudgingly, she finally decided to make her way to the boutique. From the outside it didn't look very big at all, but as soon as she entered, she saw that it was in fact much larger than she had previously thought. The ceiling of the boutique was impossibly high, given that she had just seen where the roof ended from the outside. As she continued to marvel at the spectacle that was this lavish gown shop, she saw several crystal chandeliers hanging high above everyone's heads—they shined brilliantly, even though it was light out.

As she continued farther into the boutique, she caught glimpses of women trying on gowns in front of mirrors while surrounded by falling glitter. As pretty as it looked, Lola didn't see the appeal in getting rained on with glitter—that stuff might never come off.

Even though the boutique had a lot of room, it barely fit all of the women who had managed to squeeze in. Walking to the back of the store, she continued to hear the little bell that announced the arrival of more and more customers.

"Mara!" Called Evie's familiar voice. She was standing on a platform in front of three angled floor length mirrors. Next to her were five other young women, and sitting in a chair was Jesse on his phone. Three of the ladies kept talking to Evie, while the other two recognized Lola immediately. Lola remembered that one of the two was Mara's friend Penelope who was sporting a pretty intense cut across her face. The other young woman was very lean and had shoulder-length natural red hair—Lola didn't recognize her. They both smiled widely and waved at her.

"Oh sh… Hi!" Lola said cheerfully to both of them before they bombarded her with hugs. "Fancy meeting you two here. What's going on?" Her nonchalant entrance was painfully awkward.

"We were looking for a new gown for Penny when we saw your sister," said the spirited little red head. "She said you would be here soon, so we waited for you. Penny wants your opinion."

"Giving opinions is what I do best," Lola joked terribly. She turned to Penelope and winced from looking at the healing gash on her face. "Penny what happened?"

"Oh you know, it's just that time of the month," Penelope said brushing it off casually.

"That time of the month?" Lola muttered to herself. *I need to get the hell out of here.*

"I already picked some out," Penelope told her. "I'll be back with the first one."

When Penelope walked away, the red-headed friend gave Lola another hug. "I missed you so much pookey!" She said excitedly. "I haven't seen you in almost a year. Are you excited for the ball? Who are you going with? Please don't tell me you're going with Adam. Just come with us."

"Okay," Lola said abruptly, trying to lessen the conversation. "I'll go with you two."

"Lola?" Evie called out. She was looking at herself in the mirrors in front of her while a seamstress hemmed her beautiful green gown. It was strapless, had a flowery design on the skirt, and it was beaded modestly in several places. "I asked tia Sonia if Madelyn could hem it for me, but she said she couldn't handle it alone. Darn rat needs more friends, I guess. Why did you have to be taller than me?"

Lola just smiled at her little quip. "It looks great," she said to Evie. "Better than it did on me." If Evie was anything like her own sister, she knew she would be too shy to run with the compliment.

Before Lola could say anything else, out of nowhere, flowers started blooming from the skirt of the gown. She was stunned and couldn't keep her eyes off of them, until they retreated back into the skirt like they had never been there at all.

Evie continued to look at herself in the mirror and while she did, glitter started raining down on her. Lola squirmed away trying to avoid the glitter, but immediately noticed that it wasn't sticking to anything. She slowly put her hand under the glitter and pulled it back only to see that none of it stuck to any part of her hand. It seemed to disappear as soon as it landed on anything.

"She's coming out," said the other friend as Penelope emerged from the dressing room. The dress Penelope was wearing was a simple blush-colored gown. It had no intricate beading or lace, but it was still very pretty on its own.

Penelope had her own little platform and mirrors to see herself. She stepped up on the platform with some help from Lola.

"I'm not a big fan," commented the red-headed friend. "I thought you were going to pick something closer to your style."

"Well, I didn't pick this one," Penelope told them. "Mum picked it before she left to the shop. It's kind of pretty though. Maybe I'll just set it aside for now." Penelope got down from the platform with some more help and went back into her dressing room.

Close to an hour later, Penelope had finally decided on a gown. Elaborate really didn't begin to describe this gown. It had a midnight-black corset bodice, but the real showstopper was the skirt. It was enchanted to simulate a purplish night sky with a full moon. The moon's glow reflected off of the slow-moving clouds that revolved in the skirt. It was like watching a video projected on a piece of fabric.

"This is obviously you," said the other friend.

"Doesn't it seem too cliché for me?" Asked Penelope, although Lola wasn't sure why it would be.

"I think it's more clever than cliché," said the red-haired friend, who's name Lola still hadn't caught.

"I don't know Alex," continued Penelope. "There's still going to be people there who are prejudice. I just don't want it to ruin our night."

"Screw them," shouted red-haired Alex. "Everyone in town has known for months and we haven't had any problems with them. Besides, the people who really matter don't care that you're a werewolf. Right Mara?"

"R-right," Lola stumbled. She couldn't tell if they were kidding, but assumed they weren't. She inadvertently scooted an inch away from Penelope.

"See?" Alex assured Penelope. "Get the gown already so we can get out of this prissy hell hole."

Penelope smiled from ear-to-ear. She looked at herself in the mirrors and the glitter rain started pouring. "This used to be your favorite part, Mara," said Penelope. "Now you're off saving the world. This must seem trivial."

"It's still kind of nice," Lola said, watching Penelope enjoy the moment.

Penelope decided to buy the gown and the matching gloves. After that, Evie dragged her entire posse to the shoe shop. She mentioned that she had been saving up for a pair of heels that go perfectly with Mara's passed-down gown.

The shoe excursion took almost no time at all since Evie already knew what she was going to get. Paying for the shoes is what took the most time. Obviously, a formal ball has the stigma of being a big deal, but all of this commotion made it look like it was Black Friday.

"Mara, what are you going to wear to the ball?" Asked Penelope while they waited for Evie.

Lola hadn't given it a single thought—mostly because she didn't want to go. What was she going to wear? She was pretty sure she could use one of the gowns in Mara's closet, just like she had every other item of clothing.

"I'm going to use one of the ones I already have," Lola told both Penelope and Alex.

"Oh," said Penelope sounding disappointed.

Lola knew what she was waiting for, so she took a breath and just said it. "Do you want to help me pick one?" She asked them with a cringe.

"Yes!" They both said in excitement.

Lola gave a little smile. In different circumstances the ball would have been a dream come true. Lola was a big romantic who would have killed to be in a situation like this at any other time, but it was of little importance to her right now.

After a quick lunch, which Lola sulked through while thinking of Jason, they all started to head back to Sonia's lab. They didn't make it more than a couple of feet when they noticed someone coming toward them. It was the man that had just returned with the group of soldiers. The more steps they took the clearer it became that he was aiming straight for Lola.

Alex grabbed Lola's arm and brought her in close, while Penelope and Evie snickered behind them. Lola was seemingly calmer than the other women, but something told her she shouldn't be.

"Mara," said the handsome man with an enormous smile on his face. "I'm so glad I ran into you." He gave a nod to the others, but then went right back to Lola.

Before he could say anything else, Evie jumped in front of Alex and Lola by shoving her shopping bags in between them.

"Hello Lieutenant," Evie said all giggly. "We are so excited for your ball. We just came from shopping for it." She seemed to be purposefully obnoxious.

"Evie, you don't have to call me Lieutenant," he said with a sideways grin and a little blushing. "Besides, it's not my ball and you know it, so try not to go around saying it like that."

"That's weird," Evie commented. "Because I could have sworn I heard your mom say that she was throwing a ball as soon as you came back."

"A ball to celebrate the revision of the land deal with the native Iilerrians," he corrected her.

"Sure Adam," Evie said, like the annoying little sister she was.

"Hey, can I talk to you?" Adam asked Lola, looking over Evie's head. Lola froze for a second, everyone was looking at her. Even Jesse looked up from his phone.

"I can't," Lola almost stuttered. "I'm sorry."

"Yeah, she can't," Alex repeated giving him a dirty look that felt unnecessary.

"Can we do it later?" Lola asked without thinking. She felt bad for him and hated the idea that she could inadvertently be burning down bridges for Mara.

"Yeah," Adam said. Everyone could tell his feelings were hurt, which made it just a teeny bit awkward.

The group started walking away to meet up with Sonia. Jesse gave Adam a quick head nod and then followed the women.

"I'll call you later," Adam shouted as they walked away.

"My phone's broken," Lola shouted back as they lost sight of him.

Alex didn't waste a second as soon as Adam was no longer visible. "Why does he keep doing this to you?" She asked loud enough for the whole group to hear. "He's not good for you. If I hear you two are getting back together, I will slap you."

"Yeah right Alex," Evie said as if Alex were overreacting. "You know they always get back together."

"That's the problem," Alex said, rolling her eyes. "They wouldn't need to get back together if they just stayed together, but they never stay together and then always get back together."

Luckily for Lola she followed what Alex was saying, so she was able to figure out what was going on without the details. It sounded like Mara had a pretty complicated relationship.

"I don't know," Jesse said. "I think he's kind of cool." It sounded like something Lola's brother would say just to ruffle some feathers.

When they got to the building where Sonia's lab was, they saw her waiting outside for them.

"I have to use the restroom," Lola said pushing past Sonia as she grabbed her keys to go inside.

"Make it fast," Sonia said, knowing what she was really going to do.

Lola fumbled with the keys as she tried to open the initial door. Once inside she rushed to see Jason, only to find him lying on the ground with a pillow under his head and covered with a blanket. She knelt down to give him a quick kiss on the head and then leaned in to whisper, "We're almost out of here. I promise."

Chapter 13

The whole lot of them, including Mara's two friends, made their way back to the family house. As they arrived, Lola immediately remembered she was going to help Mara's dad with fixing the other wagon, which made her feel a little queasy.

Once inside, all of the women except Lola and Sonia, rushed upstairs into Mara's room. They could hear a startled squeal from Pigsby, who no doubt was still sleeping in Mara's bed.

"Mara has a lot of gowns," Sonia said. "You'd better get started."

"How often does this happen for her to have so many of them?" Lola asked, halfheartedly still wishing this could have happened under different circumstances.

"Often enough," Sonia told her. "Mara was invited to all of them because she was always running around with Adam, but he was holding her back—she just didn't realize it until later."

"Wow, you and Alex really don't like him," Lola said, a bit humored.

"You wouldn't either if you experienced the same emotional whiplash she has," Sonia said almost emotionless. "It's too bad science can't tell us why Mara's dumb enough to keep going back to him." Lola rolled her eyes at her. "Well, go upstairs and leave me alone," She yawned as she walked toward her room on the first floor.

Lola walked up the stairs to Mara's room. She could hear the ruckus through the walls. When she opened the door to the room, she saw that the enchanted wardrobe was wide open and Pigsby was climbing his fat little butt in there.

"She should wear this one," Lola heard one of them say.

"She wore that two balls ago," said Evie.

Lola couldn't see them. Just as she was about to step into the wardrobe all three of them came out, each with a gown in hand. Evie was holding a lavender one with pink flowers, Penelope had a cosmic looking one, and Alex was holding a sheath dress that was pink and gold.

"Try this one first," Penelope said trying to hand it to Lola. "It's the one you wore to the Halloween ball right before…" Penelope stopped talking immediately and tried to fake cough her way out of what she was about to say.

"Maybe we should skip that one," Evie suggested, her eyes intensely wide. The air was awkwardly thick between the three of them until Alex jumped in. Lola didn't feel the awkwardness. She had no idea what they were thinking about but pretended she did.

"Maybe try this one," Alex insisted. "Penny, go pick another one, or some shoes—or something." Lola took the dress from Alex and gestured for them to turn around while she changed into it.

"Okay," Lola said so they could turn back around. "You can zip me up now."

Alex closed the zipper and smoothed out the gown. She straightened the mirror in front of them so that Lola could get a good visual. This gown did not have a full skirt like the others. It looked like it should have been at a red carpet event. It had a gold sweetheart neckline but sprouting from the top were gold vines that looked like they were growing upward and eventually became the spaghetti straps. The skirt was a nude-pink netting, decorated with scattered gold sequence and trickling gold leaves. To top it off there were pink flowers in various places that had gold-beaded centers.

Lola couldn't stop looking at herself in the mirror. She was speechless and dazzled by the gorgeous gown. She didn't realize how much she was smiling until Alex said something.

"Look at that face," Alex pointed out. "She loves it! It's like she's trying it on for the first time all over again. You could hit her over the head and she wouldn't notice."

Just then Lola stopped smiling. She had become aware of what she was experiencing, and it made her feel guilty. All she could think about now was how Jason was still dying and she was playing dress-up. What a jerk…

Trying to make it seem like her mood hadn't changed, Lola put on a small smile. "This one is really nice," she said wanting to be grateful for their efforts.

"Of course it's nice, but that's not something you wear to a ball like this," Evie said. "Save it for a more casual ball." She pulled her pick off of the bed and shoved it in Lola's arms. "This is what you should wear. You haven't even worn this one before."

Evie unzipped Lola without warning and made her change. The second dress was enormous and above all, heavy. She really felt the weight of the gown after slipping her arms through the cap sleeves. It was so heavy it made her hunch forward. Even the zipper was working overtime—it kept getting stuck in the fabric, but as soon as that was done Lola turned around to face the mirror.

When Lola saw herself in the mirror, the gown no longer felt heavy. Any description of the gown would never do it justice. She traced her eyes over every detail. She stared at the intricate sweetheart neckline that was covered in small pink flowers and led down to the rest of the bodice. She ruffled the lavender fabric that began at her hips and fell over the skirt like a lily flower. With a twist and turn of her hips she watched the skirt dance. It looked like the pink flowers were actively growing from the bottom and making their way to the top. There were smaller white flowers scattered in between the bigger pink ones, which made them pop out even more.

"Wow," Lola said with a gulp. "It's—I mean it's—"

"Look at the back," Evie demanded as she jerked her to turn around. She gave her a hand-held mirror and gathered Lola's hair above her neck.

The back was stunning! In place of more fabric, each end of the back was held together by three draping strings of crystals. Lola couldn't say a word. All of them were speechless.

"Looks like we're done," Alex said, breaking the silence.

"I think you're right," Penelope agreed her face beaming at Lola.

They all stayed silent for a few more moments until Lola said, "All right, get me out of this thing."

After an unwarranted debate about what shoes she should wear with the gown, they went back downstairs to have dinner. Everyone was there, including Mara's dad and Jesse's girlfriend. Manny even had to bring in an extra table just so everyone could fit. Martina made enchiladas for dinner that they could not get enough of—Lola ate about five of them herself.

All throughout dinner, they talked about the ball. The women were so excited that they kept discussing what they were going to wear and who would be there. Manny and Jesse were more concerned with figuring out how they were all going to get there. Sonia wasn't really saying much of anything and Lola was just listening intently. The women were just getting into their hair talk when Martina spoke out loud so that everyone could hear.

"When is Adam picking you up?" She asked Lola. They all stopped what they were doing and looked over at Martina like she had made a faux pas.

"I'm not going with him," Lola answered sheepishly. "I'm going with my friends." She twinged a bit at calling Mara's friends hers, but soon got over it. She actually was starting to enjoy her time with them. They offered a brief distraction from what was really going on.

"So, you're going to meet him at the ball?" Martina continued to ask.

"Ma," Evie called her out. "She doesn't want to talk about it."

"I just don't understand why you two broke up if you love each other," Martina continued to say. "It just doesn't make sense."

"Ma!" Evie said again a bit more stern.

Lola didn't really mind the exchange, seeing as how she wasn't really Mara. She actually found it a little amusing how nosey Martina was about Mara's love life.

"I'll probably see him there," Lola told her. "But I think I'll just hang out with my friends."

"I just don't understand," Martina said dramatically, like the victim in a soap opera. "Why don't you want to go with him?"

"Because he's a loser, Marti," Sonia said like it was common knowledge.

"He just came back from a dangerous mission in Anmantta," Martina defended him. "That doesn't sound like a loser to me."

153

"Nobody sounds like a loser as long as your daughter gets married," Sonia jabbed right back. All at once everyone started nodding their heads in agreement with Sonia and laughed about it. "And that dangerous mission you're talking about was a land deal that his father arranged with the people that land rightfully belongs to."

"I never said she had to get married," Martina said all huffy. "I just said I wanted grandchildren."

Everyone let out an exaggerated sigh at Martina's words. There was no way this was the first time this topic had come up.

"All right, all right," Manny said trying to defuse the odd dinner talk. "She's only twenty-six, there's plenty of time for grandchildren," he said turning to Martina. "And sometimes Adam is a loser, but not today," he told Sonia.

They both settled down and almost immediately, any tension that was there was now gone. They all went back to their respective conversations as if nothing had happened.

After dessert, all of the women went back up to Mara's room. Before Lola could join them, Sonia stopped her.

"Get a good night's sleep," she told Lola. "We're getting up early tomorrow."

"Where are we going?" Lola asked. "Wait, don't tell me—stop asking so many questions?"

"Bingo," Sonia replied. Lola rolled her eyes and went back upstairs with the rest of the women.

As nice as Mara's friends were, Lola really wanted them to leave—it was getting very difficult for Lola to dodge questions from

154

them. They wanted to know what Mara was up to on her secret assignment. Lola just kept saying it was classified and couldn't give away any information. Although answering like that was annoying, it was effective. Luckily Alex had just started dating someone new so the conversation was continuously pushed on her.

Eventually they all left before it got too late. Lola was left alone on the bed without even a pig to keep her company. She laid down and closed her eyes thinking that she would fall asleep immediately. After what seemed like only minutes, but was actually more than an hour, she opened her eyes as if she had not slept at all. The lights in the room were still on and she could see that Pigsby had joined her in the bed at some point.

She sat up and swung her legs around, careful not to disturb the sleeping piglet. She rubbed her temples feeling hazy and drained of energy. It took her a minute to un-blur her eyes but when she did, she decided to get up to go to the bathroom. She opened the door to the bedroom and saw that all of the lights in the house were off.

It must be late.

Without really thinking, she scrambled back into the bedroom and grabbed her shrinking purse. She shoved a fluffy blanket into it and then quickly snatched a navy blue hooded cape that was laying around.

Pigsby noticed that she was up and about, but made no sound —he just went back to sleep. He probably didn't care what she was doing as long as he had the entire bed to himself.

Quickly but quietly, Lola headed down the stairs and out through the front door. She made an effort to close the door as soundlessly as possible and then started sprinting without a second thought. She flew past the flowers in the front garden only to merge with the main road a second later.

Even though it was nighttime she could still see by the partial light of the moon and her non-magical flashlight. After about ten minutes of running she slowed down without stopping. She swallowed an enormous amount of crisp air, just enough for her chest to get a tight pain.

As she kept walking, she noticed that the sky was by no means clear. The clouds were preparing for at least a drizzle. The walk was serene at that point and for the first time in the last two days her headache was subsiding. The pressure that had slowly been building up was now leaking out. She imagined that if she looked like anything, it would be a cracked teapot constantly boiling over. She chuckled at the thought of the steam coming out of her head, but only because it was nothing new. Although not close to her current situation, there was always something that seemed like the end of the world. Now that she was experiencing something truly world ending, she felt stupid. She couldn't believe that Jason went along with it all for so long. If he wasn't always there to turn down the heat, she would constantly boil herself dry.

At that precise moment she realized that she wasn't who she thought she was. As independent as she always made herself believe she was, maybe she actually wasn't. She thought back to when she first met Jason—that first day of college. She had left one dependency—her parents—for another, but it never dawned on her until just then. Now there she was, six years later and she was no more independent now than the moment she was dropped off at her dorm by her lovingly overprotective mother.

"Whoa," she mumbled to herself—the sobering understanding of something so integral to her life hovered over her and made her gloomy.

I'm so stupid.

A cloud began to loom over her head—not because of her realization, although she wouldn't doubt it, but because it was just about to start pouring rain. Luckily for her, she could see that the entrance of the town was not too far away. Right at the edge was that plain and unappealing building that Sonia's lab was in.

As she got closer she felt a fat drop of water fall on her cheek, so she sprinted the rest of the way there. When she got to the front door, she tried to open it, but it was locked. She tugged relentlessly, but nothing.

"Ugh! Of course it's locked!" She said angrily to herself. "What was I thinking?" She rummaged through the purse but couldn't make use of anything in there. She stood there blankly looking at all of the shrunken vials until she realized she might be able to shrink something else that will get her inside.

She opened the little purse wide and put it over the doorknob. Instantly the doorknob shrunk to the size of a quarter and fell in. A massive sigh of relief fell over Lola as she watched her plan work. She could see the other half of the doorknob was still on the other side, so she just pushed it through and opened the door. She was feeling a little too smug for having thought to use the purse, so she patted herself on the back.

She ran up the stairs to the third floor and then booked it down the hallway to Sonia's lab. She opened her purse and shrunk that doorknob too. She was still reveling in her "brilliant" idea but soon got over it when she was able to open the door.

Her heart started pounding when she saw Jason. He was laying on the floor under a blanket and thankfully with a pillow under his head. Almost immediately she started tearing up, but pushed past the feelings before getting carried away.

Above Jason's head was a large window which brought in enough light to fill the room. The rain had picked up significantly since she entered the building, so she walked over to the window and opened it about one inch. She loved the sound of the rain. It was soothing and melodious. Sometimes she would even imagine it was just for her.

After a moment of taking in the sweet rainy air, she walked over to one of the sinks and started searching for a cup. She didn't find one and she didn't want to risk drinking out of a beaker, so she just cupped the water in her hands. Three handfuls of water were all it took to leave her satisfied. As she turned to go back to Jason, she saw a notebook on the far end of the counter. She walked over to see if it was anything of interest and saw that it had a very small label that read: *Travel Journal.*

Absentmindedly, Lola opened it up. It was obviously Sonia's because, who else would it belong to? The first page was titled: *Road Signs.* There were notes about how to decipher signs from Terre One.

Lola found it a bit comical, but then realized it was smart. She was slightly amazed at how prepared Sonia seemed to be at all times.

She kept flipping the pages and came across images of signs that were under the Terre Three tab. They didn't look much different from the ones in Terre One except for the fact that they were floating instead of being posted or hung on a pole. After seeing that, Lola's curiosity got the better of her so she kept turning pages. Mostly it was more information about Terre One, like how to use the currency and whether organic apples were better for research than regular apples (apparently they're not).

The last couple of pages didn't have a title and were filled with drawings of symbols with notes written next to them. They were very simple symbols like vertical lines that met at the bottom like a cone, or a zigzag line. The next page had a drawing of a torch and on the torch seemed to be an etched square. The scribble next to it read, *Cavalerian*. The next page had another drawing of another torch, only this one looked like it had a ring etched into the bottom. For some reason that image had triggered something in Lola's memory. She had an inkling of what she would find next.

Just as she suspected, the next two pages had drawings of torches—one with two rings at the bottom and another with three rings. The one with three rings had a note written next to it that said, *Lunding*. It dawned on Lola that this is how Sonia knew when and what to do to get out of the tunnel when they first arrived. She continued to look through the notebook to see if she could find something that would lead her to Earth, but she found nothing. "Some good that did me," she mumbled to herself.

A prolonged yawn escaped her, which was fine because she had exhausted the notebook and found it of little to no importance. She didn't need to know how to get in, but she would gladly welcome the notebook that would lead her out.

She walked back over to Jason and reached into her shrinking purse to pull out the blanket she had brought for herself. As she was pulling it out, something clunked onto the floor—it was her phone. She had completely forgotten about it. She turned on the screen and saw that it had almost no battery left. All of the notifications that appeared before they crossed over were still there—right on the left-hand corner of her screen as if to say, *can you believe you ever thought this was important?*

She sat down next to Jason as she mindlessly erased all the social media notifications—they seemed so inconsequential now. She laid down and propped her head on the small bit of pillow that Jason wasn't using. All of the notifications were dated from right before they arrived in Terre Two, except for one. That one notification was pretty old. It was the icon for a voice message that was stored onto the phone. She actually knew who it was from because she hadn't bothered getting rid of it out of laziness. Looking at the almost dead phone screen, she decided to click on the icon which immediately took her to the internal voice mail box, but also made a low battery warning come up. She stared at the six-second message briefly before playing it.

"Hey beautiful. What do you want for dinner? Give me a call back. Love you. Bye." It was his voice. It was a message Jason had left for her right before she walked into their apartment. That message was two months old at that point.

To her surprise she didn't cry, she just blankly stared at the dimming screen before pressing the play button again. The second time hurt even less than the first. She almost played it a third time, but that's when the phone gave out. She rolled to one side and threw her arm over Jason's chest, then covered herself with the blanket. She looked up at his moon-lit face as she inhaled the earthy rain air.

"We're going home," she told him. "I promise."

Chapter 14

"Hey, how's it going?" Lola heard Jason ask.

She opened her eyes and she was sitting in her favorite spot, on the patio of her favorite cafe. On the table was a cast iron tea pot full of honey-ginseng tea and a white teacup on a saucer. Sitting across from her was Jason. He was drinking an iced coffee like everything was normal and he wasn't on the brink of death.

"Good, I think—" Lola told him as she sipped from the white cup that was now in her hands.

"Do you think we'll make it back home?" Jason asked casually, leaning his head on his hand while sipping from his own drink.

"Of course we are," she responded, a bit offended that he would even question it. "Didn't you hear me promise?"

"I did," he said nonchalantly. "But you're looking pretty tired."

"Are you serious right now?" She said, giving him a some well deserved attitude.

"Yeah, you know, like you're just about to give up," he said playfully.

"I can't believe you would say that!" Lola practically yelled. Jason smirked and said nothing. Lola realized he was just trying to fire her up.

"You're a jerk," she told him, sitting all the way back in her chair.

"I'm just trying to help," he assured her. "By the way, it's time to get up." Lola felt him kicking her under the table.

"Stop that," she told him as she rubbed her shin.

"That's not me," he said smiling devilishly. She looked under the table and saw that it really wasn't him, but she could still feel the kick.

"Get up," he said. "Come on, get up."

Lola drifted out of her dreamy state only to find the kicker she was complaining about was Sonia.

"Did you have a good night?" Sonia asked sarcastically, her nose flaring up.

"Delightful," Lola grunted as she sat up and rubbed her eyes.

"Well, isn't that nice," Sonia retorted. "My night was just as good—it was my morning that displeased me."

"I wonder why," Lola said annoyingly. She didn't even look at Sonia, nor did she want to.

"What were you thinking?" Sonia asked furiously. She was agitated and it looked like any excuse wasn't going to be good enough.

"I wasn't," Lola answered honestly.

"Apparently," Sonia said. "Do you know what could have happened if I wasn't the first one to arrive here? Someone would have followed the trail straight to both of you and there would be no saving him then. Is that what you want?"

"I'm sorry," Lola said grumpily. "I just…" Sonia was right. Being this careless with so much at stake was stupid and Lola had put them all in real danger. "It won't happen again."

"It better not," Sonia said, on the verge of biting Lola's head off. "I just can't believe you thought this was a good idea." She almost looked like she wanted to grab Lola and shake her. "You get one more chance. If you disobey me again, I'm done with you. Now get up, we're late."

Lola stumbled onto her feet leaving the blanket on the floor. She walked over to the lab table and leaned on it with her elbows on top.

"You look terrible," Sonia commented, her snark worse than usual. It didn't matter, though—Lola didn't care.

"Yeah, well…" Lola tried to snap a good comeback. "I got nothin'."

Sonia tossed her a banana that almost hit her in the face. "Don't expect a proper breakfast now," she told her with no remorse.

"Yeah, okay," Lola said as she pealed the banana and bit into it while she slumped over the counter. "Let's just get this day over with."

"The day doesn't start here," Sonia told her as she turned on the projector. A three-dimensional holographic map of the area appeared and she used her hands to travel through it. "It starts here."

She pointed to a valley not too far from where they were, but far enough.

"How are we supposed to get there without a car?" Lola asked as she rubbed her eyes dry.

"Horse-back, of course," Sonia said sharply as she tossed Lola a bag. "Get changed, and don't linger—you've wasted enough time."

Lola scrunched up her face at Sonia's remark. She knew Sonia didn't want her and Jason around any longer than they wanted to be there, but her attitude spoke volumes to how she really felt about them.

After quickly changing into riding pants and a blouse, she gave Jason a sweet kiss on the forehead and left to meet Sonia outside. When she got downstairs, Sonia started walking angrily and Lola followed.

"I know you don't want us here, but you could try being a little nicer since this is technically your fault," Lola told her, allowing herself some room between them.

"Oh really?" Sonia said. "Would that help?" For someone who was in her mid-forties, she sure didn't act like it. "Suck it up. I'm not the one who almost screwed everything up."

"Fine," Lola said. "But I know why you're being mean, and I think you have some serious issues."

"Who doesn't?" Sonia shot back.

They made their way to where all the wagons and carriages were parked outside of town. They met a man handling two calm horses. The man was rocking a salt and pepper beard that he was messing with right as they got there.

"Two of my best, just like you asked," said the bearded man.

"You always come through," Sonia told him in a flirty manner, or at least as flirty as she could manage. She was still visibly irritated.

"So, about that date," the man said trying to act casual.

"Later, Arthur," Sonia said as she mounted the horse. "Get on," she told Lola.

Lola took the reins from Arthur, slightly apologetically. She mounted the horse and thanked him for letting them borrow, what she was sure *were* his best horses.

"Her name is Willow," Arthur told Lola with a smile. "Just bring her back in one piece." Lola nodded graciously at him. She took a good look at Willow and then noticed that each of the horses was carrying small saddle bags, definitely not big enough for a long trip.

"We're riding east for about two hours," Sonia informed her. "And thanks to your late-night escapade, we're behind schedule." Lola could feel Sonia's glare, like it was about to hit her in the face as soon as she let her guard down.

"I'm assuming you know how to ride a horse," Sonia said. "If you don't, it's easy enough to understand, even for you." Lola brushed off the snide comment. At this point she didn't care what Sonia said to her as long as she helped Jason.

Without a moment's notice Sonia began to ride toward the same dirt path the soldiers rode in on. Lola quickly followed suit, although not as gracefully. It was clear that riding horses was not an uncommon activity for Sonia—she could see it in her superb posture. Lola, on the other hand, was the exact opposite—she bounced erratically on the saddle and almost slipped off more than once in the first ten minutes.

"So, what's the plan?" Lola asked as she accidentally passed Sonia and then circled back around to get next to her.

"It's better if I explain when we get there," she responded. "Getting what we need is going to be more difficult this time, so I need you as rested and alert as possible, which is why we are camping out tonight. We weren't going to, but again, we have you to thank for that."

"You know what?" Lola said. "How about I just leave you alone and enjoy all of this natural beauty for the next two hours? Two long, silent hours."

Sonia inhaled deeply before speaking again. It would have been obvious even to the dumbest person that Lola was taking all of this pretty hard.

"I know you just want to go home," Sonia acknowledged. "And I know I haven't made any of this easy for you, but I will attempt to be more delicate with my words...starting two hours from now. I do welcome that silence you've promised."

Lola slumped over, knowing Sonia couldn't resist carving out one last jab—and then true to her word, she stayed as silent as possible for almost the entire ride.

About half an hour into their trek, they started to see some sort of fenced off facility, or base—Lola wasn't sure. She wanted to ask Sonia what it was but didn't want to risk another spiteful comment. When they got closer to it, Lola figured it was a military base because there were men and women doing drills outside in a large dirt area.

They didn't ride too close to the base, but they had been spotted by some of the people there—although to be fair, there wasn't anything else around, so any movement would no doubt attract at least some attention.

Just before the base was out of sight, it looked like they had caught the eye of someone in particular. It was too far away for Lola to see clearly without her glasses, but she almost thought she recognized the man looking at them. Her horse stalled and Lola tried to make out the face of the man that was watching them. It didn't take long for Sonia to realize that Lola had stopped following.

"What are you doing?" Sonia asked sounding a bit irritated.

"I think I know him," Lola said quietly. "The man behind the fence."

"That's impossible," Sonia told her. "Now hurry up, we're not supposed to stop in this area."

"That's a military base, isn't it?" Lola asked.

"Yes," Sonia said. "Which is exactly why we're not allowed to stop here." She continued on the path, making sure that Lola was following. "I was also under the impression that it would still be silent."

As they kept riding to wherever it was they were going, the time did not fly by, but at least there was always something to look at. They rode through grassy meadow after grassy meadow with the fresh breezy air dancing through their hair. They passed through one meadow that smelled of strawberries, which were undoubtedly close by but out of sight.

There was one meadow that really caught Lola's intrigue, it had a large area covered in golden, luminescent flowers. They were too far away to pick any up, but before they were out of sight Sonia told her to remind her to pick some up on the way back.

After crossing two rivers, more than a few hill sides, and what seemed like more than two hours of traveling, they finally arrived in a deep green valley surrounded by trench-like mountains. The location was serene and seemed untouched until they emerged from the other side of the hill.

Staring at them was this hideously out of place building. It was shaped like an *H* that was missing one of its legs. It was an awkwardly formed marvel that in and of itself looked like a warning, and it was also exactly where Lola was going to have to go.

Of course this is where I would end up. Nothing important can ever just be in a normal place.

Lola started to slowly creep forward, but before the horse could take another step Sonia stopped her.

"We're camping here," Sonia told Lola. "I don't want her to know you're here until tomorrow."

"You don't want *who* to know I'm here?" Lola inquired. Her mind immediately thought of all the reasons they might need to hide, none of them good.

"I don't want Simora to know you're here," Sonia said. "Not yet." She dismounted and started unbuckling the saddle bags. "Let's set up camp."

Lola got down from her horse and started unbuckling her own saddle bags. She saw that Sonia had laid one of her bags open and took out a minuscule bundle of something before quickly placing it on the ground. Within two seconds of taking the bundle out of the bag, it plumped up to its regular size. Now that it was bigger, Lola could tell that the bundle was a tent.

"Take your tent out just like I did," Sonia told her. "You should always take the larger objects out like that, you can do some real damage if you let it normalize in your hand."

Just as Sonia instructed, Lola removed her miniature tent from her saddle bag and quickly dropped it on the ground—and just like Sonia's tent, it grew to its normal size within two seconds.

They both began to set up their separate tents and to Sonia's surprise, Lola was able to finish before her—for that same reason Lola was now in charge of finding the firewood. She welcomed the task without a single complaint, anything to get some time away from Sonia breathing down her neck.

Lola got on her horse and rode in the direction they had come. It took her a little longer than she had expected to get to the area she was thinking about, and unfortunately for her the sun was already setting.

"It's not even five o'clock yet," Lola commented to herself, unreasonably exasperated. She was trying not to let the little things get to her, but it was getting more difficult when there was already so much pressure from the bigger problems.

She took her enchanted shrinking saddle bag and began to pick up twigs and branches as she saw them. She continued to collect anything she thought they could burn until she came across a section of a discarded tree trunk. Excited to know that she wouldn't have sit on the dirt floor, she rushed over to pack it up, but as soon as she got there a crow landed on it. She was taken aback for a second, but then tried to get the crow to leave.

"Shoo!" She demanded as she flailed her hands at the ominous bird, but the bird just stayed there. "Come on you, get away." The crow refused to move even an inch, so Lola decided to try and shrink the log with the crow still on top of it. She wriggled most of one end of the trunk into her saddle bag until it shrunk and fell inside. The crow landed on the soil beneath the log but seemed unfazed. Just then Lola felt a shiver go up her spine as she and the crow locked eyes. It took her a good second to look away, but she finally did.

"Well, thanks for the log, bird," she told the crow, as if it could actually understand her.

Proud of her victory over the tree trunk, she turned around and started to walk back to her horse. The crow was not about to take that exchange as a firm goodbye, so it started following her. Its little body hopped closer and closer as she walked away. Lola turned around and caught the crow right at her heels. Her eyebrows furrowed and her lips made a hard line as she watched the sneaky bird hop even closer.

"What are you doing?" She asked the crow. "Why are you following me? Was this really your log?"

The crow said nothing, as most crows do, so Lola kept on walking toward her horse and so did the crow. She stopped again and looked back at it. After several mesmerizing seconds of eye contact, she crouched down in front of it, ready for an odd confrontation.

"You're not just a bird, are you?" She asked the crow as casually as if she were talking to a human. "What are you? Why are you following me?" The crow gave a low *caw* and was still unwavering from his proximity to her.

"Listen here, bird," Lola said as she pointed her long finger at it. "I don't trust you, just like I don't trust everything else in *your* universe—okay? So why don't you just go along your business and I'll do the same?" Lola hadn't even taken three steps before the crow started to follow her again. This time she whipped her whole body around and did little to keep her anger at bay.

"No, bird!" She yelled. "Do not follow me! You don't think I know you're not a normal bird? Everything in this stupid universe is out to get me, so I'm going to tell you something right now—if you try anything, I will lose my sh…" Just then she started kicking loose leaves everywhere around the crow. She was erratic, like she had finally lost her mind. "That's what I'll do, bird! That's what I'll do to you if you don't leave me alone!"

Right as she ended her tantrum, they heard another crow cawing from afar. Both she and the crow turned toward the new bird call and then back to each other. A second later the crow opened its wings and flew toward the unseen bird caller. Lola patiently watched as the crow flew away, dodging trees and branches along the way. Even

172

after the crow was out of sight, she kept staring in its direction. Her mind had gone completely blank and she could think of absolutely nothing. She was observing the increasing darkness as she felt a crisp, earthy breeze waft past her face.

When she heard the sound of her horse from the other side of some bushes, she was revived from her numb trance. She blinked furiously and wiped her eyes from the dryness. After a few deep breaths she finally walked back to meet Willow. She placed her hands on Willow's silky coat just to make sure she was real. Her ridiculous outburst left her questioning her state of mind without much resolve.

"What am I doing?" She could barely say it out loud to herself. Her face had gone sullen and unmoving. Silent tears began to stream down her face as she stood unflinchingly.

"You're crying," Lola heard an unfamiliar tone come from Sonia's unexpected appearance. She was no doubt checking to see what was taking so long. "Why?" Lola was unresponsive to Sonia's question.

"I caught the end of your little episode," Sonia told her. "I've never seen anything like it."

"I'm so tired," Lola mumbled. "I'm so frustrated, and hurt, and... and..."

"And defeated," Sonia finished Lola's thought, sympathy nowhere to be found. She walked closer to her with a clear air of discomfort. "Listen, I know I've been hard on you and for that I'm a little sorry. There's a lot on the line for both of us and although we're in this situation because of my mistake, I need your help. I need you to stay strong and I know you can do it." As far as apologies went, that was probably the most that Lola was ever going to get out of her.

Lola gave her one small nod, but her grief was still doing some immense damage on the inside. Letting herself be a shell of a person seemed like the safest thing to do—at least for the rest of the night.

Sonia returned the nod as she mounted her horse. She began to lead the way back to their camp site with only minutes to spare before complete darkness hit. Sensing that Lola was going to be of no help in her current state of mind, she decided to say something that she was trying to avoid.

"I know you know why I've been so harsh to you," Sonia started saying. "Mara and I are not on good terms, as you can very well tell." Lola visibly perked up a bit, wanting her to continue with what she had to say about Mara. "I practically raised her alongside her parents," Sonia explained. "I never wanted children because I had her. She is the most selfless, most brilliant person I have ever known. She is the person I love most in this world, and even that wasn't enough to keep me from ruining our relationship."

Hearing Sonia finally talk about Mara made Lola gradually come to life. She already knew that Sonia's bitterness toward her wasn't really because of her, so she wanted to know every detail about the real source of the animosity.

"What happened?" Lola asked wearily.

"I used to think that it wasn't my fault, but nobody seems to forget to remind me that it is," Sonia said, giving off an arrogant vibe.

"I'm sure it's hard to tell, but sometimes I tend to prioritize my work above others."

"No—" Lola feigned surprise, not attempting to hide her sarcasm, which was received with no defense from Sonia.

"I wish I could say I did everything I could to help, but that's where I went wrong." Sonia's voice softened even more and she was becoming harder to hear.

A sad silence afflicted them both, but Lola couldn't help herself—she wanted to know everything. "What did you do, Sonia?"

Before speaking, Sonia turned around to face her, but then quickly turned back. Even in the dark Lola could see the shadows that formed Sonia's wounded, yet prideful expression.

"I didn't help her," Sonia said, not bringing herself to look at Lola again.

"Come on," Lola egged her. "What happened? What did Mara want?"

"Look, I'll tell you, but I already know how you're going to respond—so just don't." Sonia sounded like this might have been the hundredth time she had been asked to explain the situation.

"Fine, just start from the beginning," Lola said with anticipation. She even made Willow gallop a fraction of a second faster in order to be closer to hear better.

"Mara was called away to Cavalerian a couple of months ago," Sonia started to say. "They're dealing with an *ailment,* I guess you could say. It needs to be reversed and they were in urgent need of her help. She's one of the most well known aide workers for magical ailments in the country, you see." She looked so proud to say that about Mara. Lola even saw a little twinkle in her eye. "She asked me for help and I said no. I was busy."

"There's no point hiding anything now, Sonia," Lola told her, pressing for the whole story.

"I was busy," Sonia snapped. "I was on my way to finally finding a solution for the people who were losing their children." The defense of her actions probably didn't win her any sympathy points from anyone—it sure didn't with Lola.

"Isn't there someone else that could have helped her?" Lola asked, surprisingly wanting to make Sonia feel better. "If she's really that well known, why didn't she just ask someone else for help?"

"She's well known because she's a witch," Sonia told her. "The best help would really only come from other witches and warlocks. That's why she came to me—that's why she's been talking to Gwen. There aren't a lot of us and the ones that do exist don't normally follow the humanitarian route, so there's not a lot of help to go around."

Lola wanted Sonia to talk more about Mara. It was fascinating to know what her other dimensional self did in this world. It was also a little unnerving at the same time. She was starting to get jealous of Mara. How could she be so much less accomplished than her? Lola was starting to feel down on herself about her unadventurous life. This was not going well.

The silence came back for a brief moment while Lola pondered all of the new information about Mara and how great she is, but also about her role in Sonia's life. It was kind of interesting because she didn't have that kind of relationship with her own aunt.

"There's more, isn't there?" Lola asked. Her face had gone hard and looked as if she didn't trust Sonia's entire story. "I can feel it. You're not telling me the whole truth."

"How perceptive of you," Sonia remarked with snark, but as soon as she, did she remembered that she was trying to be nicer to Lola. "Sorry, force of habit."

"So, what are you not telling me?" Lola insisted. Sonia huffed loudly, clearly not wanting to discuss it further. "What are you hiding?" Lola pestered on. Sonia's refusal to continue the conversation was even more of a reason for Lola to refrain from completely trusting her. It didn't matter how many times Sonia said she was doing all of this to help get them home, something about all of these little missions kept nagging at Lola. It was making her wonder if this was really the best way of going about things.

Again, Sonia said nothing and outright ignored Lola.

"Just tell me!" Lola demanded.

"Fine!" Sonia yelled, out of frustration. "She wanted my work —" She blurted out. The words echoed around them as they got closer to the opening of the valley. Lola was taken aback, not expecting such a fierce reaction, but then it all made sense. Almost as if she had made the biggest discovery in the world. Lola finally understood Sonia's disdain for her.

"You weren't succeeding, were you?" Lola quickly became enthralled because she had figured Sonia out. "You were afraid she

177

would be able to do what you couldn't—to use your work and actually finish it. You didn't want her to prove that she was better than you." Lola's train of thought came out mindlessly without regard for how Sonia was feeling. Sonia's heart was pounding so hard, Lola could swear she could hear it. It looked like she wasn't even present anymore.

"I'm done talking about this." Sonia told her through gritted teeth.

Lola knew better than to press her on this new development, but she was still very curious. Luckily they arrived to their campsite seconds later so they each busied themselves with readying the inside of their tents to avoid awkward looks. There wasn't much to ready as far as the tents went, they just both knew they needed some time to cool off.

It's not my fault she screwed things up, Lola thought to herself. *She can't seriously stay mad at me for figuring out the truth—that's just stupid. She put Jason in this situation. I wouldn't doubt she messed everything up for Mara too. She's so self-centered. I'm surprised anyone has the patience to be around her.*

Like always, Lola's thoughts carried her away and got the best of her. One after the other, her thoughts started feeding each other until eventually it just became boring to keep going and they started to dwindle.

Neither one spoke to the other for almost an hour—not even when they made the fire, which Sonia did by snapping her fingers, nor while making dinner. As soon as the food was ready, they both sat on the log that Lola had taken from the crow and just ate. Surprisingly, the silence wasn't as uncomfortable as it should have been. They were probably both too tired to care much about their earlier conversation.

Lola couldn't stop thinking about what she had said to Sonia and how it must have made her feel. It's not like Sonia didn't already know what she had done and why she had done it, but at the same time, hearing it out loud must have really stung.

"I'm sorry," Lola told her. Sonia continued eating as if she had not heard her speak. "I shouldn't have spewed all of those accusations."

Sonia didn't say a word. She didn't even acknowledge that Lola was apologizing, at least not right away. She sort of just sat there and kept eating.

"You're not completely wrong," Sonia admitted after several dragged-out minutes.

They both went back to eating their food until Lola tried to ease the tension even more. "So, why didn't you two just work together if you were both trying to figure out the same thing?" She asked, thinking it was the obvious solution.

"That's not exactly what she's working on," Sonia said. "Our work was similar in that it required life-giving magic."

"Oh," Lola said, thinking that was all she would get out of her.

"We should move on," Sonia suggested. "We have more important things to talk about."

Just as Sonia finished speaking, something wiggled around on the inside of her coat. Lola noticed it immediately and then saw that it moved again. Before Lola could ask, Sonia held up her hand to stop her.

"It's nothing," Sonia told her and then looked inside of her coat.

"I'm sure," Lola said sarcastically, but then let it go. She didn't strain to poke her nose in places it didn't belong as much anymore. It was exhausting to ask questions and then be told you don't need to know the answer, so she just stopped.

Once Sonia was settled with whatever she was hiding, they both set aside their bowls so they could get started. Lola began to feel a lump in her throat as she awaited instructions for another ludicrous deception.

"We have to do this as soon as the sun comes up," Sonia started to say. "The entrance is inside the invisible leg of the right tower."

"Of course it is," Lola said. "I'm assuming the tower is just going to beam me up, is that it?" Sonia exhaled deeply, except this time it seemed routine for her to give that kind of reaction to Lola's smart-mouth comments.

"You're just going to have to feel around for it," Sonia explained. "There's something there, trust me. You have to slide your hands all over each wall until you find a fist-sized hole. There is a sharp point inside the hole where you have to prick your finger. Well, actually you won't." She pulled out a very small vial and held it up in the light of the fire. Inside of the vial there was a drop or two of what was presumably blood.

"You're going to pour this onto your finger," Sonia told her.

"Ugh, that's so unsanitary," Lola said with disgust. "It's your blood, isn't it?"

"No," Sonia assured her. "It's Mara's blood. The entrance won't open without it. Obviously, it can't be *your* blood or Simora will know you're not Mara, and it can't be mine because you're not me—are you following?"

"I really hope you don't just carry this around," Lola said dryly as she tipped the vial back and forth between her fingers. "Blood sacrifice is a weird power move. How are you okay with that?"

"It's not about being okay with it," Sonia responded. "I agree that it's odd, but if you knew Simora you wouldn't think this is out of character for her. I know a lot of powerful people who prey on weakness. If you weaken yourself, you've done half of the work for them, and all they had to do was give you the tools."

"Do you hear yourself?" Lola said. "You sound like a crackpot old lady." Sonia gave a huff, but didn't seem too bothered by the comment. "Moving on, what's next?"

"You're going to make your way up the stairs of the tower until you reach the bridge," Sonia told her. "She'll be waiting for you there."

Lola's breaths were becoming shallow and rapid. "What am I supposed to say to her?" She asked with her eyes just a little wider than before.

"The truth," Sonia said. "Tell her you want her piece of the experiment—her memory of it."

181

"You're confusing me," Lola told her. "You said I was supposed to be getting ingredients."

"Not this time," Sonia admitted. "She has the formula we need to make the potion. The formula that was going to help solve the anomaly before they stopped us. Technically we're not supposed to be using anything that has to do with our experiment for the time being, but also technically, you're not supposed to be here. Let's try to keep this hush, okay?"

"Wait," Lola said. "They stopped you from finishing your experiment? Who?"

"Just focus," Sonia said. "She's not going to give it to you."

"I'm so lost," Lola said throwing her arms in the air.

"What you're actually there to get belongs to her valiant," Sonia said. "I won't ruin the surprise, but it's important that you get the right feather." Lola nodded as if she was taking very detailed mental notes from a crazy person. "Her valiant is a falcon. There's only one up there and it usually stays on the outer walkway of the bridge. It likes to watch for intruders, in case you were wondering."

"I wasn't, but go on." Lola's sass tended to have a mind of its own, but Sonia didn't notice.

"I want to make it very clear that Simora can't know that you are taking those feathers," Sonia warned. "Just go to the area where the falcon perches and pick handfuls up off the floor."

"All of this sounds terrifyingly easy," Lola said. "So, this is where you tell me why I'm picking up dirty bird feathers."

"Simora doesn't have the memory of the formula," Sonia told her. "Her falcon has it. I'll conjure a spell to lure him to me so that I can extract the memory."

Lola pursed her lips as if she were sucking air through a thin straw. Her confidence in Sonia was wavering to say the least. This all sounded so bananas that she was waiting for the tin hat to come out. She took a couple of breaths with her eyes shut and lips still pursed. "Anything else I should know?"

"Yes," Sonia said. "She's a real *witch*."

"You're super classy." Lola shook her head, but Sonia's expression gave a clear indication that she knew Lola would feel the same way about Simora soon enough.

After their talk and without much hesitation, both women retreated to their tents. As soon as Lola's head hit the unshapely thin pillow, she started to drift to sleep. Although her eyes were closed, she could see a distinct pair of grape-sized yellow lights flashing at her. The lights were bouncing nearer by the second, but she wasn't scared. They came closer and closer until finally they were flashing right at her face, except these weren't lights, they were eyes. Everything around her was pitch black, except for these acquainted eyes.

"She knows," said a squawky voice that followed the eyes. They took flight and landed a few steps away. The sound of a loud switch turning on, echoed as if they were in a warehouse. A single light from above followed the noisy switch, and it illuminated a well-known wooden log and its favorite crow.

"She knows," said the birdie voice again.

Lola took a step toward it, but as soon as she did, the crow flew away and the light shut off.

Chapter 15

The morning rays bled through the tent as Lola woke up. She was slightly blinded by what little sun light was coming in, but welcomed it knowing that she was going to be one day closer to going home. As she sat up, she could hear the harmonious sounds of birds chirping and busy rustling footsteps on the dead leaves that were scattered around her tent. She undid the entrance of her tent and stuck her feet out to put her shoes on.

"And here I thought you were going to sleep all day," Sonia greeted her with fresh morning sass. Lola said nothing, instead she gave Sonia a long, flattened smile. She laced up her shoes and then got up to stretch. She was surprisingly rested even after having slept on the hard ground.

Sonia shoved a hot bowl into Lola's gut without warning. "Eat," she demanded. "You need to be well energized and focused."

Lola shoveled the contents of the bowl into her mouth without argument. She had come to the realization that if she just did what

Sonia said, they might get out of Terre Two faster. Although, not questioning everything would be hard for her to do.

"Splash some water on your face," Sonia told her as she handed her an old leather-covered canteen. "I need you as awake as possible."

Lola did as she was told—she poured the water over her forehead so that it would drip down her face, and then shook it off. When she looked up she thought she saw something small and rodent-like poking out of Sonia's tent.

"Hey," she called to Sonia. "I think your 'nothing' is trying to escape."

"My what?" Sonia asked confused.

"That 'nothing' you had in your coat last night just poked its head out of your tent." Lola knew that the thing Sonia was hiding last night was an animal, but now she knew for sure that it was a rat.

"Don't worry about her," Sonia said. "She's fine."

"Okay then," Lola said. "I'm ready." She looked over at Sonia, who was giving her the magical shrinking purse.

"Remember what we talked about," said Sonia. "Find the entrance but be careful not to prick your own finger. Make up an excuse that will give you enough time to grab the feathers from the outer walkway, and don't get caught."

"Right, don't get caught," Lola repeated. "Sounds conveniently easy enough."

"You can do this," Sonia told her right as she gave her a little push toward her horse. Lola hesitated as she slowly slipped one foot into the stirrup. The view of the towers from their campsite was ominous. Even though the sky was fairly clear, the white clouds were obligated to loom in the distance.

Lola mounted her horse and began to ride toward the enormous towers They could have easily trumped the Empire State Building in eccentricity alone and it took her longer than expected to get there. Up close, the towers were even more menacing. She was second guessing going through with the plan, but as far as she knew, this was the only way.

She stopped a few feet away from the invisible leg of the first tower. She looked up toward the bridge that connected the two towers and almost at once became a bit nauseous. She dizzily dismounted but landed firmly on the ground and retrieved only what she needed from the saddle bags.

"There's nowhere to tie you up, so I expect you to stay put," Lola told her horse, Willow. The horse snorted and shook her head toward the ground, in response. "Hey, I know you know what I said."

Lola checked her shrinking purse one last time for safe measure. She watched as the little objects rolled around playfully, all the while hoping that she wouldn't have to use any of the potions.

Trying not to delay the inevitable any longer, she stretched out her arms and walked forward toward the invisible leg of the tower. She felt an eeriness go up her spine as she got closer and saw the half of the tower that wasn't invisible, hovering over her head. She tried to shake the feeling, but she couldn't, so she resolved to find that secret entrance even faster than before.

Even though she fully expected to find a solid wall at some point, she still flinched as her fingertips touched the unseen bricks of the tower. She finally exhaled, having not realized that she was holding her breath.

As the relief of actually finding the invisible building passed through her, she quickly wasted no time sweeping her hands all over it for the secret entrance. She traveled around the base of the tower once but found nothing. Unfortunately for her the towers were not small, so finding the entrance was probably going to take longer than she expected. Her next brilliant idea was to press her whole body against the bricks hoping that would help her find where she needed to prick her finger. She could picture the bizarre sight of her own private miming show.

After two more go-arounds, her knee was the body part that found the way in. Cautiously she inserted her hand and slowly found the sharp needle-like point that was asking for her blood—or in this case, Mara's blood.

Lola dropped her bag on the floor and one hand started searching for the vial of Mara's blood, while her other hand stayed inside the hole where it would go. She pulled out the vial and unstoppered it with her teeth, trying carefully not to spill it. She pulled her other hand from the hole in order to drop the blood onto her finger. She couldn't help thinking how disgusting that was. She touched her fingertip to the mouth of the vial and two little drops came out.

Delicately, she put her hand back in the hole and gently touched her finger to the pointy figure inside. It didn't take long before she could no longer feel the needle—it had disappeared instantly and produced a now visible entrance.

It was difficult to say exactly how the entrance had appeared —whether the bricks moved back or disintegrated, but either way the blood had worked and that's all that mattered.

The inside of the tower was dimly lit and the walls were some semblance of grey, but it was hard to tell. On a good note, at least getting lost would not be a problem. There was a clear path to the stairs and on each side a door that looked like they could easily lead to cavernous dungeons.

When she reached the spiral stairs, she peered up only to realize that she might not even make it all the way. There were no railings and the steps didn't exactly seem up to code. They were more or less just extra limbs that the walls had conjured, so that daring people could try their luck. They wrapped around the entire tower and looked kind of like displaced piano keys, making the labor of escalating them, even more intense.

I'm going to die here, she thought, quite sure of herself— although, surprisingly not too bothered by it. She took the first two steps in stride, but that's exactly what caused her to fall backwards almost immediately.

They moved! The stairs began to move like an escalator right as she started to walk up them. At that point she was still on the ground, confused and a bit irritated. The stairs were not moving now, but she was sure they had been just a moment ago.

Lola stood up as she dusted herself off and began her second attempt at the stairs. Without much to hold on to, she put one hand on the wall and stretched out the other for balance. She took one step, then a second one, and then they moved—but not for long. They stopped almost as soon as she stopped climbing.

Again, she took two more steps and the stairs began to move. One step after the other they helped her climb past several doors that were embedded in the walls. Each door looked the same—no numbers, no signs, no way of knowing what floor you were on.

Getting to the bridge was taking its toll on Lola. She was getting dizzy trying not to fall off the edge. Fortunately for her, she could see a landing coming up that she was sure was the entrance to the bridge.

When she finally climbed all the way, she became even more uneasy. The air seemed thinner and there was a flow of energy that she couldn't describe. It was making her want to puke. Her legs were a bit unstable and wobbly as she attempted to shake them out.

As soon as she was feeling better, she looked up to see the door to the inside of the bridge. It was enormous and beautifully old-worldly. It was covered in mechanisms that needed to be triggered in order to be opened. Instead of trying to find out how to open it, Lola figured a knock would suffice.

Her knock initiated the movement of the exposed gears on the door. They moved in sync as if the door was assembling itself into a puzzle.

Well, that was easy.

When the chain reactions of the door finally unlocked, it slowly opened to reveal a gorgeous blonde woman in a light gray pant suit, but that's not all it revealed. Behind the woman was the sight of something out of a jungle movie. There were birds upon birds of all types perching or flying about. They were colorful and of all sizes.

"Mara," Simora said with the fakest smile Lola had ever seen on a person. "Don't just stand there."

Lola's eyes had widened almost enough to cover most of her face. The birds were everywhere. She crossed the threshold and followed as Simora walked casually past her avian pets... or friends—it wasn't clear yet.

The entire enclosed bridge was set up like a laboratory. There were glass containers on tables holding all different kinds of liquids. Upon closer observation, she even noticed that there was work being done at that very moment.

The birds were working on the experiments in the room even as they were walking in. They were mixing ingredients, heating liquids, and testing concoctions. Lola watched a blue jay with a pipet in its mouth transferring liquid from one beaker to another. She also saw a small songbird peck apart a leaf and then drop a piece of it into a cylindrical glass container that immediately produced a puff of smoke.

"This is incredible," Lola said as she continued to observe the birds.

"You're surprised?" Simora asked, stopping in front of one of the arched openings that led to the outer walkway of the bridge.

"These creatures always surprise me," Lola answered quickly. Her smile gave nothing away and for the first time that day she felt confident.

Simora looked at her for more than a few seconds, as if she were deciding whether or not to agree with her comment. She stood there with the demeanor of what Lola imagined was the most powerful person in existence. "I suppose so," she said. "I've always believed them to be more impressive than humans in every capacity."

Lola exhaled profoundly, but didn't waiver in her gaze—if anything she even stood up a little straighter.

"This is your first time here, isn't it?" Simora asked.

Lola said nothing, just smiled. She wanted to make sure she wouldn't be caught in a lie, especially since she had no idea if Mara had ever been there.

"What do you think?" Simora wanted to know.

"It's a lot more modern than I expected," Lola answered.

"Well, I'm not medieval," Simora said in a snooty tone, but at the same time jokingly. "So, are you ready to tell me the reason for this visit?"

"Yes," Lola stumbled. "I mean, not that I wasn't ready before —I mean—I'm here for the memory, but I suspect you already know that."

Whatever trace of a smile that Simora had was now gone. It was replaced with curious eyes and straight lips.

"You know, there's something peculiar about you today," Simora snared a bit. "Don't get me wrong, you've always been odd, but now you're just... peculiar."

"It has been a while since I last saw you," Lola said pretending she was trying to recall the last time she saw her. "I've changed a bit."

"People don't really change, dear," Simora countered. "Some of us just become better liars. Have you become a better liar, Mara?"

A swirl of icy air ran through Lola after hearing Simora's words. She was now visibly more worried and her confidence was leaving her little by little. Before she could answer, a cawing sound rang out from the other end of the room.

"Oh, that's right," Simora started saying. "George told me he ran into you last night."

"George?" As soon as Lola repeated the name, a crow swooped in and landed on the table next to Simora.

"He was quite upset that you took his favorite log—whatever that means," she said, making a fake pouty face as if she were mocking them both. "But mostly he was upset that you were yelling at him— saying something about *this world*? What do you mean by, *this* world? I'm slightly intrigued."

Lola's heart sank to the pit of her stomach. *Stupid bird.*

"I just travel so much that every place looks like a different world," Lola fibbed. "I'm sure you experience that sometimes."

Simora's gaze was harsh and almost blinding. There was no muscle movement on her face whatsoever. "No, not really," she said in response to Lola's assumption.

At that moment, Lola caught a glimpse of what she was actually there to get. She could see the falcon perched right where Sonia said it would be.

Lola was focusing so much that she was surprised when Simora continued to talk.

"I know what you're working on," Simora said. "Trust me, you would never be able to use my work in time to help them."

"Nevertheless," Lola said, the strength in her voice slipping away. "I'm still here for the memory."

"Did you really think I would give it to you," Simora asked, her pride glowing.

Lola took a beat before answering. "No, but I had to try anyway. I have to try everything I can to save him…them."

A sinister smile crept over Simora's face. It gave Lola an unsettling vibe. She tried to look away, but her eyes were locked.

"That's nauseatingly noble of you, but you've wasted your time," Simora told her. "In any case, I'm using it, so I'm not giving it to anyone."

Trying hard to sell the disappointment, Lola dropped her head and looked at the ground for a couple of seconds. "I understand," she said, her dismay convincing even herself. "Before I go, can I bother you for some water? The stairs were brutal."

Simora pressed her lips in annoyance, but then began to walk out of the room. As soon as she was out of sight, Lola sprinted through one of the three arches for the outer walk-way. She was running so fast that she slid and hit the railing right where the falcon was perched. The falcon was startled and flew away.

Just as Lola was about to gather up some of the feathers, she noticed how little was between her and a horrific fall. The land below started swirling and an unexplainable gravitational pull inflicted her body. Her hand wrapped tightly around the thin bar of the railing. The sounds of the birds started to creep back into her ears and that helped her shake off the vertigo. What seemed like minutes were only seconds of fogginess.

Quickly, she opened her purse and shoved whatever handfuls of feathers she could get until she heard Simora coming back. She stood up and dusted herself off as if nothing had happened.

"Wow, what a great view," Lola said a bit breathy. "You get to see this every day? That's awesome."

Simora handed Lola the glass of water, but not without suspicion.

"Oh, thank you," Lola said as she quickly took the water from her and drank it in one giant gulp. "So refreshing!" She fumbled in handing back the glass. "Well, I should really go. Thank you for your time. I'm sure you're very busy."

Lola couldn't help herself, she just kept rambling. "By the way, I'm very impressed at how well trained your birds are—you know, with them not pooping in your lab and all that. It's extremely impressive." She backed into a small table on her way to the door, but made sure it didn't fall over.

"Thank you," Simora said without meaning it. "Just please leave."

"Right," Lola said as she opened the enormous door to leave. Without looking back, she closed the door and began her decent for the exit, relief washing over her with every step she took.

Chapter 16

It didn't take long for Lola to get back to the campsite. Willow had waited just like she was told to do. Sonia was waiting patiently by the fire when Lola arrived. The smell of the burning wood welcomed them back with a nice cloud of smoke.

"Did you get it?" Sonia asked immediately after Lola dismounted.

"I think so," Lola said. "I grabbed what I could." She opened the purse so that Sonia could look inside.

"Lucky for you, most of those do belong to Simora's falcon," Sonia told her. Even when Lola did something right, Sonia still couldn't bring herself to give an actual compliment.

Lola slumped down onto the log and rubbed her face harshly. She reached over to grab a stick that was toasting bread and pulled two pieces off.

"Can we go now?" She asked impatiently and with a mouth full of toast. "I could really use a shower."

"Yes," Sonia said. "Pack up before Simora chases us out of here."

As they rode back to town, they passed the field that had the golden flowers Sonia wanted, so they made a stop. Oddly enough she didn't ride toward the flowers at all. They stopped right in the middle of the trail.

"You can stay on the horse," she told Lola as she dismounted and then began to walk in the direction of the flowers. She stopped halfway and then crouched down as she pulled something out of her coat.

It was a little difficult to see what was going on, but if she squinted her eyes enough, Lola could see a gray blob scampering toward the flowers Sonia wanted. It was so hard for Lola to see what was going on without her glasses. The blob, which Lola assumed was Sonia's rat, Madelyn, made about a dozen trips back and forth before Sonia was satisfied with her loot.

Lola hadn't realized this until they were done, but Sonia had been covering her nose and mouth with the lapel of her coat the entire time. She even tried to stay covered as she zipped up the bag that held the flowers.

When they were done, the rat went back into Sonia's inside coat pocket and rustled around until it settled into a lump. Sonia seemed pretty pleased with her find as she walked back to the horses.

"I'm glad to see this wasn't a complete waste of time," Sonia said, more happy than usual as she mounted her horse.

"Yup, that's what I want to hear after a blood sacrifice and collecting disease ridden feathers with my bare hands," Lola said back, shaking her head.

"I was referring to the commute," Sonia told her. "These poppies are expensive if you don't gather them yourself. Luckily, Madelyn is immune to poppy pollen—a trait I helped her develop early on."

"That's great," Lola said, less than enthused. "Can we go now?"

The ride back seemed shorter than before and thankfully so, given how exhausted Lola was from that morning's task. Arthur was waiting for them when they arrived. He almost looked relieved for some reason.

"I can't thank you enough for letting us borrow your magnificent horses," Sonia schmoozed him. "It's so hard to find good friends, let alone ones who will come through for you at the last minute."

Arthur blushed at Sonia's words. Out of all of the things that Sonia had done, fake flirting with a man for his horses was probably one of the cruelest.

"So about that dinner," Arthur began to say.

"Absolutely," Sonia said. "Let me look at my schedule. I'm sure I'm very busy, but I'll let you know. Bye-bye." She nudged Lola to follow her.

Lola thanked Arthur a bit more sincerely before catching up to Sonia. "You're going to lose your *good* friends if you keep treating them like that."

"I'll call him eventually," Sonia said defending herself. "I'm not going anywhere."

They made it to Sonia's office, which couldn't have come soon enough if it were up to Lola. Like every other time, she rushed over to see Jason to make sure he was still alive.

"I can't believe how normal he looks," Lola said. "Maybe you can wake him up for a minute so we can ask him how he's feeling."

"We already had this conversation," Sonia told her, slightly shaking her head. "It doesn't matter how he looks on the outside, what matters is what's going on inside."

"He just doesn't look hurt at all," Lola almost whimpered. Sonia walked over to her and helped her stand up.

"Trust me," she said. "He's not doing well, but we're almost done. The ball is tomorrow night. While you're off getting the tea leaf from the castle, I will be getting Simora's memory from her falcon. This will all be over tomorrow."

Lola chocked up a little just thinking about them being able to leave soon. "And you'll take us to the portal right away?" She asked, just to make certain.

"Yes," Sonia assured her. "Come on, we have to prepare." She pulled open a couple of drawers until she found a small snipping tool. "Here, put this in your bag."

Lola took the snipping tool and dropped it in her shrinking bag. She then pulled out all of the feathers that she had taken from Simora's tower and placed them on the table.

"I was going to ask for those next," Sonia told her. "Not here though—let's go."

They left Sonia's lab and made their way to the other side of town to Sonia's government issued lab. When they arrived, Lola wanted a couple of seconds to take a good look at the castle before going inside. She was imagining a distressed princess in one of those towers, waiting to be rescued.

"Hey, snap out of it," Sonia said trying to pull her toward the building entrance. "That reminds me, you're going to have to really focus in there tomorrow. Any kind of screw up can make everything fall apart."

Sonia continued to walk into the government building and Lola followed, trying to do just as she was told and stay focused. Sonia swiped her badge and the doors opened immediately to reveal the same paralyzing white lobby and the weird potted plant in its strange red planter. Somehow the chilly air in the lobby was more uncomfortable the second time around.

"Hello ladies," welcomed the crimson haired receptionist.

"Hello Charlotte," Sonia greeted her.

Charlotte pushed the button underneath her desk so that they could proceed to the second set of doors. Sonia swiped her badge one more time and the doors opened to the daunting hallway of potted plants. Lola began to walk to the extent that they walked last time but stopped as soon as she noticed Sonia had stopped early.

Sonia had picked the room immediately in front of the double doors that were now closed. Last time they were there, they had to pass at least twenty doors before they entered Sonia's lab. Just as Lola was approaching her, she noticed the same red planter from the lobby across from the door they were entering.

"So that's why you don't lock your door," Lola said.

"What?" Sonia asked absentmindedly.

"This place," Lola continued to say. "It's made for you, isn't it? You pick a weird planter and go into the lab it's across from. That's why you don't worry about the others coming in here."

"You're close," Sonia said. "But not quite." She walked over to her glass cabinet and called for Lola to follow.

"If someone really wanted to come in here, they could just try each door," Lola said, as if she had beat the system.

"If they wanted to risk life and limb, they could," Sonia responded. "Don't be fooled by my *weird* planters. You never know what you might find behind those other doors." Sonia gave Lola a warning look as if to say, *don't try opening the other doors.*

"Now then," Sonia said. "You need to stock up on potions for tomorrow. Security will be high, but that doesn't mean you can't do it."

"Do what again?"

"The tea leaf," Sonia reminded her. "You need to get some of it so that we can melt the crystal ginger Gwen gave you." Sonia opened Lola's purse and started dropping vials into it. This time she pulled out

202

one that Lola had not seen the last time. The liquid was a pretty sunshine-yellow and seemed to have a thick consistency. Unlike the others, Sonia only had a few of those.

"See this?" Sonia asked. "It's *my* invisibility potion. It's stronger, lasts longer, and takes a hell of a lot more time to make than the average stuff the government uses. Fortunately for us, I started brewing these a month ago." Sonia was holding one of the vials in her hand, but Lola saw that there was one more in the cabinet. "Try not to use it if you can avoid it."

"Is it dangerous?" Lola asked, cautious about using something even the government didn't have.

"No," Sonia assured her. "But it only makes *you* invisible, do you understand?"

Lola nodded her head as she took the vial. "I'm glad you have this," she told Sonia. "What kind of magical dimension would this be if you didn't have an invisibility potion?" Sonia didn't respond. She was too busy pulling out another potion that looked like liquid opal.

"Wow, that's beautiful," Lola said wanting to touch the vial.

"I'm only going to give you half of this," Sonia told her. She grabbed an empty vial and filled it halfway with the opal potion. When Lola reached for it, Sonia clasped her hand around hers. "Listen carefully—you will definitely need to use this, but you have to be quick. You're going to use this to get into the vault where they keep the tea leaf." Lola's breath became shallow. Sonia was making her extremely nervous. "The potion is still a bit unpredictable, but I'm almost positive that half a vial will give you at least four minutes."

"Four minutes of what?" Lola asked, caught up in the intensity of Sonia's tone of voice.

"Four minutes of being able to walk through the vault door."

"Okay…" Lola's skepticism meter rose the more nonsense Sonia spoke.

"You're going to touch your finger to the liquid, rub it on the vault door, and then you're going to stick it back in the vial with the rest of the potion. That's how the potion will know what to assimilate with."

Sonia walked over to the giant table in the middle of the room. She cleared all of the glass containers and equipment with a snap of her finger. The objects flew to different parts of the lab and put themselves away.

With another snap of her finger, a small blue light began to form in her head. It became a little sphere that traveled from her head to the palm of her hand. She took the marble of light and began to stretch it apart in the air with her fingers. When it got big enough, she stretched it with her hands until it revealed a holographic image of the castle.

"Take a good look," Sonia told her as she spun the image around so they could see the front of the castle. She put her finger on the entrance and the hologram traveled them into the main lobby of the castle. Sonia pointed to the stairs, "You're going to go up these stairs and to the left. At the end of the hallway you'll find the elevator—take it to the seventh floor." Sonia made the image change again to see the elevator and then to see the seventh floor.

Lola tried to soak in the image of the seventh floor to make sure she wouldn't get lost when she got there. She could see that the walls were lined by gold-framed portraits. The carpet runner was royal blue and had gold fringe all the way around.

"There," Sonia said as she pointed to the biggest door in the hallway. "You're going to go through those doors." The image changed again to show the inside of the room where the vault was. The vault itself looked intimidating and very much like an old-timey bank vault that you would see in the movies.

"Sounds like a lot of work," Lola said. "Are you sure I'll be able to pull it off?"

"The better question is, are you sure you can pull this off," Sonia said. "You can't doubt yourself here—if you do, you'll trip and there's not much we can do after that. Just tell yourself you can do it, otherwise you'll be the only one stopping yourself."

Sonia was right. Lola had to stop relying on her to make sure things worked out. As much as she blamed Sonia for all of this misfortune, half of that blame was all her own.

"Once you're in the vault you'll find the tea leaf," Sonia continued to explain. "We can't take the whole thing because they'll notice. You should snip the stem with the smallest leaf, one that's hardly even there. We want to make sure they don't suspect it's been tampered with. Put the tea in your mouth to get it out of the vault with you. There should be enough residual potion on your tongue for it to pass through."

Sonia closed the hologram by sandwiching the image between her hands. She pushed the blue light into her palm and it traveled all the way back into her head. "Not too bad, right?"

"Right," Lola agreed sarcastically.

"While you're at the ball, I'll be working on getting the memory from Simora's falcon." Sonia held out her hand and Lola grabbed the feathers from her purse to give to her. "It won't take long so I need you to come back as soon as possible."

"Will do," Lola told her.

As they were leaving the lab, Sonia gave Lola some final instructions on what not to say and to not gawk at everything in the castle. When they stepped outside of the building, Lola saw a woman she thought she recognized heading their way, but she couldn't make out exactly who it was until the woman got closer.

"Hey, doesn't that look like Simora?" Lola turned to face Sonia, but she wasn't there. The woman drew near and sure enough, it was Simora.

"Loitering around a government facility, you really must be desperate." Simora approached Lola as if they were old friends.

"I was just passing by," Lola told her and then immediately began to leave.

"Why don't you join me inside for a minute?" Simora asked, but it didn't really seem like a friendly invitation.

"I really should go," Lola said, continuing to try to leave.

"I insist." Simora's fake smile looked like it actually hurt her face.

Lola reluctantly followed Simora inside. When they walked in, Lola immediately noticed that instead of a potted plant, there was a simple wooden bird house suspended in midair. The bird house was blue with yellow stars. Lola tried to make it look like she was not observing the bird house as they passed it.

Just then Lola realized that Charlotte was going to recognize her—she couldn't have her mentioning that she was just there with Sonia. "You know, I'm in a rush and I really need to go." Lola turned around to leave, but as soon as she did, she was unable to move. She felt a force pulling her. She practically flew to Simora, her heels dragging rapidly on the floor.

"Nonsense," Simora said when Lola landed by her side. They approached the receptionist's desk together, but Charlotte wasn't there. She had been replaced by a young woman with long platinum-white hair.

"Good afternoon Ms. Wells," greeted the receptionist.

"Hello Ruby," Simora said, pleasantly enough.

The white-haired receptionist pushed the button underneath the desk so that they could continue through the next set of doors. Simora scanned her badge and just like going to Sonia's lab, the hallway was decorated with the same object that was in the lobby.

What seemed like hundreds of bird houses, were just floating in front of unmarked doors. There were very beautiful patterns on otherwise normal seeming bird houses. There was even a bird house completely covered in glitter and another one that was made of fire blown glass.

"I know what you're up to *Mara*," Simora said breaking the awkward silence. "Don't think for a moment that you're fooling me."

"Excuse me?" Lola said. "I'm sorry, but I don't know what you're talking about."

"My suggestion to you would be to leave," Simora said, not paying much attention to what Lola was saying. "Stalking me won't do you any favors, so you can forget about the memory." Although her words were menacing, her tone was cool and collected.

Simora stopped at one of the doors that was next to a shiny red bird house. "Have I made myself clear?" Lola gave one hard nod in acknowledgment. "Good. I suspect you know your way out." Simora entered the door and let it close on its own.

Lola shivered as soon as the door closed. She started walking back when she noticed the blue bird house with the yellow stars that was in the lobby. It was two doors down and one across from the door Simora had entered. She only looked at it briefly so as to not look suspicious.

Once outside and about a block away from the government building, she saw Sonia waiting on a bench near the center of town.

"Where did you go?" Lola asked angrily.

"I couldn't let her see us together," Sonia explained. "It would have ruined everything."

"Yeah, well a warning would have been nice," Lola said. "She's freaking terrifying."

"What happened?" Sonia turned her head and leaned in so that Lola could keep the details quiet.

Lola took several deep breaths before answering. "She made me walk with her so that she could tell me to stop stalking her."

"Anything else?" Sonia pressed her.

"No," Lola told her. "She just really doesn't want to see me around." They continued to make their way to Sonia's house while they talked about the encounter with Simora.

"Wait," Lola shouted. "Her lab—I know which one it is."

"I'm going to stop you right there," Sonia told her. "She made you walk with her to her lab?"

"Yeah," Lola said. "Was that not clear?"

Sonia pulled Lola to the side to make sure others couldn't hear. "What else did she say to you?"

Lola began to worry, given Sonia's tone. It took her a second to gather up the exact words before she told Sonia what Simora had told her. "She said that I wasn't fooling her and that I should leave, or something like that."

Within a millisecond Sonia's face turned from normal to a mesh of angry and nervous. "She must know," Sonia said ominously. "She must know you're not Mara."

"Wait, what?" Lola's face was now starting to resemble Sonia's worry.

"She must know," Sonia repeated. "She wouldn't have let you into the hallway if she really thought you were Mara. She probably assumed you weren't clever enough to know how to find the lab."

Lola's head started spinning so much that she didn't respond to the insult. She leaned against the wall of the shop they were in front of and rested her head on it. All at once her dream of the crow came back to her. She could hear the crow warning her—it rang in her ear like it was right next to her.

"You have to leave tomorrow before she turns me in," Sonia said.

"How do you know she won't do it right now?" Lola asked in a panic. She crossed her arms around her stomach and tried to slow down her frantic breathing.

"We have plenty of history to suggest that she won't," Sonia told her. "At least not right away. Besides, I have too much over her for her to risk saying anything without covering her tracks first."

Lola still wasn't convinced. She was running through every possible outcome in her head simultaneously. *What am I going to do? What am I going to do? What am I going to do?*

"Hey," Sonia said trying to get her attention. "Hey, look at me. We still have time, trust me." Sonia grabbed Lola's face sternly to make her focus. "Trust me."

Lola nodded heavily at Sonia's words, having no other option but to trust her. What else could she possibly do that was better than what Sonia had planned?

They continued to Sonia's house and when they finally arrived all they wanted to do was rest. They were exhausted and probably smelly from the horses.

Lola was on the verge of going inside when someone called her from the other side of the house.

"Hey, Mar," Manny called out. "Why don't you give me a hand with the wagon?"

As tired as she was, Lola secretly didn't want to pass up an opportunity like this. Sonia almost reached for her to not go, but she too was tired and figured it wasn't worth arguing.

Lola walked over to the side of the house where the horse-drawn wagon was parked. Manny was in the wagon waiting for a helping hand.

"We need to replace some of the boards," he told her. "I need you to cut me three eight-foot pieces while I take these old ones off."

Lola grew up doing this kind of stuff with her dad all the time, so luckily she didn't miss a beat. She found some goggles and ear plugs in the shed, and after plugging in the saw—which was surprisingly similar to the ones she had used before—she quickly made her cuts and had the boards ready.

"Here you go, pa," she stopped cold at her slip up, but tried to hide it. She knew pretending that Manny was her dad was a bad idea, but could anyone really blame her? She passed the boards to him as he put them in place.

"Hand me those," Manny told her pointing at the two electric drills.

Lola grabbed the drills and a handful of screws to give to him. "Aren't you going to pre-drill?" She asked him.

Manny smiled. It was the kind of smile a parent gives their child when they realize the child did learn from them after all. He pointed to a little box on the ground that held assorted drill bits. She opened the box and grabbed two tiny drill bits, then jumped onto the wagon. Manny handed her one of the drills and got to work.

For a brief couple of minutes, Lola was at peace. She almost felt like she was dreaming in a serene cloud of her own personal reality, but she knew she wasn't. This was all real and giving into the moment too much would lead to more heartbreak.

As soon as they were done, they began to clean up. Lola made it a point to avoid eye contact as much as possible.

"Is everything okay Mara?" Manny asked Lola. Of course he would notice, how could he not? It's not like she was being subtle about trying to avoid him.

"I'm okay," she lied without much effort.

"¿Estás segura?" He asked again, this time in Spanish.

She took a second to contemplate whether she should confide in him—whether it would be worth it, or even a good idea. Compromising with herself, she decided that more than ever she needed her dad.

"There's just a lot of pressure on me right now," she admitted. "I'm not going to give up, but I feel bad because I kind of want to give up—but not really. Am I making sense?"

"You want to come home?" Manny asked, already knowing the answer.

Lola's eyes started watering, but she fought back her dewy tears. "Yeah, I do."

A small, dad-knows-best smile appeared on Manny's face. He knew he was going to make a good point and was happy to make it.

"Do you remember when you left for college and every couple of months you would call your mom, crying that you wanted to come home?" It was clear he was going to be very proud of this teaching moment. "Your mom and I would always tell you to come home if you wanted to, but every time we did, you convinced yourself to keep going. I couldn't figure out what you were trying to prove to us, until I realized that you were actually trying to prove something to yourself."

Manny went in for a hug and Lola gave in. "You can come back if you want, but if what you're working on is that important, I know you won't come home until you've accomplished what you've set out to do." Lola let out more tears than she wanted, but it was no use, the flood gates were open.

"You're the most hot-headed, stubborn know-it-all I've ever met," Manny said, laughing a little. "But that's just how *we* are." It was true. If Lola was like anyone in her family, it was her dad. It must be the same for Mara and her dad.

"Thanks pa," Lola said, this time on purpose. "I'm gonna go take a nap."

Manny gave Lola a little kiss on the forehead before she made her way inside through the back entrance. She continued up the stairs to Mara's room, still wiping away tears.

When she opened the door, she saw Pigsby in the middle of the room standing across from a little white chihuahua. Both animals stopped to look at her and Lola noticed a sheet of paper in between them. The chihuahua grabbed the piece of paper with its mouth and scampered out of the room with Pigsby following.

"Whatever."

By now that sort of encounter was seemingly normal, so Lola paid it no mind. All she did was face-plant onto the bed that soon cradled her to sleep.

Chapter 17

Lola's dream was pitch black, just the way she needed it to get good rest.

"You look so tired," said Jason's disembodied voice.

"I *am* so tired," Lola retorted.

"Sorry," Jason's voice said. "I thought you could use the company." His invisible echoing footsteps began to grow faint as they moved away from her.

"I'm sorry, don't leave," she told him, despite not being able to see him. She turned around in a circle hoping to see something, but she didn't. She began to follow Jason's voice.

"I know you're trying really hard to save me," he began telling her. "But something about all of this seems rigged."

"Even if that's true, it's not going to stop me from saving you," Lola said as she walked, not knowing what was around her.

"I know," he said. "Just realize that sometimes things are out of your control." He of all people knew how much Lola hated not being in control.

Just then, Lola's outstretched hands felt a cold and tall surface. A single spotlight turned on and illuminated the object in front of her—it was a mirror. In the reflection of the mirror, but far away, Jason was standing with his back turned to her.

"Jason?" Lola called out to him.

He turned around and walked toward her. "Oh, hey."

"What are you doing in there?" She asked, but that's when she noticed that there was a piece missing from the mirror at the bottom.

"I'm not sure," he told her. "I know it has something to do with me, though."

"You're not making any sense," Lola said with little patience.

"Since when have your dreams ever made any sense?" He asked. "Anyway, try to get us out of here as soon as possible tomorrow. I have a bad feeling about Simora."

"Duh," Lola said as she rolled her eyes.

"I'm serious," he continued to warn her. "It's like I've seen her before. Also, don't freak out, but I think I'm real."

Lola was used to the people in her dreams thinking they were real. On more than one occasion she had to tell these dream people that they were just that—dreams.

"Yeah, okay," Lola said.

Jason banged his palms on the mirror abruptly, which made the glass crack and in turn made Lola jump back.

"Listen to me," he said aggressively. "It's not just Simora. Sonia is up to something too. She's not telling you the whole truth. I know she's been planning something other than my rescue when you're not with her."

Lola was almost convinced—almost. "I have to trust her. She's the only one who's going to help me get you out of here alive—the real you."

"I am the real me!" He said banging his fists on the glass again. "I know I'm me." The glass cracked even more and this time it continued to crack into thin fractures that covered the entire surface like a pattern.

"Get us out," he whispered, right before the entire mirror crashed at her feet and he was gone.

Lola awoke more disturbed than ever. She was not at all convinced by dream Jason saying he was real, but it still made her feel uneasy.

She rolled out of bed to find that Pigsby had pulled all the covers off and was curled up in a makeshift nest of blankets and sheets.

"Don't worry you little jerk, I'll be gone tonight," she told him promisingly.

As soon as Lola stepped out of the room to go downstairs, she was confronted by a peppy little sister.

"Here," Evie said as she handed Lola a pill. "Your hair could use a couple of inches for tonight."

"Normally I don't take pills from strangers," Lola joked, but mostly to herself.

"Come on," Evie urged her. "Don't you want your hair to look beautiful at the ball?"

"I seriously doubt a couple more inches of hair will restructure my face."

"Neither will that attitude," Evie responded glibly as she continued to walk downstairs.

"You don't have to feed into society's ideals of beauty," Lola shouted after her.

"Don't care," Evie shouted back.

Lola followed her parallel sister to the kitchen as she swallowed the pill. Evie was already sitting at the table with Manny when she got there.

"Ma," called Evie. "Can you tell your daughter that feminists are allowed to like makeup and being pretty?"

Lola scoffed and half laughed at Evie's words. "Can you tell your other daughter that I prefer to not spend the energy?"

Martina came over to the table with a pan in hand ready to serve her eggs. "I'm going to tell both of you, that makeup or not, you're both annoying."

"She's right, you know?" Manny chimed in with not the slightest bit of coyness detected in his voice. Both Lola and Evie rolled their eyes, but secretly thought it was funny.

Lola couldn't help but smile. She was as much at ease as she could be, but at the same time she couldn't stop thinking about the hours left until she could take Jason home. She quickly sipped her first cup of coffee and surprisingly went in for a second cup. She figured she was going to need all the energy she could get. Halfway through her second cup of coffee she heard Evie yelp.

"Mara!" Evie looked like she saw something horrific.

Lola jumped out of her seat, alarmed that something might be on the verge of attacking her. "What is it?" She asked still frightened.

"Did you just sip that coffee?" Evie asked as if Lola had been poisoned.

"Geez," said Lola. "I didn't even have a whole two cups. I wasn't going to have that much."

"Whole two cups?" Evie asked aggressively. "Are you still asleep?"

"What's going on?" Martina asked, clearly sick of their bickering.

"She took a hair growth pill and drank two cups of coffee!" Evie told Martina. Her arms were an inch away from flailing and her eyes resonated immediate danger.

"Mara!" Martina expressed, just as shocked as Evie. "Are you crazy?"

"I…" Lola said, not knowing what she was being called crazy for.

Just as Lola stopped speaking, the other three faces at the table simultaneously began to mirror each other's disgust. Lola couldn't tell what they were all looking at—she was praying it wasn't a giant spider.

When she turned her head to look around herself, she found it slightly more difficult to whip her hair in the direction she wanted. She looked down only to see mounds of hair cascading on top of more hair. She couldn't feel the hair growing, but she could definitely see it. She almost stood up from her chair, but when she did she felt a hand on her shoulder push her back down.

"Not a great idea *Mara*," said a newly appeared Sonia. "Wait it out or you'll be tripping everywhere."

"What do I do?" Lola asked, panicked out of her mind. She couldn't believe what was happening.

"Just wait," Sonia said again. "It will stop growing at this rate in a couple of minutes."

As they waited, they all heard scared oinks by the sink cabinets. Martina walked over and parted the hair that was trapping little Pigsby. He squirmed as she picked him up, but then settled in her arms.

Sonia's feet were engulfed in Lola's hair, as well as everyone else's feet for that matter. She shuffled over to a drawer and pulled out a big kitchen knife. She shuffled back to stand behind Lola and just as she predicted, the hair stopped growing like it was being poured out of a bucket. With more strength than should normally be needed, Sonia pulled together half of Lola's hair and cut it right off. She did the same to the other half but by then they were all stepping in a pool of hair. It had even knocked over the trash can, so all they saw in one corner of the kitchen was eggshells, coffee grounds, and who knows what else mixed into the hair.

"This is disgusting," Evie said as she gagged a little. Lola had never seen someone scrunch up their face and gag at the same time.

"Well, then it's a good thing you know someone who can fix it," Sonia snarked at Evie.

"No way," Evie said. "Trish is all booked up and I'm not giving her my appointment. It's not my fault she did this."

"Evie," Martina warned. "Ándale!"

Evie's eyes curved up as she looked at her mom. "Ma!" She pleaded, but it was clear who was going to win. "Fine!"

"Make sure Trish gives her the antidote," Sonia told her.

Lola felt bad—Evie was clearly looking forward to this ball more than her, but she couldn't just walk around with miles of hair.

"You better hope someone canceled their appointment," Evie told Lola as she pulled out her phone and stumbled out of the kitchen, taking some hair with her.

"Why don't you go freshen up?" Sonia suggested. "Don't forget that you grow hair in other places."

Lola blushed and got up quickly. She apologized to Mara's parents for the mess and then hurried to the bathroom.

After she took care of all of the other long unfortunate side effects, she was ready to get this problem fixed. Her hair had not stopped growing, but at least it was doing so at an exponentially lesser rate. Although, in the half hour that she had spent getting ready, it had already grown almost to the end of her lower back.

"Let's go before you turn into something woolly," Evie said, still upset at the situation.

They decided to walk into town since both Manny and Martina would need the wagons later. By the time they arrived Lola's hair was down to her knees. As they walked through the town, almost everyone they passed looked over to see who was rocking the crazy long hair.

When they arrived at the Salon, Penelope and Alex were sitting on the benches outside. They both gasped at the sight of Lola, but really didn't know what to say.

"That's a bold statement," Alex commented with a half-smile. "It looks good…" She couldn't tell right away whether this was something Lola had done on purpose.

"We're here to fix it," Evie said hotly.

"Oh, thank goodness," Penelope said. "No offense."

Lola and Evie sat down next to them. Lola's hair sat on the ground which made her feel uneasy from all the dirt that was getting into it.

They called Penelope into the salon soon after Lola sat down. It seemed to be going pretty fast, but Lola should have expected it would go fast in a place that can use magic.

"It won't be long now, ladies and gentlemen," said the woman with the appointment book. Only a few more minutes passed when the lady came back out to call Evie's name.

Lola went to stand up, but her head was jerked down by an unknown force. She turned around only to find that one guy from before, stepping on her hair. What was his name?

"Adam!" Evie said noticing him right away.

"I am so sorry," Adam apologized to Lola. "I didn't realize I was stepping on your hair." He picked up Lola's hair and tried to bunch it all together as he handed it to her, but then dropped it shy of her arms. "I'm so sorry." He awkwardly helped her pick it up again, but this time he tried to stack it on top of her head. That obviously didn't work and that's when he just ended up patting her head several times as some sort of weird apology.

"It's okay," Lola assured him with a grimace. "I've got it." She folded her hair on top of itself and cradled it in her arms.

"I'm sure there's a good story behind this," Adam said trying to make conversation.

"She drank two cups of coffee after taking a hair growth pill," Evie blurted out, still visibly angry. "The story ends with her using my appointment because she didn't have one of her own." Lola felt bad enough for ruining Evie's day, but she knew she would not hear the end of it.

"Why don't you take my appointment?" Adam said. "I don't really need it anyway."

"Are you sure?" Evie asked, probably not intending on letting him back out either way.

"Yeah," Adam told her. "I don't even know why I have one. My hair is easy. I'm sure someone at the castle can take care of it."

"But…" Evie started to say.

"Don't argue with the man," Lola cut in. "Just take it." She nudged her head slightly and that was all it took for Evie to accept the gesture. She happily sauntered into the salon without another word.

"Thank you for that," Lola said to Adam. "I felt horrible that she was forced to give me her appointment. She was really looking forward to it."

"It's no big deal," Adam said, looking nervous and having trouble making eye contact with her. Lola gave him another small smile and then turned around to walk inside.

"So, you're going tonight?" Adam asked, as if he wasn't ready to part ways.

"I don't have too much of a choice," Lola said back.

"Great!" Adam said. "I mean, great that you're going, not great that you don't have a choice—what I mean is…"

"I'll see you there," Lola helped him out.

"Yeah," Adam said, fidgeting with the back of his head. "See you there."

Lola walked into the salon and was quickly escorted into a chair next to Evie. A stylish pink haired woman and an equally well-dressed man walked over to them. The young man started brushing Lola's hair right away.

"What is this?" The man asked. His voice was deep and he had an accent.

"She drank coffee after taking a hair growth pill," Evie repeated sounding tired of the story.

"Did you hit your head or something?" Joked the man. He and Evie both laughed as if Lola was stupid.

"I'm assuming that since you have an antidote, this happens to enough people for you to have one," Lola said back with stiff attitude.

"Yes, but it usually happens to children darling," chuckled the man. "Children and their soda make up our whole antidote business." He and Evie kept laughing.

"I...I just forgot," Lola said embarrassed, even though she really didn't know this would happen with a bit of coffee.

"Well, I can see that," said the hairstylist as he handed Lola her second pill of the day. She took it right away without even waiting for the water and settled into the chair.

Getting their hair done didn't take much time after that. Like Lola suspected, there was a bit of magic involved with the whole process. None of the hairstylists were using heating tools, in fact she didn't see a single curling iron or straightener in the entire salon.

She observed as her hairstylist made a clean cut straight through her hair right below her shoulders. A considerable amount of Lola's hair was now on the floor along with some twigs and who knows what else, tangled in there.

"It won't stop growing for about another hour," said her hairstylist. "It will be a good length now that it's slowing down." He then proceeded to add texture and layer Lola's hair. "So what look are you going for?"

"I don't know," Lola responded. "Maybe some curls?" Even though she knew it was silly, she was weary of saying the wrong thing. It was *her* hair after all. The absurdity that picking the wrong hair style would somehow affect her mission, did not escape her.

"Your sister's a rebel," the hairstylist teased with Evie.

Lola didn't want to think too much into it. She knew they were all just having a small joke at her expense. None of it really mattered as long as she and Jason were home free after the ball. Everything just made her so nervous that it was hard for her not to read into things at every turn.

As these inconsequential thoughts bubbled in her head, her hairstylist reached over to the shelves by the mirror and picked three bottles with funky labels on them. He also grabbed a regular empty spray bottle and unscrewed the top. The bottles with the weird labels had equally weird-looking liquids inside. One of them had a glittery pink liquid, while one of the other ones had liquid that looked like it was boiling.

As he opened each bottle, Lola noticed that they had droppers inside. He delicately used the droppers to dispense a certain amount of each liquid into the empty spray bottle and then filled the rest with water.

After detangling Lola's hair a bit more, the stylist sprayed his concoction into her hair. He made sure to spray every strand. Then he pulled out his hair dryer as if he were almost done. As he dried Lola's hair, it fantastically began to form wide curls.

"Wow," Lola said with a breathy expression. She couldn't stop looking at the transformation happening before her eyes.

"I'm guessing you don't normally get all dolled up," he said as he fluffed her hair with his hands.

Lola looked over to see how Evie was doing. Her hairstylist was mixing up a hair formula in a different spray bottle. When Evie's hairstylist was ready to finish up, she began to dry her hair and Evie's hair began to curl. Her curls were tight, like she had left them on the curling iron for too long.

"I think you overshot it Trish," Evie said.

When Lola was done, she decided to wait outside of the Salon for Evie to finish up. Penelope and Alex were also waiting outside. Penelope had gotten a very elegant up-do and Alex went with a long wavy bohemian look with a couple of little braids scattered throughout.

Everyone coming out of the Salon seemed to be in a good mood. There was a cheerful vibe buzzing around the entire town.

"What did Adam want?" Alex asked boldly, giving Lola little time to observe the people walking around. Lola came to learn that Alex was not one to beat around the bush about anything.

"Nothing," Lola said. "He was nice enough to give Evie his appointment."

"He's just trying to get back into your good graces," Alex said, clearly skeptical of his motives.

"I think that was nice of him," Penelope said with a little smile directed at Lola. Alex flashed a not so pleasant look at Penelope.

"Just remember why you didn't work out in the first place," Alex said. "He was a jerk who left you the minute it became too serious. He's not good for you."

Lola stayed silent not wanting to say something that Mara would have to answer for later. Instead she just shrugged and inquired about lunch.

Once Evie had come out of the salon, the four of them went to a quaint café and sat outside at the intricate iron-forged tables. They were all talking about how exciting the night was going to be, all except Lola. She was getting antsy. Her right foot was tapping a mile a minute and she kept gnawing at her nails and utensils.

"Stop it," Evie told Lola. "Stop biting your nails."

"I'm not biting them *off*," Lola said with a finger still in her mouth. "I'm just biting them."

"No," Evie snipped at her as if she were a bad puppy. "Stop it, you know you're going to regret it later when they get all nasty."

"Fine," Lola conceded all huffy.

"I know you're nervous," Evie said softly while the other two women talked to each other. "But it will be fine. If you really don't want to talk to Adam, you don't have to."

"I'll keep that in mind," Lola told her. She thought it was cute how Evie worried about her as if she really were her sister, but there was no way of her knowing otherwise. If only Evie knew the real reason she was so nervous.

After lunch the four of them split so that Lola and Evie could get back to the house. At that point it was only five hours until the ball commenced.

"Oh good," Evie said. "I still have two hours until I have to start getting ready."

"It takes you three hours to get ready," Lola asked with a thread of judgment in her tone.

"We need to be ready to go by seven," Evie told her. "You know the traffic is going to be insane."

"Are you saying it takes you two hours to get ready?"

"You're right," Evie said. "I should add another half hour to that."

On their way out of town they passed Sonia's lab, the one that Jason was in. Lola stopped at the entrance to the building wanting to go in, but she had no excuse for Evie. Sonia wasn't there, so what other purpose could she have to go in?

"What are you doing?" Evie asked, trying to hurry her along.

"I think I left my pen in Sonia's lab." Lola struggled to come up with something to explain her odd behavior.

"I'm sure she'll keep it safe for you," Evie said not sure if that was something Lola needed to be comforted for.

"I hope so."

Chapter 18

Evie decided they would take a wagon back to the house. She didn't want to mess up her perfectly bouncy curls, although from Lola's understanding, these curls were indestructible. She briefly imagined the sensation that infallible curling spray would be in her world—if only she could take it with her.

As they pulled up to the house, Lola realized why Manny and Martina had told them not to take the wagons earlier that day. Parked right in front of the house were the two wagons that had now been converted into carriages.

Evie just about lost it when she saw them. Lola too was a bit speechless at the sight of these beautiful carriages. She might have been just as excited as Evie, if the ball were truly her first priority.

Without waiting for the driver to stop, Evie made the rash decision to jump out of the wagon and then ran to the green carriage. It was the one moment she had little regard for her hair. When Lola was able to join her, she could clearly see why Evie was so excited. The carriages were ornate with fine fabrics and trim. Both of them had the gold trim on the outside, outlining the doors and windows. The inside looked marvelously redone with cushioned seats and cute dangling lights from the ceiling—they almost looked like crystals covering Christmas lights.

"I thought it was too late to take them out of storage," Evie said as Manny walked over to them.

"That's why it pays to know people in high places," Manny told her.

"I didn't realize Ernie was that high up in the storage facility corporate ladder," Evie mocked him.

"Hey, they're here aren't they," Manny responded with his classic dad demeanor. "What do you think Mar?" He gestured toward the white carriage. "I threw on a fresh coat of paint while you were away."

Lola walked over to the white carriage and looked inside. She saw baby blue cushioned seats that complimented the white and gold very nicely. She saw the same crystal lights that Evie's carriage had, hanging from the inside.

"It's perfect," Lola said as she smiled at Manny.

When they made their way inside, Manny explained that he and Jesse were driving the carriages to the ball. Lola hadn't realized it before, but she and Evie would each have to take individual carriages given the size of their gowns. Even then, Lola wasn't sure if they would fit inside. Evie said nothing to indicate she was worried, and instead headed upstairs.

Just as Evie had said, she began to get ready soon after they had arrived back at the house. Lola did no such thing. She was becoming more and more nervous, so much so that Sonia had to give her something to relax so that she wouldn't act suspicious around her family.

"It's a good thing we stopped to get these poppies," Sonia told her as she carefully tweezed off a little section of one of the petals. She was wearing a face mask over her nose and mouth while she was doing all of this. "I'm a little worried that your reaction to this will be adverse, but I guess we'll just see, won't we?"

Lola was placed in front of the TV after putting the minuscule piece of poppy in her mouth. She was told by Sonia that she was not allowed to get off of the couch until she felt the effects and calmed down. After about half an hour she did start to feel less distressed, although to her, it felt like she had been sitting on the couch for a couple of hours.

She decided that she couldn't have been sitting there that long since the only thing she could remember watching was a soap opera in which an illicit love affair was discovered through a crystal ball, and a commercial for the latest and greatest in magical washing machines.

As entertaining as Terre Two programing was, she didn't want to stay on the couch anymore. Standing up made her almost lose her balance. She walked into the kitchen but there was no one there. Dazed and confused, she just stood there staring at the empty kitchen for several minutes until she saw something scurry by her feet—it was a gray fist-sized blob—Sonia's blob...

That was a weird thought.

Intrigued by what it was up to, Lola followed it out of the kitchen and to the only bedroom on the first floor. She approached the bedroom door at a snail's pace, trying not to scare the gray blob. It went into the room through an arch-shaped notch.

Normally entering someone's bedroom, especially when that someone isn't very fond of her, would be something Lola wouldn't do —but for some reason she thought it would be okay.

She turned the knob and entered as if there was nothing strange about her going in. There was a powerful aroma of incense that hit her hard and made her even more foggy. Almost immediately, a headache ensued. It also didn't help that the only light in the room was being produced by burning candles.

Lola stumbled about the room having forgotten why she was even there. She walked over to the dresser where she found a three-ring binder. She un-thoughtfully opened it like she was welcome to anything in the room. The first thing she saw in the binder was a calendar with circled dates. As she flipped through the first couple of pages, she saw a picture of her mom with a small bio and a list of dates underneath the picture. Each date had a location written next to it. Most of them said Las Vegas, one or two said Los Angeles, and only one of them said Miami. She looked at the last date on the list and the location was blank.

Not knowing what to think of this discovery, Lola continued to flip the pages of the binder. The next page had a picture of her dad...

the dates on that page had ended two years ago. Her eyes started welling up, but that didn't stop her from going on.

The page after that was a picture of her. The ones following were of her brother, her sister, her aunt Mari, her aunt's boyfriend, and some other people Lola recognized as her aunt's friends. All together there were about twelve pages of people. She took a good look at the last date on the last page and the location was blank. Immediately she flipped back through all of the pages and sure enough, the last date of each page did not have a corresponding location. That date was July 15, the day of the accident.

All of a sudden Lola became nauseous and could barely hold herself up. She stumbled backward onto the bed trying hard to gasp for air. When she looked up to the other side of the room she saw the form of a person.

"Sonia?" Lola asked trying to clear up her blurry vision.

She saw the gray blob from before, climbing all over the person in the corner. As she tried to get up on her feet, she reached for the person, but the person didn't reach back.

The closer she got the more she realized this thing wasn't a person—it was just a fabric mannequin. Her vision was now coming in and out of focus, but it was clear long enough for her to see a gray rat holding a sewing needle on top of the mannequin's shoulder.

"Ahh!" Lola yelped and fell to the ground. She scrambled on the floor and crawled all around looking for the door. She managed to run into the bed with her head before crawling over a purse and breaking something inside it with her knee.

Not wanting to leave evidence of her intrusion, Lola reached inside the purse and pulled out a handful of glass. She stood up, found the bedroom door, and stumbled out. Luckily the front door was only steps away. She opened the door and immediately threw up on the bush to the right of the steps.

Soon after she vomited, her vision cleared up, her stomach settled, and she sunk to the ground with her back against the first step. She gulped the fresh air as if she were on the brink of suffocating. All of a sudden she could feel a stinging in her hand. The shards of glass were still in her palm and she had completely forgotten why she had taken them in the first place. She was obviously not thinking clearly.

When she opened her hand she saw the bloody shards stuck in several places. The contents of the glass along with a piece of labeled tape were also in her hand. Whatever the glass was carrying, it was syrupy and dark blue.

As she slowly and delicately picked the glass out from her wounds, the blue liquid spilled into them like a magnet. To her amazement her cuts began to heal rapidly as they expelled the rest of the glass. She flipped over the piece of tape and saw the word *Sanasa* on it. This was a potion Sonia hadn't explained to her, but it looked familiar.

The more she thought about what had just happened, the more she realized that the vial she broke was almost empty when she broke it. She didn't feel a goopy mess when she took it out of Sonia's purse, so it had to have been used. She hoped Sonia wouldn't be looking for it since there was practically nothing in it.

Feeling lucky that her mistake of grabbing a handful of glass had fixed itself, Lola shook off the rest of it from her hand and made her way back inside to the couch. Almost as soon as she sat down, Evie descended to find her slumped over and looking dreadful.

"Have you been up there this entire time?" Lola asked breathy from the sickness. Evie nodded her head and patted the sweat from Lola's forehead with a washcloth she was holding.

"Okay sicky, it's time to get ready," Evie said. "I'll get you some water." She came back with a tall glass and made sure Lola drank every last drop, then helped her up the stairs.

Lola was fortunate that Evie found her when she did. Apparently she had seen Mara in a similar condition more than once before—at least that's what she assumed from Evie's ramblings about how she thought she was still on track to getting better. With the additional help of a fizzy orange drink called Nozzatea, Lola was able to quickly regain a clear head and a peaceful stomach.

"What was it this time?" Evie asked, all too familiar with her stomach sensitive sister.

"Oh, you know, the usual," Lola answered. She didn't want Evie to make a fuss over her.

Evie didn't seem to believe her, but she wasn't in the mood to pry. They were both in the bathroom, Lola sitting on top of the toilet lid and Evie managing to find counter space for every piece of makeup.

"There's only an hour left to finish getting ready," Evie said realizing what time it was. "Can you get out now? You have to get ready too."

"Your bedside manner is pristine," Lola told her as she got up to leave the bathroom.

Evie was right about Lola needing to get ready. By some miracle Lola's hair was still intact, but she expected nothing less from a magical hair solution.

Mara's own little stash of makeup was on her bedroom vanity, so Lola helped herself. It only took her a few minutes to apply the makeup—nothing fancy. The real challenge came when she tried to put on the gown by herself. Her first attempt of getting dressed failed when she tried excavating underneath the gown but ended up not being able to resurface. After that she remembered how she helped her best friend get into her wedding dress just a few months ago. All she had to do was open it up all the way and step inside. Her second try at putting on the gown wasn't her proudest moment, but in her defense, she did still have a little bit of sick brain.

The gown was so heavy, Lola immediately regretted picking that specific one and wanted to switch it for another. Evie did not agree with her and refused to help her choose another one. The amount of control Evie was exuding over something so trivial would have been funny to Lola had she not been the subject.

The last part of the ensemble was something Evie also needed help with. They were walking around bare foot looking for someone to help them put on their shoes. At first they tried to help each other, but that failed miserably with Lola practically upside down after toppling over. Finally, they heard someone in the master bedroom that could help—it was Martina, who was just getting out of the shower. Evie took it upon herself to barge into the room to ask her mother for help—Lola had a different idea. She wasn't too excited about the height of the shoes that were chosen to match the gown, so she took the opportunity to go find a smaller heel.

When she entered Mara's room, she saw Pigsby at the vanity, his two little feet on top of the table where all the makeup was and looking at himself in the mirror. He turned around to face her but didn't get off of the table.

"Hi Pig," Lola said cunningly. She realized how she could get better shoes without the struggle. "Do you think you could find me some comfortable shoes to wear?" Pigsby said nothing.

"I can pay you," Lola negotiated, almost desperate to not wear those high heels that would no doubt tear up her feet. "What do you want? Name it. Carrots? Worms? Bananas? What do pigs eat?" None of those choices fazed him so he continued to sniff at everything on the table. "I saw a piece of cake in the fridge." Pigsby turned back to face her—that got his attention. "You want cake? I can get that for you, but you have to do something for me first."

If it was ever possible for a pig to wear a look of suspicion on its face, Pigsby was doing it. He climbed down his little steps that he used to get up to the vanity chair and trotted over to the wardrobe. About two minutes later he emerged with a pair of shoes he thought would earn him that cake. He pushed the shoes out of the wardrobe and carried them one by one over to Lola, who was now sitting on the bed.

"These look great," Lola told him. "Now help me put them on." Pigsby oinked in defiance. "I can't do it by myself and you know it." He oinked again putting his pride before him. "Help me or no cake. Please."

Pigsby hesitated but ended up helping Lola with the shoes anyway. All he had to do was guide them to where her feet were. As soon as she had them on, he sprinted to the door.

"All right, I'm coming," Lola said as she balanced her way off of the bed.

She had a hard time going down the stairs because of how big the gown was, so Pigsby got to the kitchen first. When she arrived at the kitchen, he was already waiting by the fridge with a brown paper bag in his mouth.

"Where did you get… never mind." She dumped the piece of cake into the paper bag for him, closed it at the top, and gave it back. He quickly left, presumably to either eat it or hide it. As rude as he was to her, she had to admit that he was the cutest little pig she had ever seen.

Before she even had a chance to leave the kitchen, she heard Manny calling out for all of them. "Let's go everyone," he said. "Traffic is going to pick up soon."

Lola walked over to the front door to meet him and was stunned at how nice he looked. He was wearing a classic black tuxedo, something her dad would have never worn, but then again, he wasn't her dad.

"Mara, you look beautiful," he told her as they both went in for a hug. Evie was walking down the stairs right at that same moment. "Look at my girls."

"Can you help me?" Evie asked as she reached out her hand to Manny. He walked halfway up the stairs to help her come down.

"Mar, start heading out," Manny told Lola. "There's no way you're both going to fit in the doorway."

Lola squeezed herself through the door and made her way to the carriages. Surprisingly, Sonia was already out there. She was just as dolled up as the rest of them, only her dress was an elegant sheath and not an enormous gown.

"I should have worn something like that," Lola said to her.

"No," Sonia said. "You would have stood out at a ball of this magnitude if you didn't wear the right thing. The younger women wear ball gowns."

As soon as she stopped talking, Sonia mimed putting something over Lola's shoulder, but she wasn't actually miming. Lola felt something sitting on her shoulder as soon as Sonia pulled back her hands. It wasn't heavy, but there was definitely some weight on her.

"What did you just do?" Lola asked.

"I made your potion purse invisible," Sonia told her. "Thankfully it's a lot easier than making humans invisible. Do you remember what's in there?"

"Yeah," Lola told her, or at least she thought she remembered.

"Everyone ready to go?" Manny asked as he came out of the house with Evie and Martina. Jesse wasn't far behind them and he was looking just as sharp as his dad.

They helped Evie get into her carriage first. Martina was going with her, which meant that Sonia would be riding with Lola.

The sun was setting and Lola was enjoying everything that was happening around her. The carriages looked amazing when Manny turned on the little crystal lights that hung inside each of them. The horses were also a bit dressed up with decorative fabric hanging from their necks.

Sonia made herself comfortable in the carriage before it was Lola's turn to get in. Manny and Jesse seemed to know exactly how to shove these gowns into the carriages without ripping anything. Lola found it amusing that the men in this universe would have to know how to do things like that.

It took no time at all for both carriages to get going. Lola had the best view of the land as the sun continued to set. The sky bled with pinks, oranges, and purples as the wispy clouds blanketed the light. She was trying to meditate away the anxiety by just being in the moment and focusing on controlling her breathing. Sonia could probably tell that's what she was doing because she didn't start talking about the plan right away.

They were just arriving at the entrance of the town when night hit. The entrance was blocked off by white posts, most likely so that people wouldn't try to take the short cut. They could see the building where Jason was being kept as the carriage turned to go on the road that went around the town square. They stopped seconds later because of all of the traffic from the other carriages going to the castle.

Lola stuck her head out of the window and saw a carriage traffic jam. They were all moving at a walking pace. She looked over at the shops in the town. It was nice to see that they were all charmingly decorated with lights.

"Are you ready?" Sonia asked, breaking Lola out of her head.

Lola nodded and was starting to think she could actually do this. She had gone over the plan in her mind so many times that she was just ready to get it over with.

"As soon as you are done getting the tea leaf, meet me outside," Sonia told her. "I'll have the carriage ready. I'll be there after I stop off at my lab. I have to lure the falcon to us before we can get anything else started." It was odd, but Lola thought she could sense that Sonia was a bit nervous.

"What should I do if I get caught?" Lola asked, with a few nerves of her own.

"Honestly," Sonia said. "I don't know, so don't get caught."

While they were inching along in traffic, Sonia made Lola repeat what each potion was for. Lola could feel the small weight of the purse on her lap. She looked inside just to make sure everything was there and found a flip phone.

"I also put a phone in the bag," Sonia said as if she were planning on mentioning it but forgot to do so. She knocked on the roof of the carriage for it to stop. "Just in case you need to call me." She opened the carriage door and hopped out. The lab was only a few yards away from where they were stalled. "Try to make it fast and don't get stuck in your head," she told Lola as she closed the door.

After dropping Sonia off, it took them about another half hour to get to the castle. As they pulled up, Lola's heart jumped to her throat.

She was overstimulated by all of the bright lights and flashing cameras. Her palms were getting sweaty and she was already imagining messing everything up. She took one more deep breath before the carriage came to a complete stop.

Don't get stuck in your head— Don't get stuck.

Chapter 19

Stepping out of the carriage made Lola feel like she was at a Hollywood premiere. The castle was backlit with pink and purple lights to enhance the glamour of it all. The bigger flood lights made it impossible for anyone to mistake this as anything but the most extravagant ball of the year.

Manny was helping Lola out of the carriage, but even then, she practically stumbled out. She landed on the mile-long blue carpet that led all of the guests inside, past the giant wooden doors. Evie was waiting for Lola so that they could walk inside together. Just then, a hypnotic bell rang above their heads. Lola looked up and saw the bell swinging in one of the towers.

"Nine o'clock," Evie said. "Just in time! The ball only started an hour ago."

The two of them walked inside arm in arm. They passed several excited people, all in their best and most debonair attire. Everything was decorated beyond belief. There were thousands of flowers in vastly expensive-looking vases. Portraits lined the walls in their gold ornate frames. Chandelier upon chandelier draped above their heads as if one wasn't enough. It was magnificent to say the least.

As they continued to walk past all the small groups of people who were busy in conversation, Lola wondered if anyone would notice if she disappeared right away. She feared that Evie would not let her out of her sight for a second.

They reached the end of the hallway that led them to the giant ballroom. The first sight of the ballroom was absolutely exquisite! Everything was covered in gold—the tables, the walls—everything. The chandeliers were so grandiose that Lola was left speechless. Nothing she had ever seen before this, would ever compare— explaining it to anyone would never do it justice. Everything sparkled so marvelously that Lola would have gladly stared at it forever.

She kept looking around at all of the splendor, but thankfully became conscious of what she was doing and stopped. As far as anyone knew, this was nothing new to her and she had to keep pretending that was true.

At this point all Lola was hoping for was that not too many people would notice her, or at least not think much of her being there. She understood that Mara was a well-known person, which is why getting around undetected was going to be so difficult.

Without realizing it, she had caught the eye of someone in particular already. Evie pulled her away before the stranger could approach them and took her to Mara's friends.

Penelope was so excited to see Lola that she forgot they were all wearing enormous gowns that were perfect for keeping distance.

She reached over and gave Lola an extended arm hug. Her gown was even more magnificent than the first time Lola had seen it. Her skirt looked like a movie screen—the moon and clouds moved as naturally as if it were the actual night sky. A lot of the women that were there were wearing enchanted gowns.

There was a beautiful gown on a petite red-haired girl that simulated a mesmerizing coral reef, thriving with tropical fish. Evie's dress was sprouting flowers every couple of minutes and Alex was wearing one that showed a field of sunflowers blooming.

Not every woman was wearing an enchanted gown, but the ones who were wearing these mystical garments were getting a lot of attention. Although Lola's gown was not enchanted, it was still very extravagant—she could feel the crystals draping on her back and of course the more ostentatious a gown was, the heavier it was. She couldn't believe she was really expected to be weighed down like that all night.

Lola was happy that Alex and Penelope were there. She had gotten pretty friendly with them even though they both still thought she was Mara. She kept thinking how nice it would be if they could actually be friends, but of course that wasn't going to happen.

"Penny, your face healed up nicely," Lola told her, referring to the big claw mark she had endured days earlier.

"What would we do without magic, am I right?" Penelope said with a big smile. "Some regular Sanasa potion cleared it all up."

The name of that potion sounded so familiar. Where had she heard of it before? Right before Lola could put her finger on it, she noticed that Alex's face went from cheerful to disdain. Lola turned her head and saw that Adam was walking toward them. She was taken aback by how handsome he was, in what she assumed was some sort of military formal wear. His suit was white with accents of blue and gold, and he had two medals on the left side of his chest. It also looked like he did get that hair cut he was talking about. His thick brown hair had been styled back nicely with a few waves woven in.

"Good evening," he said as he approached them. "You all look very lovely."

"Doesn't she?" Evie said referring to Lola.

Adam blushed slightly, but then turned to face Lola. "I was hoping you would accept my invitation for the first dance."

Lola was nervous and glad that her friends were the only ones witnessing this exchange, but little did she know that many people around them were watching too.

"Sure," Lola agreed. "But you'll have to catch me in a bit." Just as she said it, a plan formed in her head that would help her get what she came for a lot faster. "Actually, do you mind if I use one of your bedrooms?" Everyone but Lola chocked at her words, especially Adam.

"I don't mean to be inappropriate, but I have to use the restroom," Lola continued explaining. "Preferably a private one in one of your bedrooms."

"Mar, just go in the ones down here," Evie said, embarrassed that this conversation was even happening.

"I can't," Lola said. "I've become pretty shy about it since you last saw me." They all seemed to be very uncomfortable at this point, all except Lola.

"I guess I could take you upstairs," Adam said hesitantly.

"Great," Lola said relieved. "Ladies, I'll be back soon."

Adam led her through the crowd and she followed diligently until she saw someone familiar that made her stop in her tracks—it was a woman with ashy blond hair in a sleek green gown. She looked to be about Sonia's age. Lola couldn't quite remember where she had seen her, and as she was trying to figure it out, the woman noticed she was being watched.

The woman began to walk over to her and made clear eye contact. There was no way Lola was going to get away now, but just then it hit her—it was Gwen. The same Gwen who gave her the ginger doll, only now she looked like the picture Sonia had originally shown her. Why she didn't look like an old hag anymore?

"Mara," Gwen greeted her. "I thought you would have been gone by now."

"I had to make one more stop," Lola told her confidently. Her chin tilted upward as she took a breath.

Gwen looked over at Adam who had noticed that Lola stopped to talk. "I see," she said as she took in a deep breath of her own. "What you're doing is dangerous. Have you thought about what might happen if he gets caught helping you?"

Lola didn't say anything. What could she say?

"Have you thought about what might happen if *you* get caught?" Gwen continued to ask. "I know you don't know much about Sonia, and as good as her intentions are, it will always come down to the bottom line with her. Just keep that in mind." She walked away as soon as she said her piece, leaving Lola second guessing what was going on.

What is she talking about?

Adam was waiting patiently for her just a few feet away. Lola walked over to him and continued to follow as he led her to the large lobby where the main staircase was. More than once she caught him sneaking glances at her, and as flattered as she was, it was also making her a little uncomfortable.

"Thank you," she said to him, stopping after climbing a few steps. "I think I can take it from here."

"I'm going to have to walk you all the way," he told her happily. "The guards won't let you through without me."

Of course they won't, Lola thought to herself.

The staircase in the lobby was wide enough for a dozen people, yet Adam walked an inch away from her. Neither of them were saying a word and it wasn't getting any better by the minute.

She could sense there was a lot of awkwardness on his part, which in turn made her feel a bit awkward. No one had told her why Adam and Mara were estranged, or at least that's what she gathered they were. Everyone made it seem like they used to be inseparable. Lucky for her, not knowing was probably easier. She could pretend to not want to talk to him and no one would think otherwise.

When they reached the top, they walked to the end of the hallway, exactly where Sonia said the elevator would be. There were guards placed halfway on each side of the hall. It was easy to see down each hallway because this part of the castle didn't take any corners. Lola's gown was so enormous that they barely managed to squeeze into the elevator all the way.

"You know, I never understood why these dresses had to be so big," Adam said trying his best to break the ice.

"Tradition, right?" Lola said, now wondering the same thing. As she saw what was going on in his corner of the elevator, she started to chuckle lightly. The gown was taking up every available inch of space, that it left Adam pressed against the corner of the elevator by the door. He was clearly trying hard not to step or do anything to Lola's gown. He realized why Lola was laughing and smiled. He was probably thankful that the tension had been broken, even if it was just for a split second.

When they stopped, Adam got out first. As Lola maneuvered the gown out of the elevator, she noticed that they stopped on the fifth floor—she needed to go up two more floors.

"I almost forgot how big this place is," Lola said, setting herself up. "I always liked the seventh floor the best, maybe we should go there." Adam must have thought she was messing with him because he gave her a single laugh.

"What are you talking about?" He said. "There's nothing up there but conference rooms." He began to lead her to one of the bedrooms. "You're so weird... funny weird."

Lola had to rethink how she was going to get up there. She could feel the movement of the vials in her invisible purse and she knew one of those was going to get her to the seventh floor.

"Since I have you alone," Adam began to say. "I was hoping we could talk about everything that happened before you left."

Lola was caught off guard. "Maybe," she told him. "I think that sometimes things should be put off until both parties are ready to talk." She was hoping she wouldn't have to deal with Mara's drama for her.

"Just promise me that we'll talk before you leave again," he said—his eyes were asking for her sympathy. Lola just smiled hoping he would take that as a yes.

They passed the only guard stationed in that hallway and Adam opened the door to one of the bedrooms, "You can use this one." He flicked the light switch to reveal a lavish room with exquisite drapes, puffy bedding, and expensive looking furnisher.

"Oh wow," Lola said looking at the grandeur of the room. "Is this your room?"

Adam looked at her as if she had hit her head. "Are you serious? You haven't been gone that long."

"No, I mean…this should be your room," she tried to cover. "I think I like it better than the one you have now."

"Yeah, well I'll let you get to it," Adam told her as he left to wait outside of the door. Lola could tell that he blushed a little.

As soon as the door closed, Lola hurried to the bed and dumped out the contents of her purse. The vials rolled out and she separated them quickly as her mind tried to come up with a plan. The phone had fallen out as well—she could call Sonia and she would tell her what to do.

She picked up the phone and almost dialed the only number programmed onto it, when she discovered what was underneath it—the invisibility potion. She picked it up and her head swam with excitement. She found a resurgence of confidence as she unstoppered the vial. Just as she was about to drink it, she stopped. She remembered what Sonia had said about the potion making *only her* invisible. She would have to get out of the gown...

Coming to the realization that she would need to take off absolutely everything, made her cower terribly. She began pacing furiously, not knowing if she could go through with it.

A loud bell sound began to emanate through the castle as Lola contemplated her decision. She listened to the booming resonance until it faded away. That bell was exactly what she needed to make up her mind. An hour had passed, and she couldn't afford to waste more time. Without a second thought she drank the potion in one gulp. Surprisingly, it tasted like the liquid version of a gummy worm.

Lola smacked her lips as the aftertaste lingered in her mouth, but as she did, the potion started to take effect. She could see her face and arms begin to blur in the full-length mirror in front of her. In no time her reflection was all gone.

She began to unzip the gown and stepped out of it, careful not to rip it. She immediately became chilled by the lack of clothing, but knew she had to take off every single item. As soon as there was no trace of clothing on her, she rushed to the bed to put everything back into her equally invisible purse. The problem now would be getting out of the room.

She figured that if she just knocked on the door it would be less suspicious than if she opened the door herself. She kept almost knocking and then pulling her fist back. Her stomach was in knots and she was thankful she didn't eat anything beforehand or it would most likely be coming up by now.

She knocked on the door slightly, just loud enough for Adam to hear. He opened the door slowly and peeked his head in but didn't see her. He did see the gown laying on the floor, so he closed the door fast—so fast that Lola didn't make it out.

"Ugh!" She needed a better plan.

Looking around, she tried to think of something that would pull him into the room, or maybe even make him go away. She searched the room a bit more before going into the bathroom for ideas.

On a shelf in the bathroom, above the fresh towels, were two crystal glasses—presumably for a midnight drink of water. Before even fleshing out the plan, Lola grabbed one of the glasses, turned her face away from what she was doing, and smashed the glass on the floor. She hoped the distinctive shattering sound would reach Adam's ears so that the rest of her not-so-formulated plan would work. She sprinted back to the bedroom door, careful not to step on any of the glass.

"Adam!" She called him through the door. "I'm so sorry, but I broke a glass in the bathroom and got cut on my foot. Can you bring me something to bandage it?"

"What?" Adam yelled through the door. "Are you okay?"

"I need bandages!" Lola told him again.

"Right!" Adam said realizing he needed to hurry. "I'll be right back."

"Just leave them on the inside of the door, please! Don't come in all the way."

Lola could hear his rushing footsteps fading down the hallway, and as soon as they were no longer audible, she cracked open the door —the coast was clear. She stepped out of the room, careful that no one was around to see a door opening by itself.

Even though she knew she was completely invisible, she was still very uncomfortable—so much so that she ran to the elevator as quietly as she possibly could. Fortunately for her, being barefoot really helped with sneaking around quietly.

She passed by several large mirrors hung in between the elegant paintings, and not once did she see herself in them. Nevertheless, she couldn't help covering up certain areas with her hands and purse. She was completely skittish and kept checking her surroundings, making sure that every mirror she passed reflected no part of her.

The elevator wasn't far from the room, but for Lola, getting to it felt like she ran a mile. She quickly pressed the up button over and over again, knowing full-well that the doors wouldn't open any faster no matter how many times she pushed it. Still, it made her feel like at this very vulnerable moment, she was at least in control of something, even if it was just an elevator door.

When the doors opened, she rushed in to hide and repeated the button pushing process. She could see the empty hallway in front of her and even as empty as it was, she still felt like at any moment someone would see her.

Lola was feeling so relieved that she was pulling off her mess of a plan, that as soon as the doors closed, she slumped into the elevator wall forgetting that she was naked. She jumped when her skin touched the cold metal wall. She didn't need any more of a wake up, but it didn't hurt to keep on her toes. She adjusted the purse so that it hung right in front of her as she prepared to bolt out of the elevator.

When the doors opened she did a quick sweep of the hallway and then sprinted halfway toward the room that Sonia had told her about. The only person that was there was a guard that stood two doors away from the ones that Lola was aiming for. She wanted to make sure that the guard wouldn't notice the doors opening, so she decided a bit of vandalism was called for.

She stopped next to a delicate vase that was on a pedestal and simply pushed it off with a single finger. The crash was louder than she expected, making her fear that it would draw the attention of other guards. The guard that was there was startled, but just as expected he walked over to see why the vase had fallen.

Lola took the opportunity she had made for herself and rushed to the room that contained the vault. She opened one of its double doors just enough to slide in so she wouldn't catch the guard's attention, and then closed it softly as if she had never been there.

The room itself was dark, even after Lola had turned on the lights. The chandelier in this room stayed dimmed and the dark blue curtains looked like they were meant to be closed at all times. There was a circular glass table in the middle of the room with a single red table runner.

Even though the room was interestingly distracting, Lola still went straight for the vault on the left side of the room. It almost looked like half of the room was made into the vault. She stood right in front of the vault door and didn't even bother to attempt to open it. She knew there was no way around drinking the opal potion to get inside, and she didn't want to risk setting off some kind of alarm.

She reached into her purse to scoop out all of the vials and placed them on the glass table. She kept the opal potion in her hand and stared at it for longer than she wanted, afraid that it wouldn't work. With no more time to waste she dipped her finger into the potion and then rubbed it on the vault door, then stuck it back inside the vial so that the potion knew what material she would be trespassing. She drank up every last drop and even made sure to rub the residual from her finger on the inside of the purse, the phone, and the snipping tool so that they could pass with her. Immediately after, she placed her hands on the vault door and waited.

She kept waiting for about one minute. Each second that passed made her heart race faster and faster. She began to shake not knowing if it was ever going to start working, until she noticed that the shaking was allowing her hands to sink into the vault. Even though she couldn't see herself passing through the vault door, she could sense the absence of anything solid on her palms. She sank forward until she reached the other side in one piece.

The inside of the vault had the same dim lighting as the grand room. There were shelves lining the walls and each one was storing a different item with its own little spotlight. Lola briefly noticed that there was a lot of gorgeous jewelry, and for some reason there was also a tiny fridge neatly placed in the right corner of the room. She didn't take much notice of anything else that was there because she was focused on finding the tea leaf.

She only had to run her eyes over a few stacks of shelves before she found the tea in a round glass container that looked like a petri dish. Trying to be delicate and swift at the same time, she opened the dish and snipped the smallest leaf on the stem. She then mindfully put the dish back so that it looked like it hadn't been touched and put the leaf she trimmed in her mouth.

Before exiting, she took another quick look around to make sure she didn't bump anything out of place. She walked directly at the door with her hands stretched out, but as soon as she reached it she could actually feel the metal. She pressed her hands into the door hard, trying to force herself through, but still nothing happened.

"No—no this can't be happening."

She pushed her hands even harder into the door, almost bending her wrists, but no success. Seeing no other option, she tried opening the handle and that didn't work either. She had no more of the potion and had no idea how to open the door. She was trapped in the vault without a clear solution and just as importantly, no clothes.

Chapter 20

Lola's breathing elevated rapidly. She tried to open the vault by pulling on the handle again and again. She didn't really expect it to work, but she needed to try just the same. She knew right away that she had to call Sonia.

She was lucky she had brought her purse into the vault with her or she would absolutely have no hope. As the phone rang Lola felt some relief because she was positive that Sonia would know exactly how to get her out.

"I'm not back yet," Sonia answered the phone. "I'm on my way now."

"I'm not ready!" Lola blurted out. "I'm locked in the vault! The potion wore off. What do I do?"

"What do you mean it wore off?" Sonia was noticeably upset. "You took too long to get it!"

"No, I didn't!" Lola defended herself. "You probably didn't give me enough, but it doesn't matter now, just tell me what to do."

"We only had one plan," Sonia told her. "We don't have a backup."

"What if I call for help?" Lola suggested. "I'm still invisible and Adam or the guards can probably hear me."

"It's too risky," Sonia told her. "You don't think they'll investigate to see if something was taken if they hear a girl screaming from their vault of valuables?"

Lola's confidence in Sonia plummeted instantly. She was going to get caught naked in a restricted vault trying to steal something, which in turn meant she wouldn't be able to save Jason.

"There has to be something we can do!" Lola said furiously.

"All right, all right," Sonia said as she tried to think of a plan. "Look around, see if there's anything there that can pry the door, or melt it, or something."

"They don't exactly keep fire torches in here," Lola said. She knew being short with Sonia wasn't going to help matters, but she had a tendency to do that in difficult situations.

"What *do* they have?" Sonia asked her.

"Nothing useful, just a bunch of jewelry and a tiny fridge."

"Look inside the fridge," Sonia said, sounding a bit winded. "What's in there?"

"Vials," Lola said. "A whole bunch of them. I think some of these might be blood."

"Start reading the labels," Sonia coughed trying to give her instructions. Lola could hear the semblance of running heels through the phone. "Hurry!"

"Duplichi," Lola fumbled to say. "All these blood ones have names. There's one that says Vollé. This other one says Sanasa." She recognized that last one as the same stuff that she found in Sonia's bag, but quickly skipped it. "Extraceit, Parpara, Energia…"

"Wait," Sonia gasped. "Go back. Grab the Extraceit."

Lola did as Sonia instructed. "Okay, now what?"

"Did Adam touch you?" Sonia asked.

"What?" Lola asked confused and slightly revolted by her question.

"Did he hold your hand, or touch your shoulder?" She clarified. "Or face, or something?"

"No, I don't think so," Lola told her. "I was wearing gloves the entire time." She heard Sonia curse on the other end.

"Oh, wait!" Lola remembered that earlier that day Adam *had* touched her, or rather her hair. "He did, he touched my hair when we were in town."

"How much Extraceit do you have?" Sonia asked.

"There's just one vial," Lola said.

"Okay, here's what you do," Sonia began to say. "Try to remember exactly which part of your hair he touched and then pour the potion there."

Lola thought carefully trying to recall exactly what had happened earlier when they ran into each other. She knew that he touched most of the hair that was cut off. If that was the only part of her hair that he touched, she was completely out of luck.

"I think it's all gone," Lola told Sonia. The disembodied phone started pacing the room. "They cut off all the hair he touched. I don't think…" Just then Lola remembered that he also touched the top of her head—it was an awkward pat after attempting to help pick up her hair. "I think I might have something."

She knew she couldn't just pour it on the top of her head because her hair did not stop growing immediately after it was cut. She took a guess and poured the liquid halfway down her head, close to her ears.

"What do I do after I've put it in my hair?" Lola asked hopeful that whatever she was doing would work.

"Squeeze it out on the floor," Sonia told her. "It should be turning into a goop."

Lola did what she was told and sure enough, the potion had begun to thicken after she wrung it out.

"This is disgusting," Lola said, her face scrunching up. "What is it?"

"It's everything that is not genetically yours that was in your hair," Sonia told her. "Probably whatever glitter junk you had in there, but most importantly, any remanence of Adam's DNA. The vault opens by the touch of authorized people. Just give it a second, it's going to start to separate."

The glob began to pull apart into sections of itself. When it was done there were four smaller piles of goop.

"It's separated," Lola said excitedly. "What do I do now?"

"Hopefully one of those is Adam's DNA," Sonia told her. "My guess is that it's the smallest mass. Grab it and touch it to the door."

Lola took the quarter-sized ball of goop and smeared it on the vault door, but nothing happened. "It didn't work."

"Try the second smallest one," Sonia said.

Quickly she picked up the next glob and smeared it on a different part of the door. Just as she was going to say that it didn't work, the vault door made a clanking noise. Lola pulled the handle slowly and to her surprise it actually opened.

"It's open," she told Sonia. "It worked! I can't believe it actually worked." She was so alleviated that she almost teared up.

"Don't close it," Sonia told her. "You need to clean up that mess. We don't want this ending up with an investigation."

Lola ran to the circular table in the middle of the room and took the red table runner. She cleaned up as fast as she could before closing the door. There was nowhere to put the goopy table runner, so she shoved it into her purse. She also placed the tea in one of the empty vials before she forgot she had it. She was sure to swallow it without realizing if she kept it in her mouth any longer.

As soon as she was done, she went to open the door to leave but she remembered that there was a guard outside. She cracked the door open to take a quick peek. Thankfully the guard was standing next to the person he had called to clean the glass from the vase Lola had tipped over.

She swiftly left the room and tiptoed past the guard to go straight to the elevator. When the doors to the elevator opened the guard and the cleaner looked over. Both of them had a look on their faces that Lola was dreading. She looked down at her hands and they were opaque. There were spots on her body that were becoming more and more visible in the few seconds that she was in the elevator. There was no way she would make it back to the bedroom without Adam seeing bits of her walking right past him. The elevator reached the fifth floor and the doors opened, so she hid up against the wall behind the buttons. Her hands were almost all the way visible now.

Thinking that maybe there were a few drops of the invisibility potion left, Lola ransacked her purse. She pulled out the empty vial that had contained the potion, but found that there was barely a molecule. She reached into the purse again, her fingertips now completely visible, and pulled out a handful of vials. She was holding a red one, a murky metallic gray one, a green one, and a pink one.

That gray potion would be the only one that could really help her out of this situation, but it would make a big fuss—big enough to get a lot of security involved. She knew that if she used it, the whole floor would be crawling with guards within minutes; it was either that or getting caught naked outside of the room she was supposed to be in. There really was no other choice, and unfortunately "no other choice" seemed to be the theme of her time in Terre Two.

The bedroom door was the fourth one on the right. Lola clutched the gray potion tight, closed her eyes, and then smashed it on the ground. A cloud of smoky fog emerged from the shattered glass and within seconds of it being activated, it grew to fill the entire elevator.

Lola was completely concealed in the fake smoke. It even helped her breathe a little better knowing that she was hidden.

Adam took notice immediately and just before rushing over to see what was happening, the smoke-colored cloud busted out of the elevator ferociously, and there wasn't an inch of the hallway that wasn't covered.

This was Lola's chance. She followed the right wall with her hands as she felt for each doorknob along the way. She made it to the third door when she felt something hit her outstretched foot, and then heard a thud right next to her.

"Who's there?" she heard Adam say.

Lola didn't stop for a second after tripping him. She was almost grateful that she had tripped him or she might have had the misfortune of accidentally being groped. She reached the fourth door soon enough and tumbled inside. As she sat on the carpet, still splotchy from invisibility, her face told the story of making the impossible happen. Her chest was heaving, but she still had a big smile.

After she got up, she didn't waste any time putting on her clothes. Never did she think she would be so happy to be wearing a heavy, itchy gown. Almost as soon as she finished zipping herself up, she heard a knock at the door. "Mara!" Adam called out. "Are you okay?"

Lola opened the door and found Adam standing there looking a little disheveled. The cloud of fake smoke had almost dissipated, but there was still evidence of it.

"What happened?" Lola asked feigning concern.

"We're not sure," Adam told her. "Did anything happen in here?" Lola shook her head assuring him that she was safe.

"We should go," Adam said. "Our head of security is on her way to investigate." Lola followed him to the stairs without saying a word. "Are you sure you're okay?" He asked her again.

"Yeah," Lola told him. "I'm fine, I promise."

They made it back to the ballroom without another word. As soon as they walked in, they saw that most people had already started dancing, including Evie and Penelope. From the looks of it, none of the guests were aware that anything else was going on. It was probably best to keep it hushed to prevent ensuing chaos. Lola could imagine the zoo that place would turn into if all of the women tried to run out with their enormous ball gowns.

Alex spotted them as they continued to enter and closed in. "Looks like we'll have to switch off," Alex joked as she pointed to Penelope. She looked at Adam, less than pleased.

"I'll be right back," Adam told Lola. Alex didn't bother to hide her enthusiasm for his absence by rolling her eyes.

Almost as soon as he walked away, someone else took his place. Lola didn't see this person until he cleared his throat to get her attention.

"Excuse me, Miss Soto," said a brooding voice behind her.

Lola turned to find that the person wanting her attention was the angel from the portal—only he didn't have his wings or garb. Although handsome, it didn't distract from his harsh demeanor. He was

265

just as dressed up as everyone else, but even in a well-tailored suit he still looked intimidating.

"Hello," Lola said, worried that she and Sonia had been caught.

"I'm not sure if this information is known to you," he started to say, his accent adding even more to his tough appearance. "Recently, your aunt traveled to Terre One with a mannequin of your resemblance. As it is my duty to protect the threshold, professionally I felt it pertinent that you be aware—if you are not already—of how your likeness is being used. I highly discourage what your aunt did, given the severity of being recognized in Terre One. Your namesake, although identical, seemed hardly a match. It was clearly rigid and mindless, but nonetheless distinguishable."

Lola took mild offense to that, but he probably wasn't wrong. Although, the irony of being called rigid was not lost on her.

"As well as using your mannequin in Terre One," he continued. "I am certain she used it while traveling through the countryside. This is information, I believed, should be brought to your attention for security purposes."

At that moment she realized it was him she saw at the military base they had passed. *No wonder he was looking at us,* she thought.

"Thank you," Lola told him cautiously. "I will discuss this with my aunt. I appreciate you telling me."

The angel did not say anything further, nor did he smile. He simply gave her a nod and returned the way he came.

"I think he was hitting on you," Alex joked, mildly amused.

"That was weird," Lola told her, still bemused that he talked to her at all.

"Yeah, but Sebastian's always been a stone giant," Alex told her. "I'm going to go find out if he likes you. Anyone is better than Adam. Don't leave." She walked away in the same direction that Sebastian left.

At long last, Lola had a chance to leave and meet Sonia outside. She took one step but was held back from someone grabbing her hand.

"May I have this dance?" Adam asked knowing full well how cheesy that line was.

There was no getting out of this one, she couldn't use the other women as an excuse to get away. She gave him a nod and a small smile. Adam's face lit up. It was obvious he had strong feelings for Mara. He gestured for her to take his hand and then walked her to the dance floor. The band was just starting the next song as they found a spot. Adam placed one hand on Lola's waist and straightened his posture.

Lola quickly realized that he actually knew how to ballroom dance, which put her in at a disadvantage. It also meant that Mara knew how to ballroom dance, another quality of hers which Lola could not live up to. Adam started leading her, but she was only able to follow for a brief moment.

"I forgot you don't go too many balls in Cavalerian," Adam said smug in his tone.

"I guess I have more important things to do," Lola teased, not knowing if that was the right response.

"Fair enough," Adam smiled.

After a couple of minutes Lola was actually getting familiar with the dance, especially since Adam was so good at leading. After relaxing enough to go with the flow, she finally looked up at him. She was still taken aback by how handsome he was, but got over it easily when she looked into his eyes. They were green and beautiful, and although not blue like Jason's, they still made her think of him.

Lola started to feel a bit nauseous and her face was showing it. She wanted to get out of there now, but had to resist the urge to just run away. Her palms were getting embarrassingly sweaty and Adam noticed.

"Are you feeling okay?" He asked, concern sweeping over his face.

This was her chance to leave. "It's really warm in here," she told him. "I think I should get some fresh air."

"I'll come with you," he offered right away.

"It's okay," she said. "I don't want to take you away from your own party."

"Don't worry about it, I need some fresh air too." He walked her away from the crowd to an open patio. The air outside was only slightly cooler than inside, but it was enough for Lola to catch her breath.

She wasn't paying much attention to Adam, although she probably should have. He had been waiting for this exact moment to bring up something that he had been holding in since their first encounter.

"Mara," he said wishing Lola would turn around and make eye contact. "It's pretty obvious you've been avoiding this conversation."

"Huh?" Lola said a little blurry eyed.

"I know talking about what happened last year isn't something you were planning on doing when you came back," Adam continued saying. "I wasn't planning on it either, and to be honest I tried to burry any feelings I had of making things right."

Lola stopped Adam from continuing. She wasn't trying to be rude, but she didn't know what he wanted to talk about. If anything, she might really make a mess of things if she even tried to engage.

"Listen Adam," Lola said. "I really can't have this conversation right now. Trust me, this isn't the right time."

"Then when is the right time?" He asked impatiently. He seemed somewhat jittery, which only made Lola think she would *have* to talk to him. Adam wasn't going to give up. He only kept getting closer to Lola with every word that he said.

"I didn't stop caring for you," he told her. "But I did think I stopped being in love with you. We haven't talked for months—about anything—but that still didn't matter as soon as I saw you."

Lola was moved by what he was saying, mostly because she had always wanted her own boyfriend to come to realizations like that. Nevertheless, this wasn't for her and it would be terrible if she pretended it was—even if it was on Mara's behalf.

Without Lola noticing, Adam had gotten as close to her as he possibly could without touching her.

"I'm sorry for letting you leave like that," he told her. "I don't regret it because I've learned a lot looking back, but I'm still sorry. I'm sorry I hurt you again."

She didn't have a clue what to say. She almost felt like she was violating something private by choosing not to tell him she wasn't Mara, and she felt it even more as he took her by the arms.

"Please," Lola told him. She wanted to pull away, but she didn't. "I think we should have this conversation later."

"I know you well enough to know when you're trying to avoid forgiving me," Adam told her. His eyes were sad and resembled someone who would do anything to get back into the good graces of any person he wronged.

"You're right," Lola said having decided to play along. "I am really hurt." She pulled away slowly. "I do want to talk, but don't you think it should be on my terms?"

Adam dropped his head and held an expression that indicated he knew this was coming. He looked up at her and smiled crookedly. It was charming and it almost made Lola wish she could help with the dilemma. Lucky for her, he gave in to her wishes, but not before mustering up the courage to give her a kiss on the cheek. It was gentle kiss and at the same time, notably heartfelt.

"Just wait," he told her before heading back inside. "I'll find a way to make this right."

Lola wasn't sure if she should be impressed by his persistence or weary that he might hurt Mara again. Either way, none of it would be of any concern to her after tonight. She clutched her invisible purse as he walked away. She was ecstatic that this strange nightmare was almost over.

When Adam was out of sight, she walked back inside. She kept as close to the wall as she could, hoping her group wouldn't notice her trying to leave. Lola could see that Evie was still dancing with the same dark-haired guy from before. She also noticed that Alex and Penelope were looking for her. Alex's outstretched neck and Penelope holding her phone up to her ear, gave it away.

Seeing Penelope use her phone to contact her, made Lola jump out of her skin. She was calling Mara! Any minute now she was going to get caught. She needed to make her exit now more than ever.

As she was leaving the ballroom, Lola pulled out her own phone and called Sonia again. Sonia took no time in answering.

"Are you outside?" Sonia asked.

"I'm almost there."

"Hurry, we don't have a lot of time," Sonia's tone suggested that Lola was not on her good side.

"We have a problem," Lola told her, fear resonating in her voice.

"Now what?" Sonia asked as if she were about to breathe out fire through the phone.

"I'm pretty sure Penny is calling Mara, looking for me."

"Hurry up then," Sonia told her and then hung up.

Lola was at the castle entrance within minutes. Sonia was already waiting there for her.

"Where's the carriage?" Lola asked, at the same time that she was keeping a vigilant eye out to make sure that no one important was watching.

"Change of plans," Sonia told her. "We have to find another way. Your carriage is blocked by all the other carriages."

"You can't be serious," Lola said. She was sure that one more bit of bad news would give her a full-blown heart attack.

"Hold on," said Sonia. Lola could see a flash of inspiration go over her face. "Follow me."

The two walked away from the castle entrance and followed the incoming carriages that were being parked. On the other side of the castle they found the stables and that's where Sonia started to walk toward.

Lola understood what Sonia wanted to do, but she was having her doubts about stealing horses. She was starting to think they might be digging a hole they can't get out of. They continued to sneak around the dark areas of the grounds and kept as low as possible.

"Is this really our only option?" Lola whispered.

"Do you want to walk?" Sonia countered.

"No, but I also haven't stolen so many things in my entire life," Lola said. "First Mara's identity, then the tea, and now livestock."

"We might not have had to resort to this if you hadn't messed up," Sonia said. She was clearly irritated that everything they had been working toward was almost completely destroyed. Apparently everything is always Lola's fault, which she seriously disagreed with.

When they made it to the stables, Sonia checked to make sure no one was inside before letting Lola enter.

"We're clear," Sonia told her as she waved her in. "Pick a good one." Lola didn't think Sonia actually wanted her to assess the horses, especially since she wasn't sure she would even be able to get on one.

"There's a little bit of an issue here," Lola told Sonia. "I'm not going to be able to get on a horse wearing this gown."

Before saying anything else, Sonia started to look around the stables quickly. She found a wall that had hanging equipment and pulled something off of it.

"Here," she said handing Lola a curved blade with a handle. "Cut the fabric underneath. Take out the petticoat and whatever else is sucking you in there." Lola gave a heavy sigh as she took the blade from Sonia.

"What?" Sonia asked.

"I'm not doing Mara any favors, am I?" Lola said.

Sonia chose not to speak to that because she knew Lola was right. Mara was going to have to explain for a lot of unusual behavior when she came back. To top it off, she would come home to a mangled gown that had only been worn once, and not by her.

Even as Lola was ripping up the dress, the tension between her and Sonia was palpable. She knew Sonia wanted to burst, so she decided to give her the opportunity.

273

"Can you just lecture me already?" Lola said wanting to get it over with.

Sonia peeked out of one of the stables with a stoic look on her face. She stood there silent for a few seconds before saying what she had to say.

"There's no point," Sonia said sounding like a disappointed parent that had no trust left in her child. "You're lucky the Extraceit potion was there. I hope you don't intend to keep relying on dumb luck for your entire life." Lola said nothing. She knew that arguing back was pointless. Instead she tried to diffuse the lecture bomb.

"What was that stuff anyway?" She asked, hoping that would liven the tension.

It took a moment before Sonia answered, but her ego got the best of her. Lola knew that she took a lot of pride in knowing everything.

"It's a very expensive and dangerous kind of medicine—if you want to call it that," Sonia explained. "It's meant to relieve a person of anything that isn't organically theirs—viruses, poisons, DNA, good and bad bacteria—that's why it's dangerous to consume. It's usually only used for poisons without antidotes."

With the tension close to being gone, Lola didn't hesitate to continue to cut up the gown, even though she felt bad about it. At the same time, she could feel the weight of the layers shedding off of her. The mound of material kept piling up next to her. By the end, all she had left to do was to cut off a few feet of length.

The gown, or at least what was left of it, was now up to her mid-calf. Sonia was ready with the horses by the time Lola was finished mutilating the most beautiful gown she had ever worn. She looked like she had lost a fight with a mongoose, but she didn't care as long as she and Jason were getting out of Terre Two tonight.

Sonia handed Lola the reins to a chocolate-brown horse and then immediately mounted her own. Lola reached up to the saddle but then realized she was still wearing her high heels.

"You're going to have to leave those," Sonia told her as if she didn't already know that.

"Ditching my heels after the ball, could this place get any more cliché?" Lola said taking her shoes off and then mounting her horse.

"I understand that you're making some sort of reference or joke, but your attitude about all of this almost got you caught." Sonia was unbearably annoyed with her, and Lola had no idea what to do to make things right. Lola's tolerance for being blamed was reaching its limit. It was hard for her to take, especially considering how she couldn't possibly know exactly what to do at all times—and again, this was all technically Sonia's fault!

"Stay close," Sonia told her right before dashing out, leaving Lola scrambling to catch up.

To Lola this was starting to feel like the end of the worst dream in history. The evening air flooded her face as if to say that the path was clear—at least it did, until it hit her with another dose of reality—she knew better than to assume this nightmare was almost over. There was no room for comfort until they were completely out.

Chapter 21

Sonia had led them through the back of the castle to avoid the guests and security of the ball. The muddy path took them straight to the North entrance of the town. It was blocked off by posts and chains to avoid wayward carriages, but it was nothing a few good horses couldn't jump.

The town was even more darling at night. The hanging lights and banners celebrating "Adam's" triumphant return, were outstanding. It was made clear in the previous days that Adam didn't really spearhead their operation, but the town loved him just the same.

There was no one in town, so the only thing Lola could hear was the horse's hooves stomping on the cobble stone road as they raced to Sonia's office. With no pedestrians around, they were able to get there within minutes of entering the town.

When they arrived at the building where Sonia's lab was, they discovered someone had unmistakably broken in. Lola quickly dismounted her horse to investigate the gaping hole where the door should have been. It looked like something had blasted the door right off the hinges. Lola could smell burnt wood as she passed through the door frame. She could see the edges of the frame had been torched by something powerful and what was left of the door was all over the floor.

Lola panicked and ran upstairs to the lab. When she arrived she found the door to Sonia's lab was in the same condition as the one downstairs—completely gone and thoroughly singed at the frame. She went right through and made it all the way to the spot where Jason had been left, but he was gone.

Sonia was reaching the top of the stairs when she heard a loud-pitched scream. She ran into the lab to find Lola on her knees clutching the blanket Jason had been covered in. She was in complete dismay. Her eyes had swollen up within seconds and she sounded like a heavily wounded animal.

"Where is he?" Lola wailed. "Where the hell is he?"

"I don't..."

"Don't say you don't know!" Lola screamed at her. She stood up and rushed at Sonia grabbing her by the straps of her dress. "Where is he?" She was beginning to lose her breath and her fists were holding onto Sonia's straps so tight that her nails were digging into her own palms.

It took Sonia a few solid seconds to catch her own breath before answering. She was visibly shaken as well, but it was hard to tell if it was because of Jason's disappearance or Lola's panic-stricken state.

"You know where he is," Sonia said softly trying not to agitate her any more than she already was.

Those words really put Lola over the edge. She fell to the ground and sobbed uncontrollably. Sonia was frozen and all she could do was shed a tear—although, she was able to fight back the rest.

Sonia looked around at her disheveled office and noticed that the falcon and the feathers were also taken. There was no doubt in her mind about who did this.

"Come on," she told Lola. "She's not far, the burns on the door frame are still warm." She forcefully helped Lola stand up. "Listen to me, we can still save him, but we have to hurry." Lola started wiping the tears off of her face. She looked like the victim of some top-notch pepper spray.

"I'm sorry," Sonia continued to say. "She must have followed the falcon back here. I didn't think we would be that long." Lola kept wiping her tears to no avail until Sonia snapped her out of it. "We have to go. We can still catch up to them, but we need to leave right now."

Knowing there was still a chance to save Jason was all that Lola needed to get back on her feet. She had come this far, and she wasn't about to give up now. She stormed out of the lab and back down the stairs. She could feel the debris of the doors on the bottoms of her feet as she exited, not caring that she was still barefoot.

Without even waiting for Sonia she jumped on her horse and bolted toward the path that would lead them to Simora's towers. The journey took them two hours the last time they went, but hopefully she would catch up to Simora before they could make it all the way.

Lola was making the horse gallop so fast that she almost lost control a few times. Her rage was boiling over and she couldn't stop thinking about how she wanted to hurt Simora.

Why would she take Jason? It doesn't make sense.

Sonia wasn't too far behind Lola, but she still had to try hard to catch up. The path was very hard to see. The only light they had was coming from the moon. The night was clear, which really helped, but Lola hoped she didn't make a mistake by not waiting for Sonia—she couldn't afford to get lost now.

Soon enough she recognized the patch of trees where she embarrassingly lost a fight with one of Simora's crows. She stopped for a few seconds, only to pick up a large stick for protection, and then dashed through until she came to the spot where they had set up camp the last time they were there. Far in the distance by the invisible leg of the tower, she could see some movement—it had to be them.

Lola kept going knowing she would be there soon. The poor horse was racing its heart out to get her there. When she was only feet away from the entrance, she prematurely dismounted her horse. She tripped getting off and scraped up her legs in the process, but none of that slowed her down.

She began to search for the hole to open the entrance. It took her two go-arounds to find it. When she stuck her hand inside she could feel the spike tempting her to prick her finger. There was no way of knowing how far back Sonia was, but she wasn't about to wait for her. Lola pressed her finger on the sharp object until it drew blood. She could feel the little spike passing through the top layers of her skin.

Just like before, the entrance revealed itself to her. She slowly took a step inside, trying to make sure there wouldn't be some sort of trap. As soon as she thought it was clear, she made a run for the stairs.

Almost as soon as she took those first two steps, the stairs began to escalate. Lola lost her footing and fell forward, scraping her legs even more, but she got right back up and kept climbing. As soon as she recovered her balance, she started running again, but the large stick was making it difficult to keep up the pace.

The unmarked doors that she kept passing were eerie and almost all dark on the inside. They were starting to hypnotize her, which made her slow down even more. When she finally made it to the landing, the giant mechanical doors were wide open. It seemed like Simora wasn't going to make any attempts at hiding. As riled up as Lola was, she knew better than to just walk into someone else's territory, given the situation.

"Simora!" Lola called out furiously. Her anger reverberated off of the walls. "Where is he?" She walked closer to the doors with the club-like stick leading the way. She swung it back and forth at the entrance of the lab to make sure nothing was going to attack her if she entered. As she took a step inside, she noticed that there were no birds like last time.

"Tell me where he is right now!" She shouted as loudly and as fiercely as she could.

Just then, Lola heard noise coming from the other side of one of the lab tables. She walked a little farther to see what was there and found that Jason sitting on a chair with his head hanging down to his chest. Unfortunately, Simora was standing right next to him.

"I don't know why you're doing this, but you have to stop." Lola was now holding her clubbing stick menacingly, as if she would destroy everything around her in a split second.

Simora walked around Jason to stand in front of him. She didn't look worried. Her composure was very surreal and leveled at the same time, almost as if she was at peace.

"Put that down, you foolish girl," Simora said resounding her entitled authority.

Lola did no such thing. "I'm not putting anything down until you hand him over," she said unflinchingly. She was nearing a blind rage when Sonia finally showed up. Sonia definitely had a harder time making it up the stairs, but at least she was there now.

"Simora," Sonia struggled to say. "Let him go."

"Who's going to make me?" Simora teased as if this was her favorite game.

"I know what you're trying to do," Sonia said breathlessly. "But you can't do it—it's unnatural." That seemed to have stricken a chord with Simora because her face turned upside-down.

"I don't know why you're so against this," Simora told her through gritted teeth. "We can solve this right now. I know you have Gwen's memory. You can go get it and we can do this together."

Lola was lost from this conversation. What the hell was Simora talking about? The thing she had retrieved from Gwen was an ingredient, not a memory.

"This isn't the way to do it Simora," Sonia said, slowly trying to keep her calm.

"There is no other way!" Simora shouted, letting her guard down for only half a second. "We've tried everything, and you and I both know this will work."

It was hard for Lola to follow why this was happening. Simora was grasping at Sonia for some sort of lifeline—groveling didn't suit her, but Lola had seen that look in her own eyes before. There was so much more to this than she thought, and she knew a desperate person when she saw one.

"Listen," Lola began to plead. "As soon as Sonia heals him we'll leave, we'll never bother you again."

A maniacal straight grin crossed Simora's lips. "What are you talking about?" She said. "There's nothing wrong with him."

Lola's breath hitched and she quickly turned to look at Sonia. "Yes, there is," she whimpered. "That's why we're here. That's why we're in this mess."

Simora just kept looking at Lola like she was the most pitiful creature she had ever seen. "Oh, you poor, stupid girl." Simora's condescending tone only agitated Lola more. "Do you really not know? This is sad, but I'll let you in on the secret. There's no need to heal him —at least not any further."

"What?" Lola turned to Sonia expecting her to accuse Simora of lying, but she didn't.

"Sonia, did you not tell her?" Simora asked still entertaining herself. "Hardly seems like something that would slip your mind."

Lola stepped away from Sonia, like she was a threat. "Is this true?" Before Sonia could answer, Simora interjected.

"Of course, it's true," she said as if she was pointing out something that was completely obvious to everyone else. "Look at him, not a scratch, not a bruise. Are you really that dense?"

At first Lola was drawing a blank, it was like her brain was working overtime and in-turn malfunctioning—then her eyes began to water, not from sadness, but from fury. Her arm was getting shaky from holding up the big stick, but she still managed to not let go.

"I don't understand," Lola said, barely moving her lips.

"What's to understand?" Simora said. "She was using you."

"I can explain later," Sonia told Lola. Her brow was sweating, and she looked like she had aged ten years in the last hour. Her body was struggling to hold itself up and Lola could tell.

"Why don't I explain for you?" Simora said, her cheery voice as fake as ever. "You see, Sonia has a hard time letting go. Her work would be nothing without mine alongside it, so she decided to use you to steal it—and not just mine by the way. You've also stolen Gwen's part of this experiment."

Without warning came another voice from behind Sonia. It was a voice Lola had heard before, but she couldn't tell if Sonia was happy to hear it.

"You're one to talk about letting go," Gwen said seeming to be on their side. "We're only in this situation because of your obsession." Gwen looked at Sonia as she joined them—her eyes threw darts at her and it was clear that she was mad, but it was also clear who she was

284

there to help. She must have been keeping a close watch on them the entire night. "If you hadn't gone off the rails, we wouldn't be under investigation."

Simora was getting skittish as she realized she was outnumbered. She grabbed Jason and made him stand as she wrapped an arm around his neck. She was getting even more desperate and they could all tell.

"How dare you both!" Simora snarled with more wrath than before. "How dare you criticize me. Neither one of you know what it was like to go through my loss and you promised to do everything you could to help me, but did you?" She began to back up, still holding Jason as a human shield. As she slowly walked backwards, she had her other hand outstretched reaching for something.

"Simora, please," Gwen tried to reason. "We're sorry for what happened, but you know what you're doing is wrong. That's why we were disbanded in the first place." Gwen was the only one who was walking toward Simora. "Let's stop this now and we might get another chance at saving other people's children."

"No," Simora said, finally reaching what she was searching for—a black covering on something tall and thin. "There's still time to save my son." She pulled the cover off to reveal a mirror that was a tint of blue and framed in ornate gold.

Sonia and Gwen lurched forward, but as soon as they did Simora tightened her arm around Jason's neck—his compliant, yet limp, body looked like it couldn't tell the difference.

"Simora, there's no going back if you do this," Sonia warned. "Let the him go."

"What's going on?" Lola yelled frustrated at not knowing how to help.

"Don't worry," Simora said with a crazed look gleaming from her eyes. "It's not going to hurt him. All I need is his soul." She turned Jason to face the mirror, but his reflection wasn't of his unconscious self. His reflection was awake and screaming for help. It looked like some sort of trick. They must have used magic to make it seem like his reflection was awake. There's no way that was actually him.

Simora reached into the mirror and grabbed Jason's reflection by the arm. The reflection was pulling to get away from her and pushing his foot against the mirror for leverage.

Without giving it a second thought, Lola swung her club at the mirror, and it hit full force from halfway across the room. The mirror shattered with Simora's hand still inside of it, shredding up her arm in the process. She let Jason fall to the ground as she shrieked in pain from all of the glass stuck in her arm. Her screams did not go unnoticed by her avian friends.

They all started hearing birds chirping and cawing. The bird noises became louder by the second, until they finally burst inside through the open arches that led to the outer walkway.

The birds surrounded them and even started pecking. They were being attacked by so many birds that it was hard to see what Simora was getting ready to do.

Lola had her head down, covering her face as best as she could. She was able to get one glance at Simora and could see that she was cradling her bloodied arm, but she was also trying to hold a hand out to something that was high up.

As she peeked up to see what Simora was looking at, she got a glimpse of the falcon. It was just about to take flight to reach her when a booming clap rang out. Lola looked to her right and saw that it had come from Gwen. The bird flapping stopped and they all dropped from midair like they had been frozen.

Lola knew exactly what Simora was going to do next, so she sprinted to where she had seen the falcon drop. Simora also started running toward her falcon with her finger pointing straight at it. Soon enough, a black marble-sized orb emerged from the falcon. Simora was closer to the falcon than Lola was, and just as she was about to reach it she tripped over another one of her birds. She got right back up, in time to see Lola grab the tiny black orb and then get flung back by its power, only to hit a wall several feet away. Simora was close enough to get thrown back as well, but not as harshly as Lola did. The birds started waking up from Gwen's spell and they all flew out of the lab immediately, all except the falcon.

Lola was on the ground unconscious and hardly breathing. Gwen went to help her, but when she did, she too was thrown to the side by a force of magical energy.

Simora had gotten up and was aiming straight at Lola. Even with only one hand she was able to move Gwen aside. Just as she was going to strike Lola with her magic, Sonia stood up to protect her. She was able to block Simora's magic with her own.

"Get out of the way," Simora told her as she threw another punch of energy. Sonia deflected with an invisible shield as sparks flew from the contact.

"It's over Simora," Sonia said covering herself and Lola. "We're turning you in."

Simora let out a loud laugh in disbelief. "How are you going to do that without turning yourself in? She's seen too much. They'll lock you away for exposing our world."

Just then they heard a wolf howling in the distance. It was barely audible at first, but then they heard it again. Within seconds, the howling started coming from below near the entrance of the towers.

The second surprise was coming in fast. They could see lights approaching in the distance, but they were so high up in the tower that it was hard to tell when they would arrive.

"Stand aside!" Simora said throwing another hit of magic. It sparked again as it hit Sonia's invisible shield. "I'll kill her before I let you have my formula." She continued to send strike after strike of magic while Sonia held them off.

The wolf howled again, this time scaring Simora's falcon. The lights were getting closer and it wasn't until they could hear footsteps running up the stairs that Simora had no choice but to go off completely.

"This is your last chance Sonia," Simora told her. "Give her up now or I'll kill you both."

At this point Sonia was holding on by a thread. She had cuts on her face from all the blows she was taking, but she didn't look defeated. She spit to the side because the blood was pooling in her mouth, but she didn't move.

Simora was just about to deliver her biggest attack yet, when Adam and a hoard of soldiers showed up. They were all still wearing their ball attire, but even then Simora knew exactly who they were.

"Detain her!" Adam ordered.

The soldiers charged Simora, but as they did she ran to the outside walkway and straight over the railing. She didn't fall more than a few feet before her falcon swooped in and caught her by the back of her dress, flying them both away into the clear night.

Chapter 22

By the time Lola had woken up, she was no longer in Simora's lab. She was being carried by someone, but it wasn't until she rubbed her eyes profusely that she was able to see who it was.

"What's your name?" Adam asked, stone faced. Lola didn't know what was going on, but it was probably safer to keep pretending she was still Mara.

"Mara," she answered sleepily.

"No, it's not," Adam said. "That's why we're here."

That was enough for Lola to perk up and wiggle herself out of being carried any farther. She looked around and saw at least a dozen people there—one of them was Penelope. She was wrapped in a blanket, but from the looks of it that was all she had on.

As they neared the horses, Lola finally saw Sonia. She was in hand cuffs and being supervised by one of the soldiers. Adam stopped at one of the horses and beckoned her to get on. From on top of the horse she saw that they also had Jason in custody. He was probably still unconscious.

"What are you going to do to us?" Lola asked terrified of the response.

Adam looked at her as if he were disappointed. He mounted the same horse and laced his arms around her as if he thought she wasn't afraid to jump off mid-ride. There was no mistaking that she wasn't going to be able to get away.

***

When they arrived back at the castle, they were immediately taken into a chamber room that was bustling even before they had gotten there. There were women and men half dressed in black robes that they had put on over their ball attire. They were sitting on a high bench and everyone below was also still wearing their clothes from the night before.

As they approached the bench, the people around them became even angrier. Lola cringed as they kept walking up to the front of the room, and Adam made sure he had a good grip on her shoulder.

Gwen was the next one to come in, but she wasn't being escorted. She sat down in the front row, presumably because she was a witness. People kept pouring in like there was a concert going on. Everyone Lola had come in contact with was now in this room. Penelope and Alex sat a couple of rows back with Mara's family. Sebastian was also there standing at the back of the room, statuesque as ever. The last person to come in was Sonia—still accompanied and handcuffed.

"Silence!" Boomed the voice of a petite woman in a black robe.

The soldier escorting Sonia stopped right in front of the bench. Lola looked at her hoping for some sign a reassurance, but Sonia was expressionless.

"Sonia Annette Cruz," began the woman at the bench. "It has come to our attention that you knowingly brought two inhabitants of Terre One into our world; you falsely claimed them as mannequins to threshold guardian Sebastian Veil, forced the female to impersonate your niece Mara Soto, and persuaded her to steal for an experiment that is still under investigation for unethical practices."

Lola looked around the room only to see that everyone was wearing the same expression. They were shocked to know what Sonia had done, and now everyone wanted to know why.

"Lieutenant Gartwick," the woman in charge addressed Adam. "To the best of your knowledge, please recount the events that led to the capture of Ms. Sonia Cruz."

"Yes, Governor," Adam responded. He went on to explain that the first sign of something wrong was when the smoke bomb went off and covered the entire fifth floor that he was on, but they found no trace of where it had come from.

He then continued to tell everyone in the room that the reason they went to look for Sonia and the person they believed to be Mara, was because Mara's friends were looking for her. They decided to call Mara, but when she answered she told them that she wasn't in town. Mara's friends decided to tell Adam, fearing there was something wrong or someone else was using her phone. He gathered a search party because he had also just seen Mara himself not long before.

They found the remains of Lola's gown in the stables and Penelope offered to transform into her werewolf state to track her down. She led them to Simora's towers and after Simora escaped, he got most of what happened from Gwen. He told them about how Simora was trying to use Jason to continue their disbanded experiment and bring back her son who was born in Terre One.

The entire room was captivated by what Adam had explained. It almost sounded like a terrible movie with evil witches and a helpless damsel, which Lola resented being portrayed as.

"Was anything substantial discovered at the laboratories of Ms. Cruz?" Asked the Governor.

"Yes ma'am," Adam responded. He waved for someone in uniform to come over and was handed a plastic bag with Gwen's ginger crystal doll. "We were informed by Ms. Gwen Harding that her part of the experiment was in the possession of Sonia Cruz."

That's what was in the doll? Lola felt so used she almost wanted to cry.

"Take the evidence to processing," The Governor instructed them after taking a closer look. Before continuing, the people on the bench consulted with each other, whispering back and forth.

"Bring her forward," the Governor told Adam. Lola was nudged to step up even though she was hesitant. "What is your name?" The Governor asked as gently as if she were talking to a caged animal.

Lola didn't answer right away. She tugged at the fabric that was once an immaculate gown. She hung her head enough to see her muddy bare feet covered passed her ankles. As she pulled at her tattered dress, she realized she was still wearing the invisible purse with her potions.

"Lola," she finally answered.

"Is there anything you want to tell us?" Asked the Governor.

"I just want to go home," she said, her voice cracking.

The Governor sat back in her chair assessing what to ask next, given how fragile she believed Lola to be. "You can go back," she told her. "You just have to answer our questions first. Is that okay?"

Lola didn't like the tone she was using, it made her feel like a dumb kid, but at this point she didn't care—she would do anything to leave. She nodded her head and hoped the questions would go fast.

"Did Ms.Cruz force you to steal?" Asked the Governor.

"She didn't force me to do anything," Lola said looking right at Sonia. "She lied to me. All I wanted to do was help my boyfriend."

That last part was news to everyone. Lola assumed they would have all figured out why she went along with Sonia's plan.

"Did she lure you here?" Governor Gartwick asked.

"No," Lola told her. "I followed her because I thought she was my aunt, and because I saw her do something weird to Jason when he got hit by the car."

"I think we've heard enough," the Governor said. "Prep the inhabitants of Terre One for immediate return. Wipe their memories and give them false ones to account for the missing days." The people in the room began to chatter as these decisions were being administered.

"As for Sonia Cruz," said the Governor. "She is to be detained at Aster Prison." As she said that, the room erupted in protest from half of the people there. "She is to wear magic capturing cuffs at all times as she awaits her trial."

Chaos was ensuing, but Lola was still able to catch some of what the protesters were saying.

"She's trying to save our children!" shouted one woman.

"This is a conspiracy," said another woman. "You don't care about our children!"

Adam gently pulled Lola close to him and then started leading her out. She could see the faces of Sonia's family as she walked by—they looked terrified.

"Governor Gartwick!" Sonia shouted over the crowd. Everybody went silent at once. "You can't just take her back to Terre One."

"Ms. Cruz!" said the Governor. "You do not tell me what I can and can't do."

"I apologize Governor," Sonia said. "I meant no disrespect, but she cannot just go back. She has Simora's part of our experiment."

"What are you talking about?" Asked the Governor.

"Simora's memory—the memory of her part of the experiment is inside of her." Sonia turned to face Lola and she actually looked genuine for the first time since she'd met her. "I'm sorry Lola, but you can't just go home."

"Somebody extract the memory so we can all move on," said one of the men in the black robes.

"I've already tried," Sonia told them. "Just after Lieutenant Gartwick and his men found us. It's lost or stuck—and no offense, but if I can't find it, I very much doubt any of your people can."

"Take her to the infirmary," the Governor told Adam.

"Please, you have to listen to me," Sonia warned them. "If you send her back, Simora will go after her—not to mention that you risk losing a decade worth of work if you erase her memory."

"We'll decide what's best, Ms. Cruz," said Governor Gartwick. "Guards, escort her to Aster prison at once."

After that announcement there was no chance of calming the crowd. Adam rushed Lola out of the room and to the infirmary like he was ordered. They left behind a jungle of protest and questions.

When they got to the infirmary, they saw that Jason was laying in one of the beds. He looked peaceful and thankfully clean. Adam sat Lola in the bed next to Jason as the doctor came over to them. She was still on the phone as she approached.

"Dr. Manna this is Lola," Adam introduced her as the doctor hung up the call—most likely from Governor Gartwick.

"Hello Lola," Dr. Manna said sweetly. "I'm so sorry for what you've been through. I'm going to have to do some work on you and it might take a while, is that okay?"

"How's Jason?" Lola asked impatiently. She couldn't care less about what's going on inside of her if Jason wasn't safe.

"He's in good health," Dr. Manna answered. "As soon as we retrieve Simora's memory from you, we'll send you both back." Her voice was soothing as she explained what she was going to do. She told Lola that it would be best for them to put her to sleep since they didn't know how long the procedures would take.

Lola agreed to be put to sleep—as scared as she was, she wanted badly to rest. She laid down on the bed and Dr. Manna went to grab her a blanket. As she laid down, she hugged the invisible purse over her chest hoping no one would discover it.

When Dr. Manna gave Lola the blanket and a small cup of liquid to drink, she looked her up and down and came up with a pained expression on her face. Lola looked terrible—her feet were covered in caked-on mud and she was practically wearing torn up rags.

Lola sipped the contents of the cup slowly. The liquid had no smell and looked like water but felt like gel on her tongue. She kept sipping until she realized she had been sipping for what seemed like an hour, or two…she couldn't tell.

She blinked twice and then everything moved in slow motion, which felt humanly impossible. When she managed to open her eyes the third time, she saw that there were more people in the infirmary. Her head was resting on a thin pillow and she felt strangely refreshed.

Was it over already?

Governor Gartwick and Gwen were talking silently to Dr. Manna. Adam seemed to be standing guard by the door when Sebastian walked in. At that point everyone looked over at Lola—she had a feeling things hadn't gone as planned.

"Lola," Dr. Manna called as she walked over to her. "Why don't you go take a shower? We put some fresh clothes in there for you." She helped Lola out of the bed and walked her over to the bathroom as if she were an elderly patient.

Lola took her time in the shower once she was in there. She hadn't felt that good in days. As soon as she was done showering and dressed, she got out determined to tell Dr. Manna that she needed to be released immediately. Just as she was about to say her piece, Governor Gartwick stepped right up to talk to her.

"Hello Lola," the Governor said. "I'm sorry I haven't formally introduced myself. My name is Amanda Gartwick. I'm sure you're familiar with my son, Lieutenant Adam Gartwick, as well as Ms. Gwendolyn Harding."

"Yes," Lola said taken aback by Governor Gartwick's abrasive niceness.

"We have something to tell you," Dr. Manna interjected. Lola could tell that they were all trying to be gentle with what they had to say, but she preferred that they just come out with it.

"I'm sure I can handle whatever it is," Lola told them all. "Can you please tell me so we can go home?"

They all looked at each other nervously until Gwen spoke up. "We couldn't get Simora's memory from you," she said. "We checked and it's definitely in there, but there's no way of knowing how to retrieve it."

"Why?" Lola asked a little too aggressively. "It's not like I'm an alien. I'm a person—it shouldn't be that hard, right?"

"Don't take this the wrong way," Gwen told her. "But your human race is a little less evolved than ours. Your DNA and body chemistry are a bit different, but different enough for us to be stumped at the moment."

"So what does that mean?" In her head, Lola was jumping to the conclusion that they would make her stay.

"It just means you might have to come back," Governor Gartwick told her.

They all waited in silence to see how Lola would react to the news that she would have to return. Even *she* didn't know how to respond to that news. In the end she decided that one more trip back wouldn't be the end of the world as long as she got to take Jason home right now and he never had to come back.

"Fine," Lola agreed. "Can we go home now?"

"One more thing," said the Governor. She nodded to a corner of the room that Lola couldn't completely see. Right away Sebastian stepped out of that corner but didn't come much closer than that.

"Because Simora is still out there," said the Governor. "We've come to the decision that you will need protection. Guardian Veil has volunteered for the position, given his involvement in the matter."

Sebastian didn't look all too thrilled by this self-appointed assignment. To Lola, his volunteering had nothing to do with helping her, and most likely had everything to do with redeeming himself.

"That doesn't seem like a great idea," Lola told them. "Is he just going to follow me around everywhere?"

"That's the plan," answered Governor Gartwick.

"For how long?" This plan was becoming more complicated by the minute. How was she supposed to explain a bodyguard to everyone, especially Jason?

"Until we can find a solution to your...problem," Dr. Manna said.

"I can take care of myself," Lola said hoping her tired attempt would sway them.

"It's either him, or you don't go back at all," warned the Governor.

Lola was taken aback by what the Governor said. Not wanting to risk her chance of leaving, she gave into the bodyguard compromise. Sebastian wasn't going to make life easy for her, and it didn't help that it was partly her fault that he was being reprimanded for what happened.

After agreeing to all of their terms, Lola was finally told she would be able to leave. They tried to help her guide Jason around, but she wouldn't have it. She wrapped her left arm around his waist, as her right one clung to the hand draping over her shoulder.

Before walking out of the castle, Sebastian and other soldiers created a barrier around them all. When the doors opened they could see a crowd of people waiting for them to come out. There were flashing cameras and microphones trying to get through to see the first ever reported intruders from Terre One.

It was hard to see past the bubble of soldiers enclosing them. Lola tried to peek around them, but they didn't make it easy for her. She knew Mara's family and friends had to be in the crowd and all she wanted to say was that she was sorry. She couldn't stop thinking about how she might have hurt them by impersonating Mara. It was hard for her to imagine how they must have felt, knowing they showed real love to someone who wasn't the person who deserved it.

There were two carriages waiting for them close by. The Governor and Adam went into the first one while Lola, Jason, and Gwen went into the second one. Sebastian and the other soldiers were going to follow on horseback.

From the back window of the carriage, Lola was able to see Mara's family and friends. She felt a lump in her throat swell up as the carriages started moving. She just wanted a chance to apologize to them, but she also wanted to thank them. Manny had given her some lost time even though he didn't know it, and the rest of them treated her like she was home. She knew what she had done was rotten and maybe that was something they couldn't forgive, but she wanted to say something to them anyway.

They were quickly driven out of sight, so she hesitantly pulled herself away from the window. She didn't look at Gwen, but that didn't stop her from talking to her.

"You knew I wasn't Mara," Lola said, her head hanging low. "That's what you were talking about when you saw me at the ball—when you said I didn't know much about Sonia."

Gwen gave her a little side smile. "My pesky little fairy friend kept that chunk of hair she pulled out of your head," Gwen explained. "It wasn't hard to figure out what was going on after that." She didn't say anything more, but she knew that would be enough to get Lola to keep talking.

"Why didn't you tell us you knew?" Lola asked, grateful that she wasn't exposed by her, but still curious as to the reasoning.

Gwen thought about her response carefully before answering. "I believe in our work," she said. "The way Sonia went about it was wrong—for me. I would have never done it that way, but that also means I probably wouldn't have gotten as close as she did.

"I've always known her to be consumed by her work, which is why she's one of the best. She wants to help people like Simora, but I also know that isn't the reason she agreed to this experiment in the first place. Even her helping heart doesn't compare to her need for solving the most complicated problems this world has to offer.

"Some people are so driven by their passions that their view of the lines become blurred. What she did to you was wrong, even if it was for a good cause. I don't think anyone expects you to forgive her, but maybe you can understand the need to fight for something so important in your life that you would do almost anything."

Even though Lola was still mad at Sonia, seeing it the way Gwen described almost made the anger easier to swallow. Finding out that Jason was never in any real danger before Simora took him, did bring her temporary relief. She was glad to know he wasn't in pain, but the worry of thinking that he was in pain, really broke something inside of her at the time. In any case, it was still Sonia's fault that he almost died anyway, and that was something she couldn't forgive.

"If this place was anything like an actual fairytale, this could have all been avoided with a kiss," Lola said, joking dryly.

"I don't understand," Gwen confessed.

"It's some stupid BS about love saving the day," Lola said. "It doesn't matter."

Gwen didn't need to understand fairytales to know that Lola wasn't completely wrong. "That's funny," she said. "I was under the assumption that was why you did all of this." Her observation drew an eye roll from Lola.

"I still don't get why Simora needed Jason," Lola told her. "What kind of crazy experiment requires essence of twenty-seven year old man?"

"I am truly sorry you had to witness that," Gwen said softly. "I'm also glad you didn't know exactly what was going on."

"What *was* going on?"

Gwen's eyes shifted back and forth like she was contemplating if she should explain. She looked at Lola with pursed lips and then rubbed the side of her jaw, unsure of what to say, if anything.

"Our experiment is under investigation, as you heard," Gwen started explaining cautiously. "About a year ago, Simora started to veer from our planned experiments to some of her own without telling us. In her defense, she was desperate and I can't blame her for that, but what she was getting into was dark and forbidden by law." Lola's eyes widened as she listened to Gwen. She didn't dare interrupt, not wanting to miss anything as to how Jason fit in with Simora's plans.

"I don't pretend to understand what Simora was going through," Gwen told her. "I can't honestly say that I wouldn't have done the same."

"Just tell me what happened," Lola whispered. The bumpy road was adding an element of uneasiness that made it hard for Lola to have patience for Gwen to decide if she should tell her what happened with Simora.

With a big breath, Gwen decided to continue. "She was pregnant and she knew exactly what could happen if we didn't solve the anomaly. She didn't want to take any chances, so she sought out a seer who foretold that she would not keep her child. Of course she told us, and we did everything we could to try and help, but what we were doing wasn't getting us far enough, fast enough. She suggested that for the sake of her child, we go outside of what was legally attainable, but Sonia and I couldn't bring ourselves to do it. We couldn't risk losing everything if we were to get caught using dark science—not to mention how unnatural and immoral it was. We didn't give it a second thought after that, especially because Simora never brought it up again.

"The time was getting close for her son to be born and we were all scrambling to make something work. Sonia was sure that the apples would be the key, but before we could make our next attempt, our lab was raided by city guards and we were escorted into a hearing with the Board of Magical Sciences.

"Apparently, two of our assistants came across something unfamiliar to them when they went to the lab after hours. They found Simora's notes for her own experiment while she had stepped out.

Rather than say anything to us, they rushed out and immediately reported her to the board—and that's when we were summoned.

"Because her experiment was never tested, as far as anyone could tell, we were disbanded on a temporary basis. We were ordered to relinquish everything we had on the anomaly experiment. We were even probed to make sure we didn't keep copies of everything we had handed over. All we had left was in our minds."

There was a long pause before either of them said anything. Lola was soaking everything in. Seeing as how she would one day be returning, she wanted to make sure she could gather as much information as possible to be less vulnerable in this strange world.

"What was so terrible about Simora's experiment that they had to shut you down?" Lola wanted to know everything.

"Simora, with the help of her seer, had figured out a way to protect her son from leaving Terre Two." Gwen shuttered at the thought of what she was about to say. "She was no longer delving into science as much as she was into ancient magic. She figured out a way to use someone else's soul as a shield around her baby. In theory, she could loosely connect the soul of another person to her unborn child so that when the anomaly occurred, it would take the soul and not her son."

"But she's not pregnant anymore," Lola said. "Her son is already gone, isn't he?" As soon as she said she knew how insensitive she sounded.

"She must have figured out a way to bring him back," Gwen said. "Her other dimensional self is still pregnant as far as I know. It's rotten timing too. If she had just gotten pregnant a few weeks later, the anomaly wouldn't have taken Simora's son and we wouldn't be here… you probably wouldn't be here."

It was a sobering realization to think that everything that they had all been through—Jason, Mara's family, Simora, even Sonia— could have been avoided by something as simple as timing. Hell, if Jason had just waited a few more seconds on the sidewalk, they might have never fallen into Terre Two.

"That mirror, the one I broke, did it have Jason's soul?" Lola looked disturbed, almost like she wanted to throw up.

"Yes," Gwen answered. "Souls are real. They're powerful and forbidden to be tampered with. That mirror you broke was thousands of years old. It had belonged to Simora's family since the beginning. Now that it's gone, I believe there are only a handful more left in the world."

After that they said nothing to each other. What more was there to say? Gwen had revealed so much that Lola actually felt exhausted by it.

When they finally arrived at the tunnel that took them to the portal, Lola was feeling heavy. She stepped out of the carriage and Gwen helped her get Jason out. The tunnel itself looked bigger than she remembered. She could imagine stacking two of her two-story house on top of each other and it would still barely fill the height of this tunnel.

"All right then," said Governor Gartwick as she walked toward them. "Be safe on your way back and hopefully we will see you soon." Lola's face scrunched up in displeasure at the thought of coming back. "The sooner we retrieve Simora's memory, the sooner you can forget all of this. And I'm sure this goes without saying, but do not reveal the existence of our world. A single peep and we will destroy your life." Lola couldn't tell if she was serious because she was smiling. "Apologies for the threat, but I do mean it."

Just as she was turning to leave, Lola caught Adam's eye. He didn't look mad at her anymore, not even disappointed, he just looked like he was ignoring her. Maybe he was embarrassed that he had been fooled by her. She felt bad because there was no mistaking how he felt about Mara, and she took advantage of that, but she had to.

It only took a few deep breaths for Lola to ease into the idea of going back. Sebastian started walking toward the tunnel, so she followed, Jason in tow.

"Wait a second," Gwen told her right before they passed through the film of darkness. She pulled out a vial with pink shimmery powder and dumped a little in her own hand. "Turn around." As soon as Lola turned her head, Gwen blew the powder in Jason's face. "He'll be able to wake up when he gets some sunlight up there, and when he does just tell him all about your amazing time in that city you came from." Lola knew that Gwen had blown mem powder in his face just in case he saw anything that had happened.

"Good luck," Gwen whispered to Lola right before they stepped through the film of the tunnel.

All of a sudden they were in the damp tunnel and when Lola looked back, all she saw was infinite darkness with specks of fire from the torches—they were gone. The inside of the tunnel looked just as dreary as the first time. The glistening purpley-black bricks were

307

dripping water on their heads as they walked past all the golden torches.

They were walking toward the guardian's podium and Sebastian had yet to say a word. The guardian that was protecting the threshold looked to be a bit older than Sebastian—he had a short beard and a shaved head. When they approached the podium, his wings extended all the way which made Lola jump.

Sebastian handed a rolled-up parchment to the other guardian. After the guardian reviewed the parchment, he handed it back to Sebastian and let them through to go to the elevator.

Lola could see the elevator from afar and that's when her heart started racing with joy. She was so excited she almost teared up. She even started walking a little faster. Her invisible purse bounced against her leg as she sped up.

The elevator had been fixed back to its proper nineteenth century self. You couldn't even tell that someone had accidentally pulled the lever and plummeted the elevator into destruction. Oddly enough, it still had the smell of tangy apples.

As they ascended, Lola figured she would be the bigger person and initiated a semblance of a conversation. "Have you ever been to Terre One?"

"No," Sebastian said, unamused and cold.

In her mind, that was as good a try as any, so she didn't push it. It didn't take too long for them to get to the top and reach the abandoned opera house.

Stepping out of the elevator they could smell the dusty air that floated about in the old lobby. The worn-out red carpet was just as musty as Lola remembered, and she couldn't be happier to be there. She almost ran to the doors but stopped herself.

"You're going to be hiding when you follow me, right?" Lola asked Sebastian, worried that he would interfere with her day-to-day life.

He looked extremely annoyed, but even then he said yes. There was a good chance he didn't want to be near her anyway, but Lola didn't care—she was going to bring Jason to safety and that was the only thing that mattered.

She gripped the long door handle of the decrepit door and brought them all into the light of the day. Jason started opening his eyes and all any of them could hear were cars and people bustling. To Lola, those sounds were more magical and precious than anything she could think of.

Finally, it was time to go home.

End...

60013292R00188

Made in the USA
Columbia, SC
11 June 2019